TRIPLE THREAT

K WEBSTER

D1280254

CHAPTER ONE

Landry

MY LIFE IS perfect.

It has to be because *he* designed it that way.

I am just one shiny part in the Croft world—glittering like spun gold for all to see.

And they will.

It's why I exist.

To be a trophy displayed to the world. Beautiful, polite, intelligent, poised, elegant. I'm everything he demands I be. Never do I argue or resist his impossible demands.

Why?

Because of Della.

She's *not* perfect.

At least, not in his eyes.

To me, my little sister is everything. Funny and sassy and a little odd sometimes. She's the realest thing in my life. The only thing that brings me true joy.

But for some reason, he hates her. With every fiber of his being. Nothing she does is even satisfactory in his eyes. She's a burden—an embarrassment. And if it weren't for my careful intervening, there's no telling what would happen to her.

I suck in a deep breath and then exhale all the stress that comes with living in the Croft penthouse condo in the prestigious Hudson Yards neighborhood with one of New York's most powerful men.

Our condo might be valued at nearly thirty million and always magazine perfect, but darkness lurks behind every shiny marble surface. This home is nothing more than a fancy nightmare. An illusion tied in a pretty bow.

My bedroom is where I spend most of my time. The floor-to-ceiling windows that make up an entire wall of my room are where I can escape while still trapped. The expansive views of the sparkling Hudson River and the Atlantic Ocean, eighty-eight floors above the ground, remind me that life is beautiful out there away from my harsh reality. Lady Liberty, that bitch, taunts me from afar, boasting of her freedom.

Turning away from the false getaway that my windows tease me with, I take in my room. Like the rest of our condo, my room is immaculate. Very little reveals me or my personality. Sleek white furniture, snowy white bedding, soft white rugs sitting on warm charcoal gray wood floors. No art or fancy decorations. No television or stereo. Nothing but my picture-perfect prison.

I'm a pretty doll in an even prettier dollhouse.

And *he* likes playing with *his* things.

Tonight, he'll be home, back from a two-week business trip to Tokyo. All the tension I'd managed to unknot in that time has found its way back into the muscles of my neck, twisting me up with each passing second that'll eventually bring me to the moment I'll be forced to see him again.

"Miss Landry," Noel chirps from the doorway, making me jolt in surprise. "Do you require my assistance?"

I blink several times as I steel my spine. I can't afford to let my guard down even for a second. Not because I'm afraid of Noel, but because I need to be ready for him. Lifting my chin, I give Noel a polite smile.

"Yes, please." I motion toward the silky, golden Georgio Armani textured drape dress laid out on my bed, an exquisite blip on the otherwise perfect white comforter. "I always have trouble with the zippers."

Eager to help, Noel scurries into my bedroom, a small smile curling her lips up. I like Noel, and in another life, we could be friends. But we're not in another life. We're in this one. Here, she's paid help and not allowed anything more. I'm curious what her life consists of outside the Croft penthouse. Does she have children or a husband or hobbies?

"Mr. Croft likes this color on you," Noel says, her voice reassuring. "I'm sure he'll have missed you dearly."

I try not to wince at her words. He *will* have missed me and he *will* like this dress. I'll be everything that he's groomed me to be—perfect.

It's Della he *won't* have missed dearly.

Della who will be the recipient of his scornful glares and scathing remarks.

Clearing my throat, I attempt to ready myself for his arrival. There is no room for jittery nerves or a twisting stomach. I have to be strong and distracting so Della flies under the radar. Sure, we've had a much-needed break from him, but he's back in town, which means it's business as usual.

All playfulness will be gone. Our movie and

popcorn nights in her room will cease to exist. The treats Noel sometimes smuggles in for us will discontinue under his watchful eye. Della's sleeping in my bed will be no more. We'll have to watch our backs, which means always being on guard.

Even the staff is rigid once more. They've been whisking around all day, readying the condo for his arrival. His security detail lets us bend the rules while he's gone, as long as we don't leave the condo. But with his return they'll be strict and smothering again.

"Is Della dressed?" I ask as I slip out of my clothes down to my undergarments.

"In the buttercup dress that makes her green eyes pop."

I nod and exhale a slight breath of relief. "She didn't fight you for the purple one?"

"Oh," Noel confides, "she did, but I'm twenty years her senior and outweigh her a tad."

The air between us is light, but I can't afford to be playful. Not this close to his arrival. Imagining a six-year-old trying to bully a twenty-something is quite comical, yet I'm not laughing.

"Her shoes match?" I ask, ignoring her teasing and push forward.

"Yes, ma'am." She offers my dress to me, to

which I step into and then turn so that she'll zip me up.

"Hair?"

"She looks beautiful, Miss Landry. Please don't worry."

Am I that transparent?

"Remember your place, Noel." My words come out sharp, stinging like a whip on flesh, making her flinch violently.

"Yes, ma'am."

Noel's freckled face turns crimson like that of her strawberry-blonde hair that's pulled tight into a bun. I hate that I've been rude to her, especially since she's been so kind to us in his absence, but I'm walking a fine line with my emotions tonight. If she knocks me off my game, even slightly, there's no telling how that will play out for Della.

Please be a dutiful, sweet girl tonight, Della. Please.

"I can finish on my own," I clip out in a cool voice that sounds so much like him. "You're dismissed. Send Della my way."

"Miss Ellis is with her."

I nearly recoil at the mention of Sandra's name. Sandra Ellis is our house manager and fills in the nanny role, when required, for Della. Neither Della nor I can stand that meddling tattletale witch.

"Send her anyway," I grind out. "Tell Miss Ellis she is relieved from her duties for the evening."

She nods once and then hurries from the room leaving me to my twisting gut. My makeup is painted on expertly and my silky, golden hair is pinned loosely so that tendrils escape, framing my angelic face.

That's what he says.

I have the face of an angel.

Twisting my features into a scowl, I appreciate, for a moment, that I'm not the perfect girl he's molded me to be. Sometimes, the real me can escape, even if only for a brief glimpse in the mirror.

After indulging myself for a few seconds, I relax my features and neutralize my expression. All the simmering anger that's ever-present will have to be pushed back down and covered by the lid of pretend.

One day, I won't have to pretend.

But, for at least the next twelve years, I'll be an actress, playing a part in this ridiculous play because at the end of it, I'll take Della far away from here. She'll be eighteen and the law won't force her to be his prisoner anymore. We'll live a life filled with laughter and freedom and happiness. This hell will become a distant memory.

Glancing at the clock, I take note of the time. Della still hasn't shown up, which means Sandra is keeping her for some reason. Dinner, when he's home, always starts at seven which means I'll need to finish up and locate Della myself before he arrives. Quickly, I rummage around in my jewelry box, overlooking Mom's old rings and necklaces, before seeking out the bracelet he gave me on my eighteenth birthday last March.

I hate this bracelet. I hate him. Yet, I slide it onto my wrist and turn my arm, watching the light glint off the gold.

"You look stunning," a deep voice rumbles from the doorway. "A spitting image of your mother."

Every hair on my body crackles to life and stands on end as if awoken by dark energy clouding around me. His familiar voice alone is enough to tell me who is prowling into my bedroom, but when I catch whiff of his expensive cologne scent, it solidifies the answer.

Daddy's home.

"Thank you, Dad," I say, flashing him an ear-splitting grin. "We've missed you."

He opens his arms, waiting for me to greet

him with a hug. I walk into his strong grip. His embrace is brief before he quickly lets go of me. A wolfish, calculating smirk tugs at his lips as he holds up a fisted hand.

If Della were here, that fist would be a weapon.

But, for me, his beloved older daughter, it's a gift.

It wasn't always this way. I've just gotten really good at performing perfectly for the most vicious critic in the world.

"You brought me something?" I bounce on my toes in girlish eagerness despite the sourness in my gut. "I can't wait to see."

He lets loose a rumbling chuckle. "You're spoiled, sweetheart."

My smile falters and it takes effort to tighten the muscles, forcing it to stay in place. "You spoil me," I sass back. "It's your fault."

Pleased with my words, he twists his hand and uncurls his fingers to open his palm. Sitting like a coiled golden snake, a necklace shimmers beneath the overhead light. His gifts feel like weights, dragging me to the bottom of the abyss—a constant reminder of why he gives them.

"It's so pretty," I breathe, reaching for the dainty necklace.

"So impatient," he chides. "Allow me. Turn around."

Swallowing down my unease, I twist and face the window. In the reflection, Dad towers over me, a menacing presence. With gentle, delicate movements, he unclasps the necklace and then reaches around me to dangle it in front of my face.

"How was Tokyo?" I ask, trying and failing to keep the shakiness from my voice.

"After several days of negotiations, we finally came to an agreement on the building purchase price. The sale went through without issue and it's officially mine. Croft Gaming and Entertainment will now have a presence in Asia." His fingers brush along the outside of my neck as he brings the clasps together behind my neck. "It's a multi-billion-dollar expansion that's turning the heads of some impressive people, specifically in this city."

"Incredible," I murmur. "Congratulations."

"With the money I'll make from this global expansion, maybe I can retire. Sell the company and spend more time with my daughter." He kisses the top of my head. "What do you say?"

My knees quake but I keep them locked. Spending all hours of every day with him would be an absolute nightmare for me and Della both.

"I see a lot of trips to Greece in our future," I tease, unable to fully hide the terror in my tone. "Della loves traveling."

The air grows chilly at the mention of my sister. Immediately, I regret my words. What did I just do? Did I screw up everything over a few misspoken words?

"Perhaps," Dad says icily. "Or perhaps we'll find a sitter. She can be quite…unruly. Vacations aren't meant to be spoiled by unruly children."

I swallow down the bile creeping up my throat. Now is not the time for weakness. I'm here, rather than away at college, because of her. Because she needs me. I am the wall between them. Her only line of defense. I'll be damned if I crumble now.

"Will we be having another costume party this year for your birthday? You've been so busy with work, so…" I trail off, hoping to change the subject from Della to something that brings my father joy. Himself.

Predictably, his rigidness melts away and a smile crawls across his face. "There's always time for a Croft party, my love. Have you thought about what you'll dress up as?"

"A princess."

"You're a princess every day." He chuckles, his dark blue eyes twinkling. "You'll think up something clever. You always do."

Dad cups my cheek and winks at me before striding out of my bedroom. The air that I'd been struggling to breathe rushes in and out of my lungs in ragged pants. Tears prickle at my eyes.

There's no time to have a mental breakdown.

Not now. Not ever.

I have to protect her.

Always.

With one last exhalation, I lift my chin, affix my practiced smile, and set out on my mission to play a complicated game against a cruel, hateful man…my father.

CHAPTER TWO

Sully

IT'S NOT OFTEN we're summoned by our...*uncle*, but when it happens, we show up to the Morelli mansion. No questions asked. Ready to do his bidding.

Bryant Morelli isn't a man you fuck with.

Period.

Sparrow groans in boredom, swiping through his phone too quickly to be reading anything. He, like myself, hates these damn "family meetings." Our brother, Scout, is the only one who remotely takes interest in them, which makes me wonder where the hell he is.

"You seen Scout?" I ask Sparrow, lazily shaking the ice in my empty glass. "Like since Christopher's party?"

"Nope." Sparrow pops the "p" and doesn't bother to look up. "Not his keeper."

I roll my eyes, dropping my glass to the table beside my chair with a loud clank. Sparrow cuts his dark-eyed stare my way. He's antagonistic by nature and enjoys whenever he can find a way to poke at one of his brothers. It's earned him his fair share of fists to the face for it, too.

"Technically you are," I remind him. "We made a promise."

Sparrow scowls. "That was a year ago."

"Yeah, well it doesn't have an expiration date."

Not with Scout. Ever since our brother got us into some major shit with the fucking Constantine family that ruined our lives, he's been put on watch. He can't be left to his own devices because our brother is a psychopath.

"Scout is fine," Sparrow grumbles, already bored with the conversation, returning his gaze back to his latest Tinder hookup quest. "Besides, he's Bryant's bitch now."

As if that makes me feel any better.

Bryant isn't exactly role model material.

I scrub my palm over my face, trying and failing to swipe away my misery. This shit sucks. My life sucks. College was stolen from us by a Constantine, prison stole our mother, and our freedom was stolen by the Morellis. We're puppets now for Bryant Morelli to tug on whenever he sees fit.

This is our life.

For. Fucking. Ever.

I walk over to Bryant's well-stocked bar and help myself to a few shots of what I hope is expensive and irreplaceable.

"Do you ever want to do more than this?" I mutter, not exactly caring if Sparrow joins the conversation or not.

He scoffs. "Dude. We live in a fucking penthouse."

A penthouse that comes with many, many strings attached—all tethered to Bryant and this mansion.

"And?"

"And have you seen our cars? Dude, this is the best outcome we could have hoped for."

Best outcome? We're pampered dogs. Bryant dangles treats in front of us before he commands us to do his bidding. It's bullshit.

Sparrow's hard gaze bores into my back, scorching me like the heat of the sun. I'm feeling emboldened by the alcohol freely burning through my veins. Anger bubbles up inside me, threatening to make me explode.

"Sully," Sparrow says, softening. "This is our

life, man. It is what it is."

The three of us have all lost things we wish we could have had. I know I'm not alone, but sometimes it feels that way.

I turn to find him sitting forward, no longer interested in his phone, elbows on his knees and hands clasped in front of him. His dark hair is slicked back, looking severe and aging him a few years. He reminds me of the rest of the Morellis. Sparrow even dresses like them—always donning an expensive suit unless he's pounding it out at the gym with me and Scout.

"Our life should have been Harvard." I grit my teeth, frowning hard. "We could have had so much more than this."

If our lives hadn't gone to shit, we'd have gone off to Harvard and actually be making something of our lives now. It sucks knowing our path took such a sharp turn, landing us in the arms of the Morellis.

"Bitterness is an ugly look," Sparrow states. "Also, Scout will eat you alive if he hears you whining."

"I'm not fucking whining."

Sparrow shrugs before leaning back in his seat. Sometimes, I think Sparrow is the bigger of the three of us, but then I remember it's just his arrogance that makes him seem that way. His ego is a giant goddamn mushroom cloud above him, looming over everyone, including myself. But, since he's my brother, an identical triplet at that, I know physically we're built exactly the same. The three of us are way too competitive to allow one of the others to surpass us on muscle mass.

Deep voices can be heard, signaling the approach of men. I immediately tense up, hating the idea of dealing with Bryant. When it's business as usual, dinners and private parties are something I can endure. However, when he calls us in for a special meeting, I want to crawl out of my own skin.

I hate being his little bitch.

Bryant strolls into one of the many sitting rooms in this massive mansion that we've designated as our meeting space. His air of authority is stifling. Where Sparrow seems larger than life with his arrogance, Bryant gives off this powerful regal vibe. Like he's the fucking king of everything or some shit. Behind him, Scout enters—no, prowls is the better word—following stealthily like a pet panther just waiting for the command to destroy someone.

His limp is almost unnoticeable.

Almost.

When Scout catches my gaze scrutinizing his gait, he shoots me a scathing glare. I'm used to him being an asshole, though, so it doesn't bother me. After all, it's his fault he has the damn limp in the first place.

You fuck with a Constantine and they fuck you up. Literally. As though tuned into my thoughts of how Scout incurred not one but two broken kneecaps at the hands of one of Winston Constantine's men, his jaw tightens and his dark eyes flicker with rage.

"Boys," Bryant greets, offering both Sparrow and me a smirk. "Hope we didn't keep you waiting."

Before I can gripe that we've indeed been waiting for forty-five goddamn minutes, Sparrow cuts me off with a sharp expression.

"Just shooting the shit," Sparrow states, waving it off as if it's not a big deal. "What's up? Got another job for us?"

Bryant, pleased with Sparrow's compliance, chuckles. "Always so eager, son. We haven't even gotten our pleasantries out of the way."

For fuck's sake.

"I need another drink," I mutter, needing desperately to numb every part of my body.

Bryant cocks his head to the side, eyes narrowed on me. "I believe you've had enough."

A flash of irritation ignites and travels up my spine to my head, burning my neck and cheeks. Getting chastised by Bryant, as though I'm a child, rankles me beyond belief. I grit my teeth and fist my hands, desperate to lay into him, but manage to offer a clipped nod of compliance instead. Bryant smiles before taking the seat beside Sparrow. I fall into my seat, eager to get this over with. Whatever bullshit job Bryant wants us to do, we'll do, and then we can get back to trying to squeeze one ounce of pleasure from our stupid life.

"As you boys are well aware, a lot goes into making us one of the most powerful names in the city," Bryant starts, his authoritative tone vibrating with ire. "In order to remain an immovable force, certain people's business interests need to be…" He sighs heavily, waving a hand in a dismissive gesture. "Eliminated."

Scout perches on the arm of the chair beside me, shooting Bryant a questioning look. "The Constantines?" His jaw ticks and his eyes darken with fury. "If it were me, I'd have destroyed that family last year. Winston can eat shit."

Bryant scoffs. "As much as I appreciate your eagerness to knock that pompous prick down a few pegs, Winston is a necessary evil."

It's Scout's turn to bark out a derisive sound. "Necessary?"

"Money makes the world go round. You, Scout, of all people know this." Bryant bounces his gaze from Scout to me to Sparrow before landing back on Scout. "And with the right amount, you can make it spin faster and faster."

I arch a brow and exchange a look with Sparrow. He still wears an uninterested expression, but his body is tense. Not one of the three of us can stand the Constantines. Calling them a necessary evil is almost insulting. As though Bryant accepts the ruthlessness of Winston and his family but isn't at all bothered by it. The Morellis and the Constantines have been at war for forever. As the secret bastard nephews, we've become collateral damage.

But, then again, Bryant didn't get his kneecap crushed in such a way that took a few surgeries and a year of physical therapy to regain some semblance of normalcy like us. Scout has it worse than me and Sparrow since he took a bat to both knees instead of just one. Bryant also didn't get college ripped from his grasp. He didn't have his mother dragged through the mud by Winston fucking Constantine who only wanted to prove a point—that he was on top.

No, Bryant Morelli had none of that, therefore he isn't bothered.

I know I can speak for my brothers when I say we're *really* fucking bothered.

"You'll do as I ask," Bryant continues. "That's what family does. And you, boys, are family now. Not to mention, you know I will reward you handsomely."

Scout grinds his molars together, his anger obviously bubbling up with each passing second. Good, I'm not the only one growing annoyed at Bryant's nonchalance.

"Reward," I mutter, hoping this old fuck will get to the point already. "What do you want us to do? If it's not about the Constantines…" *Then why the fuck do we care?*

Bryant studies me for a long beat, his penetrating stare cutting through me like a hot knife through butter. Effortlessly. Smoothly. Effectively. I swallow, trying like hell not to wither, even a little, under his scrutiny. Because if he looks too hard, he'll see how much I hate him and this family—how much I want to run away and never look back.

"Oh, it's about the Constantines," Bryant rumbles, smirking. "It's always about them, but I prefer to stab in the places they don't expect. Bleed them from the inside out."

My muscles relax at those words.

"Halcyon Corporation is looking to purchase tech giant Croft Gaming and Entertainment, which is dominating the technology industry for the foreseeable future. It's a massive corporation with global reach. Word is the CEO of Croft, Alexander Croft, will be making a power grab at a place within the Constantine family." Bryant glances my way. "Through marriage."

"He's going to marry the psycho bitch who heads that family?" Scout asks, voice dripping with disgust. "And, if so, why do we care?"

"Caroline would never remarry." Bryant shakes his head, a villainous smile curling his lips. "Besides, it's not him. It's his daughter."

I do a quick run through in my head of the eligible bachelors in the Constantine family. Winston is out because he recently married our stepsister—ex-stepsister—and I thought the other brothers had girlfriends or some shit. That leaves other, less important Constantines.

"So this dude's daughter is supposed to marry some rich-ass distant cousin of the Constantine pricks and we care because…" Sparrow trails off. "Make it make sense, boss."

"We care because we love a good scandal," Bryant says, smirking. "And by a good scandal, I mean a nuclear bomb to drop in the Constantine public relations laps. Something that will ruin their investment and destroy their relationship. Croft has the potential to grow into a trillion-dollar global empire. The Constantines know it and are trying to hop aboard that train, riding it all the way to the bank." He clasps his fingers together, resting them in his lap. "I want to derail it."

"A scandal," Scout reiterates with a scoff. "Come on, uncle dearest, we know there's more to it than that. Spill the beans, man."

Bryant eyes him for a moment before nodding. "Let's just say Croft has secrets, because frankly, every man in power does. The kind of secrets people like me pay good money to uncover. I want to know everything that man is hiding. I *will* find out everything that man is hiding. He might appear to be clean as a whistle, but those men are usually the dirtiest."

Most of the jobs Bryant sends us on involve good old-fashioned ass whoopings. The three of us, when we gang up on someone, are a lethal combination. We make sure our "jobs" know how much it physically hurts to irritate the patriarch of the Morelli family. He may no longer run the show, officially, but he still demands everyone's respect.

"So we're going to spy?" Sparrow clarifies. "Get information?"

His nostrils flare. I can tell he's already bored of our new job. I'm the only guy around here who uses his brain. I made the best grades in school, made the better decisions between the three of us, and actually think ahead.

Sparrow is super fucking smart but he has just enough of Scout's reckless energy to make him trouble. He lives for seeing what he can get away with. I think that's why he likes putting on the suit and playing the rich people games...because he's good at it.

And Scout is the crazy psycho. He doesn't understand boundaries.

He just does whatever the fuck he wants. Which is usually something destructive.

"Infiltrate is a better word," Bryant answers with a dark chuckle. "Infiltrate. Infect. I want you to involve yourselves in every aspect of their lives."

"Sounds...easy," I say, confused as to why we're even being asked to do this. It's just so...dull.

"Easy," Bryant drawls out. "No, locating some

asshole and beating him within an inch of his life because he owes a Morelli is easy. What I'm asking you to do is the next step."

"The next step," Sparrow repeats. "To what?"

"Harvard."

My blood runs cold. It's a harsh, cruel reminder of what we've lost.

"That's what you always wanted, is it not?" Bryant offers a wolfish grin that makes every hair on my arms stand on end. "You've proven you're good at obeying commands and have been loyal. Now, I want you to do more for me. This is an extension of my faith and trust in the three of you. Take this step, and I'm willing to give you what you truly want. Your future back."

Our future?

I hate that my heart pumps faster at this prospect. This life is shitty. The chance to do more—anything—is enticing. Bryant's not an idiot. He knows how to dangle the right carrots in our faces to get us to do his bidding.

Scout rises to his feet and makes his way over to the bar, his limp more noticeable this time as he walks. I trail my gaze after him, wondering what his thoughts are on this new proposition our uncle is offering.

"If the Croft guy has plans to marry off his

daughter to a Constantine, I seriously doubt he's going to allow us to waltz into his world and to start shaking shit up," I grind out. "Seems a little out there."

Bryant's shoulders stiffen and he cuts me a sharp glare. "It's not out there. My source has done his part diving into Croft and uncovering his next moves. I want to have a hand in every twist and turn he decides to take. I'm still the captain steering his ship."

Again with the narcissistic metaphorical bullshit.

"What's our in?" Scout asks after sucking down a shot and slamming the glass on the bar top. "We're pretty notoriously known as your nephews. Not exactly undercover material."

"Not as the Mannford triplets," Bryant agrees, "or even Bryant Morelli's triplet nephews."

Get. To. The. Point. Old. Man.

"But," Bryant continues, a sly grin tugging at his lips, "as someone entirely new, you can ease into their world, manipulate the tech princess, and find out every goddamn thing you can about Croft and his association with Winston. His daughter, from all reports, is practically a prisoner in her home. No friends. No outings. She's sheltered and naive and ripe for the manipulating.

I want you crawling all over Croft and his eldest daughter's lives, never easing up on your efforts. Together, the three of you will work as one—one *man*."

I roll my eyes, but inside I'm wary. This feels big. And big, when Bryant Morelli and my brothers are involved, means dangerous. "Why send three guys, then? If you only want one."

"Because I want all three of you invested. I want you working with each other, building on each other's work—even competing with each other. You'll do more than one man, or even three other men, ever could."

"That's true," Sparrow says, as if this entire thing is reasonable. "Especially with Harvard on the line. No one can stand in our way when we work together."

"A triple threat," Scout says, rejoining us. "One blade but three times as sharp."

"Precisely," Bryant agrees. "Now cut those pricks and make them bleed."

CHAPTER THREE

Landry

D ON'T PANIC.
    Don't panic.

Too late.

I stare at the empty seat across from me at our enormous dining room table that's capable of seating eight, but only usually seats the three of us. Our dining room is one of the most visually pleasing rooms in our penthouse. It's nestled in a corner, showcasing floor-to-ceiling panoramic views of the city. For such a stunning setting, it's the room I hate the most. It feels as though we can't hide from Dad. Under the sparkling chandelier that cost more than most people's apartments, we're magnified and exposed for his careful scrutinization. I can barely remember the good times here when Mom was still alive, back when dinners were filled with love and not dread.

Where's Della?

Dad is distracted by replying to emails on his phone, but that won't last forever. Eventually, he'll realize Della isn't here. His mood will plummet within seconds and then the entire condo will feel his wrath. The staff, me, and especially Della.

Darting my gaze to the opening that leads into the living room, I search for any sign of my sister peeking around the corner.

Nothing.

The savory scents coming from whatever our chef is preparing no longer has me salivating, but instead has me wanting to gag.

I could excuse myself and hunt her down. But he'd see right through that. I've tried before and it never works. No, the best option when it comes to Dad and Della is to distract him.

Come on, Della. Stop messing around.

The sound of a phone being set down on the mahogany table has me jerking my stare from the living room to my father. His narrowed eyes are fixated on the empty seat across from me. I note the clench of his jaw and slow change of color on his skin. From healthy tan to red, and soon to furious purple.

Distract. Distract. Distract.

"So, this new—"

"Della," Dad calls out, cutting off my sad attempt to make conversation. "Don't keep us waiting."

Silence.

Of course there's silence. There's always silence.

You don't just call out to Della and expect her to come running. It doesn't work that way. He knows this, but does it anyway. Always setting her up for failure.

"She, uh, was feeling under the weather earlier," I say, fear for my sister making my voice raspy. "Maybe she fell asleep. I should go check on her."

When I begin to push my chair out to stand, Dad slams a hand down on the surface so hard, it makes me cry out in surprise. Slowly, he rises from his seat, the familiar purple fury painting his skin with every passing second.

Oh, God.

"Sit tight," he instructs. "I'll fetch the child."

The child.

I hate him for this.

He stalks out of the dining room, his footsteps thunderous. I'm frozen, unsure what to do. I could rush in there and intervene, but last time I did that, I only made it worse. Tears prickle my eyes. I pray like hell she doesn't give him any trouble that would cause her pain.

A crash makes my heart jump into my throat. I curl my fingers around the knife beside my plate, wondering if I could actually use it if forced.

Can I do it? Can I take him down?

He storms back into the dining room.

Della, all dolled up and dressed for a party, squirms as she tries to free herself from Dad's iron grip around her tiny bicep. Her green eyes, filled with tears and confusion, slam to mine.

The pleading in them kills me.

Save me, Landry.

If only it were that easy.

Dad drags her chair out, tosses her onto the seat of it, and then shoves it back. His body vibrates with venomous rage. I attempt to catch my little sister's gaze, but her chin drops to her chest to hide. Golden-blonde hair curtains her face, strands finding their way into the wetness on her cheeks and sticking there.

"Tell your sister why you kept her waiting," Dad grinds out, his voice booming and angry. "Now."

No answer.

"She can't hear you," I whisper. "You know

that."

Ignoring me, he repeats himself. Same result. No answer. Finally, he brings his fist down onto the table so hard, the water from her glass sloshes out. This gets her attention.

With her hands she signs: *What?*

I close my eyes briefly hoping he doesn't see her answer as disrespectful. Rather than using ASL, her only method of communication, Dad speaks to her as if he's forgotten the fact he has a deaf child. His voice grows louder and louder as he rants about her tardiness.

Peeking my eyes back open, I watch Della as she attempts to read Dad's lips. She's precocious and busy, so learning how to sit still long enough to read someone's lips has been something she's failed to master, much to Dad's disgust.

"So Tokyo was a success," I say, interrupting him from his tirade that's seconds from turning nuclear. "What's next on your agenda?"

A beat of silence fills the room aside from Della's soft sniffling. Dad visibly relaxes, peels his glare from my sister, and regards me, a smile forming. When I was a child and Mom was still alive, I thought him to be majestic like a king. Dad had all the answers and brought me lots of gifts. He hasn't always been...a monster. At one time, he was good.

But Mom's pregnancy with Della was complicated. Her body was depleted, she lost an incredible amount of weight, and was dying by the time she gave birth to Della. The doctors had hoped she'd recover once the baby was out, but after a few weeks, she died of a sudden heart attack. The strain of carrying Della had deteriorated her organs, specifically her heart. One day she was here, and the next she was gone.

And in those six years since, Dad has clearly blamed Della. Time only made the wound fester.

"I'm going to be taking on a protégé," Dad says, smirking. "Apparently, according to my CFO, it's long overdue."

The news is surprising to me. My father doesn't usually make time for such things. He's a shrewd businessman who threw his entire self into the company after Mom died. It's always about making the next dollar—hence his Tokyo endeavor—but never about teaching others.

"That's not the only thing Gareth had to say." Dad pauses as Noel bustles into the dining room with a tray filled with plates. "Thank you, Noel."

Noel's cheeks burn crimson and she nods. "It's a pleasure, Mr. Croft."

He flashes her a wolfish smile that turns my

stomach. It's as if everyone around us is blind to his monstrous behavior. I hate that no one else sees him the way his children do. While he blatantly flirts with Noel, I glance over at Della. Her tears have been swiped away and she's scowling. If it were just us, I would tickle her until she smiled. Since I can't exactly do that, I make a silly face at her before quickly schooling my features. The corner of her lips twitch. An almost smile. Better than nothing.

After Noel deposits each plate in front of us and pours our wine, she slips away quietly. As soon as she's gone, the heaviness of Dad's anger clouds the room. Della is not-so-quietly clanging her fork against the china as she shovels green beans into her mouth.

"What else did Gareth say?" I urge, drawing his attention to me once more. "You've piqued my curiosity."

He relaxes, offering me a teasing grin. "He had much to say. Actually, some of it involved you."

My brows pinch in confusion. Me? I've only met Gareth a few times, all of which he was preoccupied talking business with Dad. None of those times did he ever even take the time to notice me, much less speak to me.

"He wants me to intern for you?" I ask, guessing the only plausible thing I can think of.

Dad barks out a laugh. "Don't be silly, sweetheart. You're a Croft, not some unpaid college intern brat."

"Then what could he possibly have to say about me?"

"There are…influential people in this city. People he thinks you should meet."

I study Dad, frowning. Since when? He rarely lets me out of the building. Now he thinks I should meet influential people. A sick, uneasy feeling turns my stomach.

"It's time," Dad says, darting a glance over at Della, "that you leave the nest. Get out there and meet new people. Schmooze and represent the Croft family as the goddess they no doubt will see you as." He beams at me. "Gareth says one of the Constantine cousins is single and recently moved back to the city. A young fellow, fresh out of college and looking to make something of himself, which is admirable. Perhaps we could arrange a meeting."

I blink at him in shock.

"Don't look so surprised." He cuts into his filet, his lips still curled into a smile. "I can't keep you as my little girl forever, though I know we both would love that."

Panic shoots through me and the room spins. I should eat to chase away the dizziness, but I can't move or breathe or think.

"But who will watch Della?" I whisper before swallowing hard. "She needs me."

It's not that she needs me to care for her, because technically that's what Sandra is for, but Della needs me emotionally. I'm the only person who truly gets her. The only person she trusts and loves. I know that she sometimes acts out when she's tired or overstimulated and just needs a second to herself. I know how she likes her snacks arranged on her plate or which bows are her favorites. It's all those little things she needs me for.

Of course, I can't say that to him. He already thinks I baby her too much.

Dad takes a bite of his steak and chews, his features darkening. I want to reel the words back in, but I've already cast them into the depths of his resentment toward her.

"This little attachment she has to you is unhealthy," he says after he chases down his meat with a healthy swig of wine. "You're not her mother, Landry."

His words strike like the belt he's used on me

and Della both in the past. I visibly flinch, and then hate that he saw my reaction.

"Besides," Dad continues, "Della has Sandra."

Sandra is an uncaring robot. She flits about, doing Dad's bidding, and adds no extra emotion or care. I might not be Della's mother, but I am her family. I can give her what no one else can. Love.

Della only has me.

"But, Dad—"

"I know this is hard for you," he barks, slicing my words off the end of my tongue like a sharp blade, "but you'll get over it. Della will be starting school soon. I have tutors lined up for her beginning next week."

"She won't go to the private school I went to—"

"Landry, she can't go to school with all the damn elites in this city." He snarls, whipping his head in her direction. "She's a fucking embarrassment."

Anger flashes hot inside me. My tongue burns with the need to lash out at him. To tell him *he's* the embarrassment. The waste of a human being we call Dad. We deserve better than this.

Della bangs on the table with her utensil. I snap my head up to see her staring fiercely at me, her fork gripped in hand like she might use it on Dad. Forcing a smile, I sign to her that everything's just fine and to eat.

"Eat," Dad booms. "Now."

Her nostrils flare. She's so tiny but filled with a lot of anger. Thankfully she goes back to eating without a fuss. I swipe away my tears, my mind reeling. He wants me to date? To get out there and meet wealthy guys? And then, what? Marry one of them?

The thought of leaving Della here all alone for the next twelve years is almost too much to bear. I wish I could wait until Dad is at work, load her up on a bus, and disappear somewhere across the country. We could be safe and happy. She would be loved.

But Dad would find us.

I know he would. His resources are endless and his wealth runs even deeper. We'd be plucked from whichever obscure town we landed in and planted right back in this condo. But his wrath would end up destroying us in the end. Especially Della. His trust and adoration of me—my only tool in my arsenal—would be completely wiped away.

But twelve years feels like forever. We can't last that long. I have to figure something else out.

My mind fights to go back to a night not long after Mom passed away. That night he struck me for the first time. I was in his office, trying every number combination possible on his safe, looking for pictures of Mom since most had disappeared after her death. It took weeks for the bruise on my face to heal and I wasn't permitted to leave my room until it did. All my teachers thought I had the flu.

No, I can't bring that on us both. I'll figure out a way to get us out of his crossfire.

"I suppose a few nights away each week won't hurt," I say in a shaky voice, forcing a smile. "You always know best, Dad."

His features soften and his blue eyes twinkle as he looks me over. "Good girl. Your father does know best. I have another surprise for you. It's what you've wanted for a long time."

I frown, unsure of what this could possibly mean. The only thing I want, and have for a long time, is freedom for me and Della. Nothing else.

Well, there's one thing, but he doesn't know about it...

He pulls an envelope from his inside pocket and slides it across the table toward me. I glance down at the emblem on the envelope with Landry Croft scribbled in someone's neat handwriting across the front.

Oh my God.

I reach for the envelope. NYU. College. I didn't even bother applying. Not because I didn't want to, but because I couldn't leave Della. Mom was a stay-at-home mother and Dad always told me my trust fund would make it so I'd never have to work a day in my life.

"What's this?" I ask, already knowing the answer.

"You've been accepted." His eyes flash in a knowing way. "You know I always keep tabs on my little girl. You're too precious to me for me to let anything ever happen to you."

He's been spying on me—my computer search history to be exact. What else could I have looked at that he might have seen? Terror burns in my gut. I hope to God I didn't look at anything that might come back on me and Della.

"I didn't apply." I gnaw on my bottom lip to keep it from shaking.

"I pulled a few strings. Anything for you, my love."

"Thank you," I force out. "I didn't think it was something you'd allow me to do."

"You're eighteen now, sweetheart. You're a woman and you're going to do great things."

I nod as if to agree.

But I don't.

Because leaving to "meet people" and to "do great things" means leaving Della. I don't like this sudden need to separate us. It feels like the beginning of something far more sinister.

CHAPTER FOUR

Sparrow

DOGS ON A leash.

That's what Sully calls us, but fuck, we're spoiled little bitches.

I prowl through the parking lot at NYU in my brand-new Audi R8 Coupe, like a panther stalking his prey.

The Croft princess.

Seek. Defile. Destroy.

Easy. If simple tasks like fucking around with some chick gets me gifts like my hot as sin new car, then so be it. I'll be Bryant Morelli's little bitch. Pride can take a damn backseat. I'm not like Sully. I can grin and bear it because the rewards Bryant often tosses our way are too good to pass up.

We were going to draw straws on how we'd divide and conquer, but Bryant had specific assignments for each of us. I'm to be in a couple of her classes three days a week. Sully, on the other hand, got the boring as hell task to do some job at the Croft home. Scout, naturally, is going to be the snake that slithers into Croft's world and bites when they least expect it.

Not sure how Bryant finagled us into these positions or what strings he had to pull in order to make it happen, but I'm just fine with my task.

College.

It's the one thing I really wanted...before. Before Scout got weirdly obsessed with our stepsister, dragged us into his shit, and earned us the beatdown of our lives. Back then, when we were spoiled assholes, I was on the track for success. Our mother was a renowned plastic surgeon to the elite and had hella connections, but I was smart and athletic. I didn't need for her to buy my way anywhere. I'd planned to do it all on my own.

Now, Bryant is offering Harvard back to us. Again, Harvard is something I wanted to achieve all on my own and resented the fact Bryant wanted to hand it to us on a silver platter. But, when I'd seen the despondent look in Sully's eyes, I knew we had to do this. He's been spiraling for a year now, lost without his Harvard dreams. At least, with this job, I can help give it back to him. Even if I have to accept Bryant calling all the shots. And Scout doesn't give a shit about Harvard, but he does give a shit about us, which means he'll play along too.

My mood suddenly souring, I pull into a parking spot but don't shut off my car. It still has the new-car leather smell, which is surprisingly calming. I inhale a deep breath and exhale my irritation. Scout is a dick of epic proportions sometimes, but he's my brother. It's not his fault he's a little fucked in the head. I probably stole all the good shit in the womb. He may have conned me and Sully into terrorizing our stepsister, which ultimately led to her boyfriend handing our asses to us in the worst possible ways, but we did it together. Always. That's what we do. We're triplets.

Like now…

We're in this thing with Bryant Morelli together. We'll continue to be his "dogs" until he decides to let go of the leash. Or until Scout bites *him*.

Smirking at that thought, I turn off the vehicle, grab my bag, and climb out. Students are rushing around since it's nearing eight this morning. I'm not too worried about being late.

It's not like this fake college gig is going to last forever.

Harvard is on the horizon. Mom would be so proud.

Thoughts of Mom have me gritting my teeth. Because of the Constantines, she's serving some hard time. Malpractice. It's not her fault ugly people got uglier after their surgery. She was a plastic surgeon, not a fucking miracle worker. Winston Constantine, though, in his bitchy endeavor to ruin our lives, made sure to pull together quite a collection of people who could testify against my mother. His power, influence, and money sealed her fate.

Which is why I'm all too pleased to help fuck up his world again. Even if it's through less direct means. Stirring up shit for his family in an indirect way will feel like we're getting some retribution.

As though on cue, my knee twitches in pain. I went a little too hard on the treadmill this morning. I'll probably deal with the aftereffects of that fated day until I die.

Goddamn Constantines.

Ignoring the ache in my knee, I stride across campus to where my English class is located. Several hot chicks glance my way, coy smiles on their pretty lips. I acknowledge each with a smirk and a chin lift. Maybe I'll have better luck in finding a piece of ass at college. Tinder is a waste of fucking time.

I'm not here to hook up, though. I'm here to meddle in the Croft girl's life. Landry is her name. Like what the hell kind of name is Landry?

When I reach the classroom door, I peek in, searching for the girl I'm supposed to be following. Bryant had given me a physical description, but only had an older picture of her when she was like ten or eleven—all big teeth and frizzy blonde hair. Apparently, this chick doesn't have social media. So, I'm guessing I'm looking for a total nerd, because seriously, who doesn't have social media these days?

People chatter, the auditorium-style classroom echoing with the dull roar, while they wait for the instructor to begin, but my eyes are scanning the place for my target. Lots of nerds and lots of blonde ones, but I'm not getting spoiled rich girl vibes from any of them.

Until her.

One chick, toward the back, stands out in particular. She sits in a regal way—back ramrod straight, chin lifted, fingers clasped on top of the tabletop. The chick isn't exactly a nerd, but I wouldn't say hot either.

Her sleek golden-blonde hair reaches about shoulder length, grazing her delicate collarbone as it curls inward. Nice tits are hidden behind too much clothing for this time of year, much to my annoyance. At least if I have to bother with her, having a nice rack to look at would be a perk. It's clear she's wound tight and has a stick jammed so far up her ass, I'll never have a chance at pulling it out. My cocky smile and great physique are usually enough to get a woman to bend to my will, but something tells me Landry Croft will be different.

Some guy beside her with a lame-ass curly bush sprouting out of the top of his head is chirping things at her that only garner forced, polite smiles from her. He's clueless. She won't even look at him. The girl on her other side eyes me with interest and then leans in to whisper to a friend on the other side of her. I attempt to make eye contact with my mark, but she ices me and everyone else around her out, only looking ahead toward the professor's podium.

I drop my bag on bush boy's desk with a loud thunk, my laptop inside responsible for the sound. He jolts in surprise and quickly sizes me up. The wince I'm met with tells me he knows he's no match.

"You're in my seat, bro." I casually thrust a thumb behind me. "Move."

His mouth gapes open. "We don't have assigned seats—"

"Man, I didn't stutter."

Iciness prickles over my skin. It takes all of two seconds to realize the chill isn't coming from the air conditioner, but instead from the glare of the Croft girl. Good. She needs to understand I'm a part of her world now.

The dork at her side grumbles under his breath but complies with my demand. After he storms off, huffing insults under his breath as he passes me, I slip around the table and drop into the seat beside who I'm assuming is Landry.

"'Sup?" I give her my signature chin lift and smirk that makes women weak.

Her lip curls up in disgust. "You're an asshole."

So she has bite. A smile threatens to break free, but I stifle it. "And, after three seconds of being in here, I deduced you're a bitch. Guess that makes us partners."

She ignores me as she opens her notebook and neatly writes today's date at the top of her paper. I watch each precise move with interest. As soon as she's finished, she shoots me a sideways glare.

"Are you going to stare at me the whole time?"

I shrug and lean back in my seat, stretching my long, jean-clad legs out in front of me. Unfortunately, in order to fit in with the college vibe, I had to trade my suits in for this shit. "Probably. I hate English, so chances are I'll be bored as fuck within ten minutes. Looks like I'll have to settle for staring at you instead."

"I wouldn't waste your time," she mutters, somehow sitting even straighter than before.

True to my word, I let my gaze sweep over her small, upturned nose and down to her plump pink lips. For a stuck-up princess, her mouth is tempting. No fucking lie. I bet, if coaxed just right, she could suck dick like a champ. My cock twitches in my jeans at the thought of this icy princess on her knees between my parted ones.

"Ford," I lie, offering her my hand. "Ford Mann." A play off my last name, Mannford. It was my suggestion to Bryant when he was handling the behind-the-scenes crap like creating a false identity. Sue me for unoriginality. "And you are…"

She cuts her attention down to my hand and denies my touch altogether before turning her brightly blazing blue eyes to mine. "Landry Croft."

I was right.

Of course I was.

"Mmm." I smirk at her. "Laundry. An unusual name."

"*Landry*," she corrects in a scathing tone. Her nostrils flare and pink races across her creamy cheeks. "Find someone else to bug. Not interested." She turns forward and starts copying down into her notebook the stuff that's been written on the board.

I watch her try to evade me all of ten seconds before I can't stand it. The urge to poke at her is intense. Swiveling in my chair, I face her side and lean in so close I can smell her sweet perfume that clings to her shirt. Her entire body freezes and she doesn't move away.

"You," I murmur huskily near her ear, "don't have a choice. It's inevitable. Don't act like I'm not the hottest guy you've ever laid eyes on."

She scoffs, but it's such a lame attempt to cover up the fact she does find me attractive. I grin, leaning closer—so close I could nip at her earlobe if I chose to. I'm considering it when her hand moves swiftly. Something pointy pokes my dick.

This crazy chick is really about to stab my dick with her fucking pen?

Slowly, she turns toward me and uses her other hand to push at my chest. Considering she has a weapon aimed at my junk, I obey, retreating a few inches. Her eyes are flashing like bright blue electric lights. She's clearly taking pleasure in her upper hand.

"You're not going to stab me there."

She presses harder against my jeans. One slip and she's going to skewer one of my goddamn balls. I tense and grit my teeth, glowering at her.

"Won't I?" she taunts, a golden brow arching in obvious amusement.

Our stares lock, neither of us backing down. The longer I look at her, the more I decide she's completely fuckable. Once I melt the ice a bit first.

"Truce, Laundry?"

Despite her irritation, her lips quirk on one side. "Does that mean you'll stop talking to me for the duration of class?"

"Yeah. I like my balls."

"You'll give up just like that?"

"It's not giving up. It's a truce."

"Then what are you getting in return for said truce?"

I slowly reach down and curl my large hand

around her slender wrist, giving it a warning squeeze. She bravely jams the pen harder until I hiss at the sensation of the thing threatening to rip through my jeans and do real damage.

"I said we'll have a truce, woman. Fuck."

"And I asked what you'll get in return."

"Coffee later."

She shoots me a bewildered look. "Seriously? You think I'd actually have coffee with you or go with you anywhere *willingly*?" A dark laugh escapes her. "I don't have a death wish, dumb boy."

Boy.

What the fuck ever.

"You'll give in." I catch the eye of a girl gazing at me and wink at her. She blushes and turns away. "They always do."

"Maybe one of your groupies," Landry hisses. "But I'm not one of your groupies."

The professor walks into the room and light-ning quick, Landry jerks out of my hold, taking her wicked pen with her.

"*Yet*, Laundry. You're not my groupie yet." I grin devilishly at her. "But don't worry. We've got all semester."

We're going to turn your world inside out, little ice princess, and it's going to take a helluva lot less time than a semester.

CHAPTER FIVE

Landry

A NOTHER CLASS IN the same day with this idiot?

Ford Mann.

Ugh, great.

If my life were normal and he wasn't such an epic asshole, he'd be the kind of guy I'd be interested in. He's assertive and commands a room, but not in the same way I'm used to with my father. Something about Ford assures me that, even when being a douchebag, he could probably make me laugh and show me an epically awesome time. I think, if allowed, he might be the kind of guy who grows on me.

His cockiness aside, Ford is extremely easy on the eyes. Dark brown—nearly black—overgrown hair on top of his head is gelled back and the sides are trimmed short. The curve along his jaw is severe, compelling your eyes to travel its sensuous line. Dark facial hair sprinkles his cheeks as though he were too lazy to run a razor over it this morning, but it somehow looks stupid-hot and gives him a bad boy edge.

Everything about Ford seems effortless. Like he doesn't have to try too hard to look like a god who accidentally stumbled onto a college campus. It's just natural for him.

When his eyes—the color of dark maple syrup—meet mine, they flash with mischievous delight. I want to ignore him, but he makes it impossible. I manage to tear my gaze from his face and let it roam down his body as he approaches. At well over six feet, and muscles barely hidden behind a black T-shirt, he's a fine specimen of a man.

He'll ruin it by opening his mouth, though, in three…two…one…

"Are you stalking me, Laundry?" One of his dark eyebrows arches up in amusement. "I knew it'd only be a matter of time."

I bite down on the inside corner of my bottom lip hard enough to stab some sense into me. The sharp pain of the bite has me jolting my attention from him and back to my notebook— the same notebook I took pages of notes on in my

English class while Ford just stared at me.

"And it'll only be a matter of time before you fail," I grumble, trying not to tense when he drops into the seat beside me. "Time to go back to the Jersey Shore, douchebag."

He snorts out what sounds like a surprised laugh. "Bitch."

I shrug, doing my best to ignore him. But, that's nearly impossible when I can't seem to breathe without inhaling him. Whatever expensive cologne he's wearing makes my mouth water—like the scent of the sea with a hint of spice.

"Go away," I grumble. "You're annoying."

"I've been called a lot of things by chicks, but never annoying."

"Well, if you're using words like 'chicks' to describe the women you encounter, I seriously don't understand how you haven't been called worse than annoying."

"I like a *woman* who can verbally spar with me."

"Lovely. Bye."

The heat of his stare burning into the side of my head makes me fidget. I try not to squirm or even glance his way. Minutes pass by as we wait for class to begin. I'm almost able to pretend he doesn't exist until he reaches over and grasps the back of my chair. A shriek of surprise bursts out of me when he starts dragging me closer.

"What are you doing?" I snap at him. "Are you insane?"

"Nah, that's my brother." He flashes me a wolfish grin but it quickly melts away as a glimpse of some unidentifiable emotion passes over his features. "I told you. I'm not letting up until you give me what I want."

The gall of this guy.

If Dad knew I had a stalker, he'd flip out. Guys like Ford Mann are no match for my father. Dad's unlimited financial resources give him an epic position of power. It makes him a formidable opponent.

But, even as annoying as Ford is, I would never wish my father's wrath on him. My sister is subjected to it daily and it's a nightmare.

"Coffee?" I mutter. "You're still on that?"

"Yep."

"I already said no."

"I'm waiting for a yes, Laundry."

Pushy bastard.

"Not happening, Chevy."

A laugh bursts out of him, teasing one from my own lips. Ugh. He's bothersome. I don't like his laugh, so why am I softly laughing too?

"I'm growing on you," he says in a smug, satisfied tone.

"Yeah, like a tumor," I throw back.

"Look how much fun we're having." He waits until I peek his way to flash me a crooked grin that heats my blood. "See? You're not like them."

I follow the bored gesture of his hand to a few girls openly ogling him. They're all sexy and quirky and young. Dressed comfortably and casually. Obviously enjoying their college life. Those girls are everything I'm not.

And while probably their same age, I feel like I've lived decades—an old, weary soul trapped in a young adult's body.

"You make me work for it." He leans forward, his grin turning boyish. "I like the chase."

A thrill shoots down my spine. The idea of this big, beautiful man chasing me anywhere is almost too much to think about. It's a moot point anyway. I can't fantasize about some hot, obnoxious Jersey Shore wannabe frat boy when I have much more important things to worry about.

Like keeping Dad happy so he'll stay off Della's back.

And attempting to socialize with his fancy colleagues.

Despite my original fears of going to college and leaving Della to do so, it's actually a good thing. I might be able to meet some people who could help me if ever I needed it. I'll also have access to the university's media center. I can do all the research and planning I want for me and Della's future without fear of Dad spying on me.

The last thing he needs to discover is my dying need to escape him for good.

But, at school, I can do it safely.

Where would I take her? She'd love going to the beach. Or, better yet, someplace with animals she could visit. It'd have to be a small town where we could disappear into. I'd need fake identification. I'm not even sure how I'd go about obtaining something like that. Planning an escape—when you have to hide your tracks from your evil father and while you have no access to money—is slightly overwhelming.

Every time I think about running away, I wind up going in circles in my head, never coming up with something solid and actionable.

I bet Ford is a man of action. I bet he'd know exactly what to do in my situation. My heart squeezes as I wonder if I could eventually become close enough to anyone—like Ford or someone less douchey—here at college that I could confide in.

"This all isn't some effort to lure you into my bed," I tell him in exasperation. "It's to push you away indefinitely. I'm not a hurdle to jump."

"And yet I still want to jump you…"

Another stupid laugh escapes me and he joins in.

"Ford—"

"It's okay to secretly like me," he says as he reaches up to toy with a strand of my hair. "I think we could be great friends."

Friends.

The word almost seems foreign.

According to Dad, friends are people who want to use you in order to gain something for their benefit. They use people like him for his money and means and access to information. And by default, because of who I am, they'll use me too.

Does Ford know I'm the heiress to a tech fortune?

"What? You're disappointed that I'm not actively trying to get into your pants? I'll admit, Laundry, you're a tough nut to crack."

"I'm not disappointed," I spit out. Okay, so maybe slightly in a deep, hidden secret fantasy kind of way. "I just…" A sigh rushes from my lips. "I don't have many friends. It'd be a wasted effort on your end."

"With that pitiful attitude, it's no wonder why," he deadpans.

I elbow him in his chest, needing desperately for him to move the hell away from me. The giant beast of a man just laughs and slings his arm across the back of my chair. A guy on my other side darts his gaze to me, then to Ford, and then quickly peels it away.

"Are you glowering at that guy?" I turn to look at Ford. "You are!"

His narrowed eyes leave the guy and fall back on my face. I can't help but watch as his lips curl into a seductive smile that twists my stomach. "Just marking my territory."

"Your territory?" I shake my head in disgust. "You're gross."

"I'm too needy of a...*friend*...to share." He grins at me—wide and brilliant like the sun. "You're all mine."

I shudder at the way his words work their way through my veins. I shouldn't like those last three words so much, but I do.

"What will make you leave me alone?" I utter in defeat.

"I already told you. Coffee. After class."

For a split second, I imagine the two of us cozied up on a sofa at the nearest coffee shop, sipping coffee and trading barbs. It actually does sound kind of fun. Too bad I'm not allowed any of that. Even if I let my guard down for a minute, Dad certainly wouldn't allow it.

"I can't," I admit. "My driver will be here right after class, and I'll need to get back home to my little sister."

"You can't, but you'd like to?"

Truth isn't going to hurt anything.

"It wouldn't be a date." I narrow my eyes at him. "Not that it matters. But, if I could, it would just be coffee with a friend. Nothing more."

His syrupy eyes draw me in and hypnotize me. "So you do admit you're mine."

My jaw unhinges. "What? No."

"My *friend*," he clarifies. "And it's too late to take it back."

Thankfully, the professor walks in, ending our conversation. Something tells me, though, that he won't let up after class. Maybe I just need to accept that I've made a school friend. A stupidly hot, super annoying school friend, but a friend nonetheless. Della will be interested in hearing about this guy. I chew on my lip to keep from letting a smile escape.

It sneaks out anyway.

✧   ✧   ✧

"YOU KNOW," FORD says, smirking as he sidles up beside me in the hallway after our second class of the day, "I could give you a ride."

"You're a perv."

He laughs, the sound warming parts of me I'd never known existed. "Technically, *you're* the perv. I meant an actual ride. In my car. Not on my cock."

The mention of Ford's cock has a flood of heat coursing through me. I elbow him hard in his side and storm ahead of him. Based on his stupid laughter, I'd say he's enjoying tormenting me.

You enjoy it too…

I don't let myself dwell on that thought for too long.

A heavy, muscled arm wraps around my shoulders as Ford catches up. He's so touchy-feely. I hate that I barely know the guy and my body responds as though he's familiar to me.

I roll my eyes but don't shake him off. For a second, I can pretend I'm a normal college-aged woman with a good-looking guy who's interested in her. There aren't controlling, abusive fathers or little sisters who need looking after. There isn't pressure or stress or drama.

Several people glance at us as we walk by. I'm not sure what's drawing their attention. My money's on the sexy beast of a man who seems to be staking a claim on me. A flutter in my chest indicates just how much I like that idea.

Which is completely dumb.

I can allow myself a friend, but nothing more. Not when there's so much at stake. Blatantly going against Dad's expressed wishes at having me date someone in his power circle would be the worst possible thing I could do. Not only could he backtrack and keep me from attending college, he might somehow punish Della with his anger.

I'm feeling quite somber and dismayed that it takes me a second to realize we've stopped and Ford is speaking to me.

"This is the part where you're supposed to be impressed," he grumbles, waving his hand toward a sleek vehicle. "Seriously. We can't be friends if you won't even acknowledge my baby."

He's pouting.

Over a dumb car.

For some reason, this amuses me. It is, in fact, a gorgeous car, but the fact I haven't gushed over its beauty and he's pouting about it, has a bubble of laughter escaping. One attempt at smothering my giggling leads to an unladylike snort, which has me erupting with more laughter.

Ford releases me, muttering under his breath, and hits the fob. I bite on my bottom lip to contain my cackling. He flings open the door and gestures in overemphasis as if to prove the inside is just as pretty. It's the look of pure exasperation on his face that has me losing it again.

"You're a real bitch, Laundry," he grits out, though there's no real venom in his tone. "No one's ever laughed at my car before."

"You said I was different and you were right. I bet you're rethinking making me your friend." I arch a brow at him now that the giggling has faded. "See you around, Chevy."

His maple syrup eyes slowly peruse down my body, lazily drinking up every detail of me. I try not to squirm but when someone like Ford Mann is practically devouring you, it's hard not to.

"Let me take you home," he urges, his voice dropping several octaves and managing to reverberate through me. "I'll go slow."

The fire in his eyes says he's talking about more than just a ride in his car. He's talking about the ride of my life. All I'd have to do is give in.

Gravel crunches behind me and a sleek, black

Mercedes SUV pulls up. I recognize Trey, one of Dad's drivers, sitting behind the wheel. Time to go.

"My ride's here." I motion toward the Mercedes. "Maybe some other time."

Like never.

Unfortunately.

Ford peels his stare from me to give Trey a once-over. When his eyes find their way back to mine, they're harder than before and glint with something almost calculating. The warmth between us is snuffed out and a chill works its way down my spine.

"Goodbye, Ford."

"See you soon." He winks at me but the action is almost taunting. "That's a promise."

CHAPTER SIX

Sully

I COULD LEAVE New York.

Take my mustard-yellow Ford Bronco—a car I purchased with my own damn money I've earned here and there—and leave this stupid fucking city.

Leave Mom and my brothers.

The motherfucking Morellis.

Constantines and their superiority bullshit.

I'd pack up and head out west. Drive the scenic route the whole damn way, stopping to smell the roses at every chance. I always wanted to go to Cali. Maybe I could learn to surf. I'd be good at that shit, I bet. I'm not a suit like Sparrow, so I could be content working above a souvenir shop, spending all my hard-earned cash on surfer gear or whatever it is California dudes spend their money on. It'd still be a thousand times cooler than what my life consists of now. I'd be a helluva lot happier, that's for sure.

There's no California dreamin' for this big city boy, though.

Truth is, my dream of living my own life is just that. A dream. I know, deep down, I'll never leave my brothers. We're not just regular brothers. We're triplets. One third of something whole. Leaving would mean severing two of my limbs. I just can't do it.

So, I'll live in constant mental turmoil.

Or at least until I can convince Scout and Sparrow there's more to our lives than being Bryant's bitch trio.

Which is why I'm taking my badass Bronco toward the Hudson Yards. My yellow beast stands out like a sore thumb next to all the Maseratis, Bentleys, Bugattis, and other shiny sports cars Sparrow would nut over.

My surfer dreams will have to wait.

It doesn't take me long to reach the stunning eighty-eight floor building where I'm to take over my "shift" with the Crofts. This place is much nicer than anything I'm used to, and that's saying a lot considering my upbringing. I'm a little eager to check out the inside to see if it's even half as nice as the outside.

For fuck's sake.

Eager?

I want to punch my own self in the nuts for being even remotely eager about a fancy-ass building. *Get a grip, man.*

God, it's so lame that I'm stuck with this job. Naturally, Sparrow and Scout got the good assignments while I'm left with the stupid one. My job is to teach speechreading to the youngest Croft girl. Apparently, upon some quick internet research, it's basically teaching a deaf person to lip read. Seems easy enough and she's a kid, so I think I can pull it off, but it still sounds boring as fuck. I bet neither Sparrow nor Scout spent all night attempting to learn the basics of another language like I had to. I can sign the alphabet, but that's where my skills end. This ruse might end before it begins if I can't convince these people I'm an expert.

I'm honestly unsure what to even expect when I get in there. Of course my brother was worthless on communication. According to our chat when Sparrow got back home from class, he had an interesting and entertaining day with Landry.

That was all the information he gave up.

Interesting and entertaining.

He wouldn't even tell me if she was hot, but

based on the way he smirked, I'd say he thought so. Hell, knowing Sparrow, he probably fucked her already. This job Bryant has us doing is ridiculous, especially if Sparrow plans to be tightlipped about his encounter with her. Though we're triplets, we're so very different. The first time she faces off with Scout, that will be glaringly obvious.

Whatever.

If she finds out, then this charade will be over. Bryant can find some other way to fuck with Croft and the Constantines. Maybe he'll find something else to obsess over and leave us alone. It might be easier to convince my brothers to leave this hellhole of a city if we aren't on one of Bryant's little missions.

I try to imagine Scout as a surfer. He'd probably try to feed Sparrow to the sharks. That makes me smile despite my annoying predicament.

I turn into the C-shaped drive in front of the building the Crofts live in and push the button down for the window. A valet man dressed in a crisp navy uniform rushes my way, his face pinching with distaste when his gaze sweeps over my Bronco.

Fuck him.

Yellow looks cool as fuck.

"May I help you, sir?" he asks, standing a safe distance away from my vehicle.

I grab my wallet and flip it open, revealing the fake driver's license Bryant gave to each one of us. Same name on all three: Ford Mann. "I'm here for an appointment with, uh, Sandra I think."

He plucks my wallet from my grasp, studying the identification card. Finally, he gives me a curt nod as he hands it back. "Of course. She's expecting you, Mr. Mann. When you're ready for your car, just ring this number and I'll fetch it for you." He passes a ticket to me and then steps out of the way.

I slide out of the Bronco and head inside. I'd tried to mimic what Sparrow had been wearing—jeans and a black T-shirt—but I couldn't get my hair to do what his does since not everyone spends three quarters of their day in front of the fucking mirror and settled for a baseball cap instead. Close enough.

The building is swanky. I'm getting a few nasty looks since apparently there's a fucking dress code here. Everyone's wearing suits and dresses like it's a damn ball, not a residential building. I'm not some poor loser, though. I grew up wealthy, so I eyeball each and every asshole who attempts to look down on me until they avert their gaze.

A man in a security uniform approaches me to check my ID. I'm forced to stand there for several minutes while he scrutinizes it. I know Bryant's ID guy is good, because he works for the Morellis, but goddamn does it still make me feel like this security officer is seeing me for the fraud I am. After far too long, he eventually hands my ID back to me and points to a bank of elevators.

I wait for the doors to open along with an elderly woman holding a teacup poodle. It cocks its head at me as though it, too, is aware I don't belong here. If Scout were here, he'd probably growl at it. Since I'm not a total asshole, I reach over and scratch him on the top of his head. The old woman shoots me a dirty look. When the doors open, she purses her lips and steps onto the elevator, making sure to step all the way to the far corner.

"Miss Franks," a man in the elevator says in greeting. "Sixty-second?"

She gives him a clipped nod, not even bothering to acknowledge him. He looks my way after he mashes the sixty-two.

"You, kid?"

"Eighty-Eight."

The dog yaps at me and the woman scowls.

"That's the penthouse, mister."

"You have to have a code," the man says, frowning.

Since Bryant set all of this up, I do, in fact, have a code. With a smug smile at the bitchy woman, I punch in the numbers on the keypad and then hit the "P" for penthouse. The man smirks at me.

I pull out my phone, needing to do something for the long ass ride to the top. When the man and woman and judgmental pup are finally gone, I breathe a little easier. This place is so fucking stuffy.

I eventually make it to the designated floor and the doors open with a ding into a grand lobby area with high ceilings, marbled floors, and a tinkling fountain in the center. Across from the elevators, beyond the fountain, is a massive door to the penthouse, which happens to be ajar.

Something black flashes out the door and runs past me.

Rat?

The thought is so absurd for such a nice building, I almost laugh. But, a bigger creature with golden hair chases after it, momentarily startling me.

From within the residence, a woman is barking out the name Della over and over again, each time growing more agitated. Rather than heading toward the sound of the woman's voice, I turn left and follow after what must be Della, if I had to guess. I find her at one corner of the lobby area, crouched beside a plant, reaching her arm behind it.

The black flash I'd seen sounds much like a cat based on the furious hissing it's making. Despite the angry cries of warning, the little girl keeps up her attempt to grab the cat.

"Hey, kid."

No response.

A heavy sigh escapes me.

I tap the girl on the top of her head, since she won't be able to hear me. She whirls around, fire gleaming in her green eyes. Her hand swipes across my forearm, scoring the flesh hard enough to sting but not draw blood. Glowering at her, I shake my head. From the intel Bryant gave me, I learned she's deaf. No means no in every language, though.

She flips up her middle finger which would be comical if not for the fact she's like six or something. What the actual fuck. And, yeah, it too means the same damn thing in all languages.

"Back at ya," I growl, offering my middle

finger back.

Her eyes widen and her mouth parts as though she's shocked. She'll learn real quick, I'm not about to let some ankle biter push me around.

"Your momma is calling for you," I say, gesturing toward the sound of a voice around the corner.

Della snarls, baring her teeth. Feral little shit. Her hands move rapidly, no doubt signing something I'm meant to interpret. But, unlike my glowing fake resumé, I don't know American Sign Language. Something, despite my desire not to, I'll have to get more proficient at if I intend on keeping this ruse up.

Slowly, I sign to her one of the only things I've learned past the alphabet. *Hi, I'm Ford.*

Her eyes narrow, sharply watching my movements. Then, slowly, she spells out Della, punctuating each sign with irritated gestures.

"Della," I say, enunciating her name which earns me a nod.

She points toward the plant and then does more of the signing—which I'm pretty sure she's mocking me based on the sneer on her face—the letters C-A-T.

"If I get your cat, will you go back inside?"

She nods again, flashing me a devilish grin

that I don't believe for a second. No one warned me I'd be babysitting Satan's little princess.

I grip her delicate shoulders and manhandle her out of the way. Then, I kneel down to grab the poor cat that doesn't want anything to do with the evil brat. The cat meows in that creepy, leave me the fuck alone way, but I've already come this far. I curse when claws pop at my hand.

"Son of a bitch," I growl under my breath. "We both know this kid isn't giving up until she has you in her grip. May as well come willingly, heathen."

The cat continues its low, warning rumbling sounds, but it does inch my way. When it's close enough, I stroke a palm over its matted fur. Kind of strange for a cat to be in such a sad state when he appears to be the pet of one of the richest kids in the city. After some coaxing, the cat finally allows me to pull him into my arms.

"There you go. That's a good boy," I croon as I rise up on my feet.

The devil kid kicks me hard in the shin. Then she does that slow signing and spells out G-I-R-L. I roll my eyes and cuddle the cat closer. "You're a mean little shit. You know that?"

Della cocks her head to the side, blinking furiously. I'd been mumbling when I said the words, so she probably missed what I'd said. Probably for the best.

"Inside," I say sternly and pointing to her door, making sure she has no problem understanding that word.

She crosses her arms over her chest and lifts her chin. The defiance rippling from her is powerful. Della may have come into this world at a disadvantage because of her hearing impairment, but she makes up for it by being a baby tyrant.

But, I know all about being a brat. Me and my brothers were the world's worst at her age. Definitely takes one to know one. Takes one to be able to deal with one. With my free hand, I gently clutch the back of her neck and guide her alongside me. At first she resists, but then she gives in, walking willingly. We nearly run into a woman as she bursts out of the door.

"Della," the woman exclaims, making sure to also sign the words. "You are in big trouble, missy."

I take note that the devil spawn doesn't shoot her mommy the bird. Though, as I take in this woman's appearance, I don't think she's her mother at all. The woman is probably in her fifties, with dark hair streaked with some gray pulled into a no-nonsense bun. Her makeup is flawless. If it weren't for the wrinkles between her brows from apparently a lifetime of excessive frowning and old lady hair, she could pass for younger.

"Thank you, young man, for finding her. This one is precocious. Most days, she drives me insane." She studies me for a beat. "I'm Sandra Ellis. Mr. Croft hired me to manage the household. Are you the speech reader tutor?"

"That's me. Ford Mann." I glance down at the way I'm still gripping Della as though she might run off if I let go. "I'd shake your hand but…"

"I understand." Her nose scrunches. "Please tell me that's your cat and not hers. I've had to take the last three strays she found to be put down. Her father won't allow her to have a pet and she knows it. Not sure why she keeps trying."

Della stiffens, the muscles under my touch tightening. I decide to throw the kid a bone because Stepford Nanny here looks all too eager for another cat murder.

"Heathen's mine." I scratch the cat behind the ears. She growls in warning, like the little psychopath her real owner is. "It's good therapy for the kids." Whatever. It sounds legit.

Sandra purses her lips and nods slowly as

though she doesn't quite believe me. "If Mr. Croft has a problem with the animal, you'll need to take it elsewhere. Understood?"

"Yep."

"Excellent. Now, let's go inside. Della can have her snack while I show you around."

Sandra turns on her heel with robotic precision and glides into the penthouse. Creepy as hell if you ask me. I glance down at Della who glowers at the woman. When she catches me staring at her, Della looks up and smirks. Then, she flips off Sandra to her back.

Stifling a laugh, I guide Della through the door. The condo is lavish and expensive, nicer than any home I've ever been in. It has at least twenty-foot ceilings in the living room and glass for walls all along the far side. The view is pretty spectacular, I have to admit. Sandra closes the door behind us and then shoos Della off. The cat—Heathen, I guess is her name now—doesn't try to escape but remains tense in my grip.

"Mr. Croft believes that it's imperative for Della to improve her lip reading skills. Not everyone out there in the world will know ASL and he wants her to be able to effectively understand those around her," Sandra explains as she shows me to a space set up like a classroom.

"This is where Della takes her lessons. Your main point of contact will be myself, but in the event Della misbehaves or ignores you altogether, you may also seek assistance from her older sister. Landry is one of the few people she listens to."

Noted.

An easy way to access Landry. Maybe this job won't be so boring after all. Based on the way Della's acted thus far, it's obvious I'll be calling on Landry at every turn.

"Any questions? If not, I'll grab Della once she's finished her snack and return her to you. Feel free to look around and make yourself at home."

With those words, she pivots in one fluid motion like before and seems to float away like a goddamn ghost.

"If I set you down, you better behave," I tell Heathen. "Don't give that woman an excuse to put you down."

Heathen growls in what sounds like defiance, but I set her down anyway. She scurries away and slips between a desk and the wall. Just in time, too. The door opens with a creak. I turn around, expecting to see Della demanding to know where her cat is.

Instead, I see *her*.

Landry Croft.

Silky blonde hair. Pouty pink lips. Wide, bright blue eyes.

The shock on her face is amusing. A thrill shoots through me. Though I hate most jobs Bryant sends us on, I feel as though I might find a tiny bit of satisfaction with this one. Sparrow understated how beautiful Landry was. He'd used the word fuckable, and while the curves of her body are tantalizing to look at, there's something about her that is captivating.

"Ford?" she blurts out, a flush of pink stealing over her cheeks and throat. "What are you doing here?"

I flash her a wide grin. "It's my job."

"Your job?"

"I'm Della's speechreading tutor."

Her bewildered expression only makes her cuter.

This job just got a whole helluva lot better.

CHAPTER SEVEN

Landry

HOW?

How is Ford Mann in my home?

He watches me, a brow arched slightly. The way he studies me somehow feels more probing than from before. Not in the taunting way. This time it's more…intimate.

Is it because we're alone?

In my home?

"Are you even qualified?" I demand, swallowing down my surprise at seeing him and allowing concern for my sister to rise up. "You have to take this seriously. My little sister isn't some joke."

Clearly affronted by my words, he frowns, a crease between his brows forming. I can't help but drop my gaze to his mouth. Earlier, it'd been twisted into a boyish, teasing grin. Now, his lips are practically pursed in agitation. It bothers me that our easy banter from before has seemed to disappear. The air between us cackles with uncertainty.

"I can handle it," he bites out.

"You're acting…different."

Aside from the small tick of his jaw, he doesn't react to my words. Just stares me down like an asshole. With the dumb baseball cap on, he looks like even more of a douchebag than from before. It makes me want to knock it off his head.

"I've had a bad day," he says finally.

I flinch at his words that feel like a blow. In our classes, he seemed like he was having a great day. Was this because I rejected a ride home from him?

"Mine hasn't been so great either," I spit back, hoping to sting him with my venomous words.

His features soften and his lips quirk on one side. "Liar."

The rumble of his voice as he says that one taunting word has me forgetting why I'm annoyed with him in the first place. He takes a step toward me but it's hesitant. As if he's testing the waters with me. I don't budge. I'm not about to back away from him and have him thinking he has the upper hand here. The challenge in my stance must call to him because he continues his approach—no, his prowl—toward me until he's so close I think I can feel the warmth of his chest against mine.

"You have a problem with personal space, Chevy."

He darts his eyes back and forth. Earlier, they'd been the color of maple syrup, but with the late afternoon sun shining in through the windows and bathing his flawless features, they're lighter. Like melted caramel. I'm in trouble if I keep associating sweet foods with this guy.

"Chevy?" he asks. "A play on my name?"

Oh, God. He's a dumb jock who probably took one too many blows to the head on the football field or something.

"Forget it," I mumble. "I'm serious about what I said. You better not be using Della to get to me. Because if you are, that's really freaking creepy, Ford. First stalking me in my classes and now this?"

"Stalking you?" His lips twitch. "I literally just met you. Careful, if your head gets any bigger, honey, you're going to have problems getting back through that door."

I scoff at his words, ignoring the use of honey altogether. Has he graduated from Laundry to honey? Jesus, this guy moves fast.

"Maybe I should observe," I threaten. "To make sure you're not up to anything weird."

"Now who's the stalker?"

I poke his solid chest right in the center. "Whatever game you're playing, I'm going to figure it out. I'm not some stupid heiress you can toy with."

His hand lifts and he curls it around my wrist. The grip on it tightens, but not to the point of pain. Possessive, maybe.

"If I were playing a game, you'd be powerless to stop it." His smug grin is nauseating. "You'd lose, honey."

Again with the honey.

"Remember," I bite back, jerking from his grip. "I'm on a first name basis with your balls."

"You've met my balls?"

My God he's an idiot. I snag a pencil off the desk nearest to me and swing my hand up. The moment the tip presses against him through his denim, he stills, his face paling.

"What the fuck, woman?"

"Clearly you needed reminding."

He studies me for a long beat before nodding his acquiescence. "I promise to be a good boy. Happy?"

Despite having a pencil pointed at his balls, he

smiles. The kind of smile that starts small but increases with power the more it grows. Kind of like the sun rising above the horizon. A small ray of light and then it becomes warm, blanketing every inch of your skin and soaking into your bones. Certainly a smile he's never shown me until now.

I hate that I like it. A lot.

The warmth that radiates from him burns my skin, especially at my cheeks. It's annoying that he'll be able to see how he affects me. Based on the growing radiance of his grin, he knows.

"Happy?" I grumble, stepping back and no longer aiming at his balls. "Not sure I even know what that means."

The truth I've just blurted out tastes bitter on my tongue. This smiling, gorgeous douchebag gets a front row seat to my ugly truth. Lovely.

He lifts a hand and I freeze, wondering what he plans on doing to me. Shock jolts through me when his finger hooks under my chin and gently lifts until his eyes are boring into mine. My heart stutters and then stalls altogether when he leans in.

Is he going to kiss me?

Am I going to let him?

"You can trust me," he murmurs, his breath

tickling my face. "Promise."

I've never wanted to believe a lie so badly in my entire life. His whispered, tender words tease me into a false sense of security, but underneath, something hides. I can sense it with Ford. Beneath what he allows me to see, darkness lurks.

I know this because I live in the abyss.

What kind of monsters are you hiding, Ford Mann?

"Kind of early in this relationship for me to believe your words at face value," I say, taking another step away from him. His hand falls and his smile transform into a smirk.

"Relationship?"

"Don't be a tool. Friendship. We're friends. I guess."

A deep, rumbling laugh erupts from him. "You guess? Do you make it difficult for everyone to get to know you?"

Yes.

I don't have time for people or distractions.

His softness is different than before at school. Unexpected but not hated. It's warm and inviting. I have this overwhelming desire to step closer so he'll wrap me in a hug like a human-shaped blanket.

Ugh. He didn't suddenly turn sweet on me

and he's not some potential boyfriend. He's still the grade-A douchebag I met at school.

Ford Mann has layers and he's dangerous to someone like me, because he has this crazy way of disarming me with his charming smiles and unpredictable words.

"I have homework. I'm leaving now," I state in the iciest tone I can muster despite the heat flooding through me. "Be good, or else."

With those words, I turn on my heel and escape the room before I divulge more inner parts of myself that don't need exposing.

There's just something about him that makes me want to tell him everything. He draws me to him. Even his secrets call to me.

I want to know him.

And that scares the hell out of me.

IT'S ALMOST BEEN an hour and Della hasn't scared Ford off yet, so they must have connected in some way. Every now and again, I hear his low voice speaking to her, but it never raises or seems agitated. I'm perched in an armchair with a book in the living room under the guise of reading, but really I'm just keeping an eye—or an ear in this case—on things. As much as I want to trust Ford,

I don't.

I can't.

The clacking of Sandra's heels on the wood floors draws my attention. All the hairs on my arms stand at attention. I pretend to be engrossed in my book, making an obvious show of turning the page, even after the sound of her heels stop. If she knows I'm micromanaging the new tutor, she'll tell Dad. If she tells Dad, he'll dig in and want to know more about this tutor. It'll put a microscope on Della and I can't have that.

Plus, if Dad realizes the tutor is incredibly hot, he might fire him on the spot.

No, it's better to feign disinterest.

"Miss Landry?"

"Hmm?" I don't look up from my book.

"Your father wanted me to let you know that tomorrow night you'll be entertaining a guest at dinner."

My eyes fly to hers, brows knitting in confusion. "Me?"

"Yes. He said he'll have Lucy bring by some appropriate dress options."

Good ol' Lucy. My personal shopper. Because heaven forbid I'm allowed to actually shop on my own. That would require letting me off the leash and Dad has a strong hold on it. If he'd let me loose, even for one day, to shop, I could probably buy and return enough stuff to stash away a good amount of cash for an escape.

But since that isn't an option, I'm still penniless and without a plan.

"Who's the guest?" A prickly uneasy feeling spreads across my flesh. "Do I know them?"

Sandra flashes me a brilliant, practiced smile. "It's his new protégé, dear. Ty Constantine."

Constantine.

As in the influential and seriously wealthy gods of New York City.

"Wait. Dad's protégé is also the guy he wants me to have dinner with?" I clarify, irritation churning my gut.

"You know how your father likes to control all the moving parts and ensure the end result is to his satisfaction." She waves a manicured hand in dismissal. "It'll be better this way. Allowing anyone access into the Croft empire is risky and dangerous. You know this."

I want to pick her apart for more answers regarding this topic, but all thoughts come screeching to a halt when Ford enters the living room with a cat in his arms and my little sister at his side.

I gape at him.

A cat?

He gives me a half shrug, not at all bothered by the way the filthy feline is clawing long snags in his shirt. Dad would have a cow for so many reasons right now—cute boy, mangy cat, and my deaf sister. The idea of Dad walking in on this gives me such anxiety, the room tilts and bile rises in my throat.

I'm vaguely aware of Sandra shooing Della to her room and telling Ford goodbye before she disappears back to her office within our home.

Then, silence.

I snap out of my daze and rise to my feet. After sliding on my shoes, I slip out of the penthouse, hoping to catch up to Ford.

Why?

Because I want to talk to him—to learn all there is to know about him. Like why he's doing this job and why he's so interested in me. I want to know what he's hiding.

Mostly, I want to know if he meant it…that I could trust him.

As much as I know it's a bad idea, I want to. I don't have friends or people I can rely on. It's just me and Della in this big, awful world. Having a person to count on seems almost too good to be true.

By the time I catch an elevator to the lobby of the building, I'm sure he's long gone. I shoulder past some men in suits lingering near the entrance, trying to catch a peek. When I make it outside, I don't see Ford's shiny Audi he loves so much.

What I do see confuses me.

An obscenely yellow Bronco idly rumbles as Ford hands one of the valet men a wad of cash. Ford doesn't notice me as he climbs into the vehicle. He guns the engine, squealing as he takes off. I stare after the vehicle wondering just how many cars Ford Mann has.

More questions.

No answers.

The urge to look him up on the internet is a temptation I nearly fall victim to. But, searching him out means leading Dad right to him since he watches my digital activity like a hawk. Right now, no matter how much he annoys me, Ford is something in my life that's mine.

My "friend."

My secret.

Mine.

CHAPTER EIGHT

Sparrow

I T'S TOO FUCKING quiet.

I hate when it's quiet.

When we're all three home, our twenty-three hundred square feet apartment in the heart of Tribeca doesn't feel big enough, and it's loud. There's always a game or movie on the television in the living room. Someone is always talking or bitching.

I rock in my recliner just to hear the squeak over and over again. Our two brown recliners are ugly as fuck but super comfortable. This apartment, a nearly five-million-dollar gift from our uncle, Bryant, had some hard-ass pretentious armchairs once upon a time. As soon as we moved in a year ago, we took them to the dumpster and bought these instead.

This might be Morelli property, but to us, it's

home.

Just like every guy, I've wondered what it would be like to be on my own. I wouldn't have to clean up the messes Scout leaves in the kitchen every goddamn night or put up with Sully during football season. But then it would always be too quiet and really fucking lonely. It's comforting having them near me. I feel like it'll always be that way.

Growing up, I've always had my brothers right there by my side every step of the way. We played lacrosse together ever since we were old enough to hold a stick and were placed in all the same classes because money talks. Back then, because of Mom, we had lots of it. The three of us ruled every setting we were in because we ruled as one.

After all the shit that happened when we were stupid eighteen-year-old dicks, we've been fractured. The close bond we once had has been severed and we haven't seemed to find a way to glue it back together. Sometimes, I wonder if it was Mom all along who held us tight, and now that she's rotting away in prison, we're drifting apart toward our own corners of the universe. Still, despite all the crap we've been through, I can't imagine my life without them.

Needing to get my mind off depressing shit like being alone and missing Mom, I flip through my phone. There's nothing to be discovered about Landry, but I'm cool with plucking those threads of information from her each time I see her. It's her father I want to know more about. He's the key that'll unlock access into the Constantine world. The three of us have been desperate in our own ways to seek retribution for what Winston did to us.

He fucked us on so many levels. So many goddamn levels.

This job Bryant has tossed our way is the most entertaining shit we've been allowed to do. It fulfils an emptiness I'd been struggling to get a hold on. I have purpose.

Maybe Sully was right…

We've been existing but not living.

Puppets in the Morelli show.

I scroll through every news article I can find on Alexander Croft. Everything I read, they all kiss his ass and praise him for being the next Steve Jobs. A brilliant tech genius with a knack for turning gaming code into billions of dollars. He's loaded and his wealth continues to grow exponentially each year.

It takes some digging but I learn that his wife,

Evie, passed away not long after the birth of her second daughter. The reporters gloss over the shattering loss in a rare show of respect for the family's privacy, and instead, focus on the mastermind himself.

And Landry?

It's as though she and her little sister are ghosts who don't exist. There are photos of Alexander, Evie, and Landry when she was younger, but then they cease to be for the past six years or so.

She's definitely being protected by that daddy of hers.

Why?

My dick stirs at the reminder of our encounters today. I fucking know why. The press would eat her up. Sassy and smart and sexy as fuck. Media outlets love their billionaire heiresses. They're more than happy to follow them around, documenting every second of their lives.

In a way, I kind of respect the guy for protecting her against the pricks of the world. Unfortunately for the both of them, the worst pricks find their way in anyway.

Like me and my brothers.

We're an infection, slowly spreading into the Croft world.

Alexander and his precious daughter are simply a door for us. An opening to damage our real opponent. Winston Constantine and the whole damn family. Our ex-stepsister, Ash, included.

I'm not obsessed like Scout is, so I don't check in on Winston and Ash, but I've heard him rant enough to know the current status. They're happily in love and living the billionaire dream.

Scout wants nothing more than to destroy that man.

Winston is untouchable, though. We learned that the hard way. His family, however, are not.

Retraining my thoughts, I dive back in on my hunt for more Croft shit that might be juicy or useful. So far, everything is squeaky clean. We'll just have to get the nitty gritty from Landry herself.

My dick twitches again.

I'm willing to do whatever is necessary. Getting that mouthy girl naked and beneath me sounds like less of a hardship and more of a job perk—one I'd be really, really good at. Lost in my fantasy, I barely notice when Sully walks in through the door. It's the strange, unhuman sound that emanates from him that has me darting my gaze his way.

"Heathen, meet Sparrow. Sparrow, this is

Heathen." Sully is scowling and there's a cat clinging to his chest, hanging by its claws, and angrily lashing its tail. Blood dots his flesh up and down his forearms.

"You have a cat?" I arch a brow, unable to bite back a laugh. "What the fuck?"

"*We* have a cat." Sully's jaw clenches and he gestures at the growling creature. "And *we're* going to give her a bath."

"Nope." I give him a sharp shake of my head. "Hell no."

"I wasn't asking, dickwad. I can't do this by myself. This cat is an asshole."

"Then why'd you get it?"

Ignoring me, he storms off down the hall. I rise to my feet, unable to stay away despite my words, and follow him into his bedroom. It's more fun to watch your brother suffer than to imagine it. I peek my head in his bathroom to find him struggling to pluck the cat from his shirt while the water in the tub fills.

"Seriously, man. Why'd you bring home a cat?" I grip the top of the doorframe and lean in. "Since when do you like cats?"

"Since never," he grumbles. "The kid likes cats."

The kid?

"Landry?"

He scoffs. "No. Her little sister. It's my job to get in good on that front. Spy and whatever. Remember?"

"She's fucking hot, isn't she?"

"Kind of a bitch if you ask me." He manages to free the cat from his shirt, but it claws the shit out of his arm in the process. "Jesus, Heathen, calm your tits. I'm trying to wash this filth off your scrawny ass."

Feeling sorry for my brother, I take pity on him and sidle up next to him. That cat is going to flip its shit the second its paws hit the water. It'll definitely take the two of us.

"Landry is a total bitch," I say, grinning. "But it's kind of her best quality."

"Her lips are her best quality," Sully argues, not missing a beat. "I'll hold Heathen down. You wash her. Watch your fingers. She'll probably bite them the fuck off as payback."

I grab the shampoo bottle, readying myself as he lowers the cat into the warm water. It lets loose a howl straight from a fucking nightmare. Creepy-ass cat. "Lips, huh? You're such a bleeding heart, man."

"Dick sucking lips," Sully throws back. "You know what I mean."

"You act like I don't know you, Sull. It's okay. You think she's pretty."

"Does it matter what I think?" He dunks the cat, earning more claw marks down his forearms and his subsequent cursing. "Shampoo."

I squirt a lot on the disgusting cat. She needs like ten baths, not just one. "Did Landry suspect anything was up?"

"She was skeptical and wary." He wrestles with Heathen when she tries to make her escape and manages to pin her. "Seriously. A little heads-up next time about this chick would be nice so I don't fuck us over with one encounter."

"She hates being called chick," I supply with a chuckle.

"Really helpful, Sparrow. Super fucking helpful."

He asked. Not my fault he doesn't like my answers.

"She tried to stab me in the balls," he mutters. "Like I said. Bitch."

"The chick went after mine, too." A grin steals across my face. "I thought I was going to lose one of my nads. Maybe both. It was touch and go there for a bit."

Sully scowls at me. "This shit isn't going to work. I don't like it."

Sometimes Sully can be such a baby. He doesn't like when Bryant keeps us tethered to him. He doesn't like when Bryant sends us on jobs. He doesn't want this life. Yet, he's still here. Bitching about it every damn day to make me crazy.

Heathen makes a break, slipping from Sully's grasp. I manage to grab the dirty beast before she escapes the tub, but not before earning myself the sharp end of her claws down my forearms.

A lot of cursing and struggling ensues, but we finally manage to get the cat washed and somewhat dried in a towel. The next time she makes her escape, we let her go. She bolts out of the bathroom and disappears, meowing loudly and in a way that sounds like a kitty version of a "fuck you both."

We take a few minutes in silence to clean up our scratches before heading back to the living room. I'm a little surprised to see Scout's made it home. What's more surprising is that he's sprawled out on the sofa on his side with a damp, purring cat curled up against his chest, staring at the double-sided custom quartz fireplace that's lit and flickering despite the fact it's like seventy degrees outside.

"Is that cat fucking purring?" Sully demands,

slight outrage in his tone. "After I saved its damn life?"

Scout settles his palm on the bad cat's back and strokes his fingers through its wet fur. The purring grows louder. "The cat is fucking purring," Scout says in a mocking tone. "Don't be mad, little bro."

Sully's not little and the same age as Scout, but his words always hit their intended mark, successfully rankling him. He flips Scout off before throwing himself into a recliner. His scowl is comical to me, reminding me of when we were little and he wouldn't get his way.

Fuckin' baby.

"You two look like twins," Scout unhelpfully points out, darting his gaze between me and Sully's matching outfits.

"We're triplets, douchebag," I grumble. "Just wait until it's your turn to dress just like us. It's kindergarten all over again."

Scout's features darken and my stomach tightens. Mentioning the way Mom used to love dressing us alike was probably a bad move. Triggering for damn sure. Sully stiffens uncomfortably. Neither of us are in the mood to stop a Scout psycho meltdown.

"Speaking of our job," Scout says, speaking

coolly as he glosses over my comment, steering the conversation to this bullshit Bryant signed us up for. "I went to mine today. I'm a pee-on associate a floor below the execs."

I plop down on the end of the sofa, shoving Scout's feet out of the way and shoot him an expectant look. "And? Learn anything useful?"

"So far, nothing." He absently strokes the cat. "But, don't worry, I'll get there."

His dark eyes glint in an evil way that never fails to unsettle me. Based on Sully's silence, I'd say he feels the same. I'm secretly thankful Scout's not going to be dealing with Landry. For one, she'd know something was up right away. At least me and Sully can pass for one another, but Scout?

Fuck no.

Neither of us is that insane and cold.

Plus, if he had to interact with Landry, he'd probably snap the first time she gave him lip. While I find it hot as hell, Scout will lose his mind. Then…

It will be Ash all over again. Our stepsister was supposed to be a game. We were to toy with her. Scout's obsession changed everything. It took us to levels in a game we had no business playing.

If he were to zero in on Landry the way he did with Ash, it could fuck everything up. Last time nearly cost us our lives.

I catch Sully's stare. He must read what's on my mind because he offers me a slight nod. We need to keep this gig the way it is—Scout away from Landry so we don't find ourselves repeating the past.

"I ordered some shit for Heathen," Sully says, tossing his phone aside. "Maybe she'll remember who saved her and reassess her loyalties."

Heathen hisses at him.

What a bitch.

A loud bang in the hallway outside our apartment sends Heathen jolting from the couch and under a bookcase. In the next second, Scout flies off the couch toward the sound. It takes me a second to realize Scout has a black Glock in his hand to answer the door.

Holy shit.

"What?" Scout snarls after opening the door and pointing the weapon at the guy's chest. "Who the fuck are you and why are you trying to beat your way inside my apartment?"

The dude in the hall is wasted and obviously confused. Not someone trying to break in or whatever the hell Scout believes. Slowly, I rise to my feet and inch toward our unhinged brother.

"Thisss isn't my place," the guy slurs, a confused expression twisting his features as he looks past Scout at me. "Whoops." He cracks up laughing. "Don't shoot, bro." More laughter.

For fuck's sake, Scout might shoot him just to shut his annoying ass up.

Scout doesn't lower the gun. His finger is curled around the trigger. One sudden sneeze and the drunk guy's brains would paint the wall behind him.

"I'll walk him to the elevator," I tell Scout in the calmest voice I can muster. "Dumbass got lost."

Scout doesn't resist when I gently push his arm down. When the gun isn't pointed at the guy's head, I breathe a little sigh of relief. Not for the drunk's sake, but for ours. I'm not about to let our lives get fucked over this piece of shit.

"Be right back," I assure Scout. "Order Thai. I'm fucking starving."

The trance Scout had been in seems to fade and he blinks before nodding. I glance back at Sully. The relief on his face is palpable. We dodged a bullet. Literally.

I drag the guy to the elevators, having to keep him from busting his face several times along the way. Knowing Scout won't have to encounter Landry settles my erratically beating heart.

Because if I didn't know my brother owned a gun—that he clearly wasn't afraid to use—there's no telling what else I don't know about him.

This job to fuck with Landry is fun.

I don't need my crazy-ass brother spoiling my fun.

Chapter Nine

Landry

THIS EVENING IS going to be a royal disaster.

Dinner with some guy my freaking dad is setting me up with. He could be a total nerd or a giant douchebag. Worse, he could be someone just like my father.

Controlling. Cruel. Cold.

Every nerve in my body is electric and alive in anxious anticipation.

Breathe, Landry.

I refocus my attention to the mirror. My blonde hair shimmers in the light, the ends bouncing at my bare collarbone with each movement I make. The Paco Rabanne floral print dress that Lucy recently brought me hugs my curves yet is still tasteful with a below the knee length. I've paired it with my favorite pair of patent leather Louboutin pumps. I might feel sick to my stomach with worry, but I at least look put together.

A long sigh rushes past my lips, exhaling the last of my unease. It's time to put my game face on and play the part of perfect daughter. At least tonight I won't have to worry about Della. I'd helped her get ready for bed and then I read her one of her favorite stories. She fell asleep without putting up a fuss.

I can do this.

"Something bothering you?"

The deep timbre of Dad's familiar voice vibrates and can be felt in each bone in my body. Like an aftershock of an earthquake, my teeth chatter noisily and against my will. Gritting them together, I turn and face my father, a forced smile on my face.

I expect to see his adoring expression.

But that's not at all what's looking back at me. It's the same cruel stare he uses on Della. I freeze mid-step toward him, at a loss for words.

"Landry, sweetheart," Dad says, words sharp and biting, "I'll tell you what's bothering me instead."

Swallowing, I barely manage a nod. He slowly steps into my room and then walks—no, stalks—my way. I fist my hands at my side to keep the trembling at bay.

"W-What's bothering you?" I whisper, unable to lift my head and meet his stare now that he's only inches from me.

Please don't say Della…

"This." He motions at my dress. "This is dinner you're going to, not a hotel for paid sex."

I flinch at his words, jerking my head up to gape at him. "But, Dad, this one was one of Lucy's picks. You bought me this dress—"

His hand seizes my jaw, and spittle hits my face as he growls, "I bought you every goddamn dress in your closet. This one is all…wrong. I'm going to have a serious fucking talk with Lucy about what she thinks is acceptable."

Struggling to keep the tears at bay, I blink furiously. Every day is a minefield in this home. You never know which misstep will obliterate you. Clearly, I've put my foot on the mine and the second I try to escape, it's going to blow.

"I'm sorry," I croak out. "Which dress should I wear instead?"

"The black Shoshanna puff sleeve dress will do." He narrows his eyes which are slightly bloodshot. Based on the scent of liquor emanating from him, I know why, too.

He's drunk.

Or at least, fast getting there.

And he always promises he'll never let it happen again. Just wine. Wine is safe. Whichever hard liquor he's tried to drown himself in is anything but safe.

"I love that dress," I agree, my voice a mere whisper. "I'll go change."

"Good girl." He doesn't release his grip on my jaw. "You need to understand something about tonight. This dinner is nothing more than a power move. It's a chance to align ourselves with one of the wealthiest families in the world."

"I understand."

He shakes his head slowly. "No, you don't. You will not make this easy for him. I will not have my daughter whoring herself out on the first date." His eyes narrow. "You'll take your time and drag this out for as long as I say. I want to make sure this arrangement is beneficial to us in every way. You winding up pregnant or ending up on the cover of every tabloid magazine in compromising photos will not happen."

"Dad…"

"Change your dress and wipe that goddamn lipstick off. I can't look at you right now."

Without another word, he releases me and storms from my room. Tears well in my eyes, blurring the room in front of me, as I try desperately to get air to enter my lungs. It's as though a vise is clamped around my throat, keeping me from taking a breath.

I remain frozen for God only knows how long and am only jolted into movement at the sound of the doorbell. The sound of men speaking to each other can be heard which means my dinner date is here. Quickly, I rush into my large closet and strip out of my dress. I exchange it for the dress Dad wants me to wear. Once I've pulled the material into place, I leave the closet to make my way to my vanity.

The girl staring back at me doesn't feel like me. This girl is haunted. Terrified. So tired.

I use a makeup pad to remove the lipstick and exchange it for a soft pink gloss instead. Since my eyes keep threatening to spill over with tears, I take a minute to touch up my eye makeup. Finally, I feel like I could be presentable and acceptable in my father's eyes.

Yesterday, I let Ford distract me at school, but tomorrow, I'm going to try and slip out of class early to do some research in the media center since I won't have security breathing down my neck like at home. Maybe I can figure out a way to access my trust fund without him knowing. As it stands, the second I attempt to withdrawal any of it from the bank, they'll notify him to make sure it's allowed. Which it's not. The twenty bucks he gave me this week for coffee and snacks at school won't get me very far. I know he probably keeps a stash of money and jewels in his safe, but that's a risk I can't take again. What's in there that's so valuable anyway?

At this rate, I'm never going anywhere. He's smarter than me and always ten steps ahead. Every time I think I have some grand idea, reality squashes it.

The quicker I can figure out a plan to get me and Della the hell out of here, the better. I thought I had more time, but after the way Dad acted just a bit ago, I realize I was foolish to ever think anything was in my favor, especially time.

His cruelty isn't often pointed at me, but when it is, it always ends badly.

Calling the police won't help since they're all deep in his pockets. Reaching out to people like Noel or Sandra or even one of the drivers, like Trey, won't work because they're all completely intimidated by him and are always doing their best to impress him.

Money talks.

Dad has endless piles of it.

I'm at a complete disadvantage here.

Lifting my chin, I stride out of my bedroom, hoping for an air of self-confidence. All depressing thoughts of my future are shoved into the corners of my mind when I am mentally prepared to deal with them. I'll be the polite, demure heiress Dad wants me to be, and make my way through this dinner without any further damage.

I can do this.

Following the sound of the voices, I walk into the dining room where both my father and a man in a fitted suit stand chatting amicably. Funny how only moments ago, Dad was in my bedroom, his anger washing over me like a tsunami. Now, he's seemingly normal, putting on his pleasant show for our guest.

Clearing my throat, I alert my father to my presence. Both men turn to regard me. Dad's features are tight but he's wearing his business smile reserved for boardroom deals. The man beside him, despite my not wanting to look at him, draws my attention anyway.

Oh, wow.

Definitely wasn't expecting someone so…handsome.

Unlike Ford, with his devilishly sexy good looks, this man appears to have fallen from heaven—all golden skin and perfectly styled dark blond hair. His blue eyes sparkle as he rakes his gaze over my form. A smile curls his lips up and reveals a perfect row of pearly white teeth. He takes a step forward and offers a hand.

"Tyler Constantine, er, Ty." His grin grows wider. "You must be the lovely Landry Croft. I've heard a lot about you."

Dad's irritation clouds the air around me. I don't have to look at him to know he's fuming with it.

"Nice to meet you," I say, as I take his hand. "I've heard lots about you as well."

Lies.

Ty's hand is slightly clammy in mine as he squeezes it and gives it a shake. Something about the fact that he might be nervous too calms me considerably. There's a kindness in his expression that's disarming.

And I absolutely cannot afford to be disarmed when in the presence of my father.

Jerking my hand from his, I force a wide smile. "Thank you for joining us for dinner." Dad steps between us and his palm finds the small of my back. He guides me over to one of the dining room chairs. It feels like a blatant show of possession. As though he wants to remind everyone in the room that I'm his and he's allowing this other man to be present. Dad pulls out the chair and I sit in it. He takes the seat on the end and Ty sits in Della's usual spot across from me.

"So," I say too cheerily, "you're working with my dad? How are you liking it?"

Noel slips into the dining room with a bottle of wine. We all pretend she isn't here as she pours our drinks and Ty prattles on about how excited he is to work with my father.

"Mr. Constantine is doing a wonderful job thus far." Dad drains his wineglass and gestures it toward Ty. "He's a natural."

Ty's cheeks turn pink and he offers me a sheepish grin. "Thanks, Mr. Croft."

"It's Alexander in my home," Dad says, smirking. "Tomorrow morning, though, it'll be business as usual."

While dinner is served and the two of them discuss some things they worked on today, I keep sneaking glances over at Ty. He's really cute, but the fact that he seems nice, too, is a huge relief. I find myself relaxing and joining in on the conversation much more easily than before. Dinner seems to pass quickly as Ty regales us with funny tales of college life and that of his place in the Constantine family.

Dad's phone rings and he excuses himself from the table and stalks across the living room to his office. Ty smiles at me, his blue eyes gleaming with interest. I blush at his attention, biting back a smile of my own.

"I'd like to take you out, Landry. Just the two of us. I think…" He glances toward the doorway. "I think we'd both feel a lot more comfortable without him breathing down our necks."

A cold sweat trickles down my spine.

"I don't know if that's a good idea," I murmur, body tensing. "Dad is…overprotective."

"You think?"

Ty is definitely a lot more playful when not in Dad's presence, but that just puts me on edge. With Dad, you always have to be on guard. You can't be playful. You just can't.

"Hey," he says when I don't answer. "You okay? You're white as a ghost."

Swallowing down the ball of stress in my throat, I nod vigorously. "I'm fine. It's just—"

My words are cut off when Dad strides back into the room. I dart my gaze to my food hoping like hell I don't look guilty. But, he sniffs out guilt like a dog with a bone. The air thickens with furious tension.

"Mr. Constantine," Dad clips out. "I hate to cut the evening short, but it appears my daughter isn't feeling well. You'll forgive us for not extending our evening to a nightcap after dinner, right?"

Ty glances at me but then slowly nods. "Oh, sure. Yeah, no problem, Alexander." He rises to his feet. "I guess I'll get going. Dinner was great, but the company was better."

Though they're both standing, I wisely remain seated. I wriggle my fingers at Ty in farewell, but don't dare try and shake his hand again. The two of them walk out of the dining room, leaving me to my spinning thoughts. When I'm sure I can stand without my knees buckling, I make a hasty exit, heading straight for my bedroom.

I hate this place.

I hate *him*.

I've barely made it into my room when thunderous footsteps can be heard behind me. I swivel around to face my father's furious glare.

But this is more than an angry look.

He's pissed and he pounces before I can prepare for it. The strike of his hand across my cheek is startling and powerful. It sends me careening into the wall. A cry of surprise bursts from me. My ankle screams in protest when it tries to twist wrong and I fall hard to my hands and knees.

Owww.

I reach up and touch my cheek that's burning from the smack. The tears I'd been holding onto all night escape their confines and race down my cheeks. I can't help but snap my head up, shooting him a horrified, accusatory look.

Whatever hateful alcohol-induced fury had been possessing him melts away and his features pinch in a pained way, like he suddenly realizes what he's just done. He takes a step toward me and I cower in response.

"D-Dad," I croak out. "Y-You hit me."

He grabs hold of my shoulders, hauling me to my feet. I yelp when I'm dragged into his forceful hug.

"I'm sorry, sweetheart. Dammit, I'm sorry." He strokes my hair and kisses the top of my head. "I drank too much and you know what that does to me."

A sob that won't be quieted garbles its way out. I shudder in his grip. He strokes my back, clearly attempting to calm me.

Why is this my life?

At least it was me and not her this time.

But when he hurts me, it's different. It's worse.

"Please forgive me," he begs. "Please."

Never. I'll never forgive him.

"I forgive you," I lie.

"That's my good girl. My sweet, sweet girl."

CHAPTER TEN

Scout

Wednesday

*T*ICK. *T*ICK. *T*ICK.

The second hand on my black BLVGARI Octo Finissimo skeleton watch—one of the last gifts from my mother before she went to prison—moves silently, only the slightest jerk as it moves from second to second.

Tick. Tick. Tick.

I supply the ticking sound inside my head. Just like when I was a child. We'd had an antique grandfather clock I used to sit and watch for a full hour straight just to hear it chime when it hit the top of the hour. It was even more spectacular whenever it'd turn noon or midnight, the sounds going on for what seemed like an eternity. Those audible, constant ticks were soothing to me. Warm and comforting.

Tick. Tick. Tick.

These days, not much soothes or warms me. The cold darkness I'd been afraid would consume me when I was a child has slowly crept its way inside me as time wanes on. I'm barely able keep it out anymore. If it weren't for the constant nearness of my brothers, it'd probably swallow me whole.

I suppress a shudder at that thought. Being separated from my brothers would be my ultimate demise.

They probably think I hate them. Worse yet, don't feel anything for them. It couldn't be further from the truth. My brothers have always been in the center of my world, no matter how dark and demented it gets.

Dark and demented is an understatement. Sometimes, I lose control. Completely. My anger is like a flame on a matchstick, seemingly harmless and not at all bright. But it always explodes. Hits gasoline and spreads until it consumes…everything. I don't actively set out to destroy everything in our lives.

It. Just. Happens.

The gun last night was an example. I saw Sully and Sparrow have their silent "he's fucking crazy" talks about me. They forget I can hear. I'm in on the whole triplet mental communication.

I honestly thought it was some asshole I beat the shit out of for Bryant. The prick said he'd find out where I lived and pop a cap in me when I least expected it. Since we're hidden from anyone actively searching from us, I wasn't too worried. Yet, when I heard the banging, I had this awful fear that spineless prick was going to shoot one of my brothers in the damn face.

I lost it.

It turned out to be nothing and now my brothers think I'm even more of a head case than I already am.

The darkness that thrives inside me can fuck off if it thinks it's going to scare my brothers off. I'll keep it at bay in order to keep them. I have to.

My phone buzzes, tugging on the tether I've managed to keep my hold on of reality, and drags me to the present. The murky darkness fades and the interior of my car sharpens into view. I inhale a deep breath, letting the scent of new leather ground me before picking my phone up from the cupholder and checking my messages. It's the group text with my brothers.

Sparrow: *Your cat's a bitch, Sull.*

Sully: *I know, but so are you, so I guess you're both even.*

Smirking, I add in my own two cents.

Me: *She's my cat now.*

Sparrow: *Are cats allowed in Hell?*

I'm about to tell him to go fuck himself when I see movement from my periphery. I settle for a quick middle finger emoji before shoving my phone in my pocket and sliding out of my vehicle.

This morning I feel like Sparrow—donning a bespoke Tom Ford suit and looking like a million bucks. I prefer when I can dress how I want, but this new job Bryant has us on requires a little more than the usual from each of us. We're no longer fists and muscles and terror. We're sly and sneaky and manipulative. It's not what I prefer to be doing, but it keeps things interesting.

Not to mention, it gets me closer to him.

Winston motherfucking Constantine.

With each limped step I take, fury builds higher and higher like a fiery tsunami of lava born from the depths of hell. I want to make that man pay for what he's done to my family.

But I can't.

I've looked at it from every angle. He's too powerful. Too fucking rich. We've had our pissing match and he proved he's got the bigger literal dick. So, since I can't cut the head off the king cobra, I'll just hit where I can.

In this case, Ty Constantine.

Bryant says Winston wants to buy Croft Gaming and Entertainment, or at the very least, partner up. This means giving Alexander Croft something of considerable value in return—the Constantine name by way of marrying off his cousin to Alexander's daughter. Ty, just a nobody in that family, is expendable to Winston.

Ty, to me, is important.

He's a blade, though seemingly insignificant, I can use to poke at Winston.

"Hey," I call out to Ty as he enters the parking garage elevator. "Can you hold the elevator?"

He sees me approaching, limp and all, and shoves an arm out to keep the doors from closing. I grit my teeth together, forcing a frown into a smile. Ty has the Constantine signature looks— golden hair, sharp blue eyes, powerful aura. It's hard not to keep from punching him in the face.

I'm playing a long game here, though.

A fist to the face is something I would have done a year ago, but not now. I'm smarter than that teenager who got bested by Winston fucking Constantine. I'm a goddamn snake now too.

"Thanks, man," I say as I step into the elevator.

He flashes me a megawatt smile, much friendlier than any Constantine I've ever known. Poor sap. We're going to fuck with his life and he has no idea.

"You work here?" he asks, nodding his head up as he mashes the top floor button.

I hit the button to the floor below his. "Yeah. Started this week."

"No shit? Me too."

"Working for the big man?"

His cheeks turn pink like he's embarrassed to admit that. Arrogance is a Constantine trait, so this is new.

"I'm a glorified intern." He stuffs his hands into the pockets of his slacks. "Probably not as cool as whatever you do."

I scoff. "I'd rather be some rich dude's coffee bitch up at the top than pushing a pencil in my cubical from eight to five."

"It's kind of awkward shadowing Mr. Croft—"

"Mr. Croft? As in the CEO?" I let loose a low whistle. "Lucky bastard."

He shakes his head. "Nah, man. Not so lucky. He's just...he makes me nervous. Last night, he invited me to his house for dinner—"

"You fucked the CEO?"

His face turns from slightly embarrassed pink

to mortified crimson. "W-What? Hell no. Dude, I'm straight. He introduced me to his daughter."

The elevator dings and then the doors open to my floor. I step in front of the doors to keep them from closing. "Was she hot?"

He smirks. "Hot. Shy but seriously hot. But the dinner itself with Mr. Croft was tense." A sigh rushes past his lips. "I've honestly been eager to hang out with someone who isn't family. I didn't grow up here or go to college here. I don't know anyone. It's boring as shit when you don't know anyone but your damn cousins."

This guy just makes it too easy.

"I could give you my number," I offer with a grin. "We could go bar hopping or some shit. You could tell me all about this tense dinner and the hottie. Hell, maybe we could invite her to come along without her daddy."

His blue eyes sparkle and he nods emphatical-ly. "Yeah. I'd like that." He thrusts his phone at me. "Plug it in. Sorry, I didn't catch your name…"

"Ford. Ford Mann." I type in my name and number before handing it back to him.

"Ty Constantine."

"I best get back to the boring-ass cubical. Go have fun with Daddy CEO."

His face doesn't redden this time now that he knows I'm just giving him shit. "I'll text you later. Nice meeting you."

"Likewise." I tip my head at him before moving out of the way. The doors close and then he's off to the next floor.

After waiting a good five minutes, I hit the button to go back down to the parking garage. Bryant got me this in with the company so I could get closer to Alexander and Ty. Since Alexander is on the top floor and hidden away from people who work in cubicles, my only attainable person is Ty. I managed to get an in with him inside of five minutes, so I'd say my work for the day is done here.

When I reach my car, I pull out my phone to see I've missed an actual picture of Sully flipping me off and then a video of Sparrow in his car singing "fuck you" to the tune of "Twinkle, Twinkle, Little Star." Idiots.

This is what's at risk if I allow my darkness to consume me.

Losing them.

We've been together since conception, and being separated, because of the crazy shit that goes on inside my head, would fucking kill me.

Me: *Met Ty Constantine.*

Sparrow: *Do tell…*

Me: *Desperate for a friend. Lo and behold, I was available.*

Sully: *You? A friend?*

Me: *I found out our boy here had dinner last night over at Alexander's. Met Landry. Said she was hot.*

Sully: *She's not hot.*

Sparrow: *She's all right.*

Fucking liars. If it's anything like Ivy Anderson—a girl we all wanted *and had* back in high school—then I know they're downplaying things. As if I can't sense their interest. Sometimes they're so obvious it's ridiculous.

Me: *I invited him to go bar hopping.*

Sparrow: *Did he actually accept???*

Sully tries to call me, but I hit decline because if I wanted to talk to him, I'd call him.

Me: *Yeah. We swapped numbers.*

Sully: *You can't beat his ass, Scout. This job is different than our usual.*

For fuck's sake. Like I don't already know that. They really do think I'm a lunatic. It rankles me.

Me: *I get real sick and tired of you always handling me with kid gloves, Sull.*

Sully: *And I get real sick and tired of you blowing up our lives!*

Sparrow: *Guys…chill.*

Sully: *I can meet Ty for drinks.*

Me: *Already tired of babysitting duty? Are you sure I'm fit to tutor some little girl?*

Sparrow: *He's being an idiot, Scout. We know you're not going to kick Ty's ass.*

Me: *Does Sully know this?*

Not sure what's crawled up Sully's ass lately, but it's starting to piss me off.

Sully: *Fuck off.*

Me: *Fine. Since your panties are in a wad, you go for drinks with Ty and I'll tutor the runt. Although, I must say I'm more likely to be found out considering I haven't been spending hours learning sign language like you have…*

I know he'll cave. For some reason, he's really into his role in this operation. A damn ASL book came in the mail today for him. And, since he can't be in two places at once, he'll have to choose. Ty or the girl.

Sully: *Whatever. Have fun getting plastered with a Constantine. Don't call me when you* *accidentally kill him and get hauled off to jail.*

Sparrow: *Yeah, don't call me either. I have more important shit to do than deal with cops.*

They continue slinging insults, but I'm no longer interested in our conversation because Bryant is calling.

"Hey," I grunt out, answering on the second ring. "What's up?"

"I got you a little intel. On your…obsession."

My hackles raise and I suppress a growl. "What sort of intel?"

He chuckles, deep and a little evil. "The good sort. Date, location, time."

"Legit?"

"Confirmed and legit."

"Go on…" I grit my teeth, hating how eager I am for this information. Bryant's "intel" comes at a high price. He's had me do some shit that my brothers don't even know about. The kind of stuff that really would get me sent away to prison for life.

"I'll need a favor, of course," he croons. "You understand. Family takes care of each other."

Family.

This fucking guy.

He might be running through my blood, but he's not my family. The only family I have is my mother, who was wrongly taken from us, and my brothers. Everyone else is irrelevant to me.

"Of course," I mutter. "What do you need?"

"A property needs dealing with. The Morellis have many enemies and I make sure they're cut off before they become a problem."

"Deal with…how?" I implore. "Break in? Vandalism?"

"The latter."

"Elaborate."

"I want you to burn their building to the fucking ground."

That's a little more than vandalism…

"If I were to get caught…" I trail off. "Your intel better be good."

"Don't get caught. Look but don't touch or Winston won't be the only man who will rip you to shreds," he clips out. "And my intel is well worth the risk."

Look but don't touch.

Sure thing, Uncle. I'll be on my best behavior…

"I'm listening."

"Winston's little wifey. She'll be at a baby shower this weekend for a friend of the Constantine family."

Ash.

My ex-stepsister.

It's about time we've caught up...

"I'll do your dirty work. Now tell me everything."

"Thatta boy, son."

I'm not his son, but I'll let him call me whatever the fuck he wants as long as he gives me the information I need.

CHAPTER ELEVEN

Sparrow

I THRUM MY fingers on my desk, my stare fixed on the doorway to the classroom. Energy buzzes beneath my skin and I'm not sure why. Maybe I've had too much coffee this morning.

Or maybe you're just excited to see Landry…

A derisive snort escapes me and the dude beside me whips his head my way. Ignoring him, I continue to wait for my target to arrive.

It's not excitement to see her…it's excitement to get back to doing my job.

Fuck with her.

Make her fall in love with me—us.

Scout learned that Ty Constantine went to her house last night. Alexander Croft isn't wasting any time. I suppose trying to marry off his daughter to one of the wealthiest families in not only the country, but the world, would be high on his list of priorities.

My mind drifts to fantasies of defiling her in the backseat of my car. I'd keep her bratty mouth quiet with my dick. If Ty is already on the move, going to dinners and shit, then I need to up my game. I don't usually have to work so hard to get a chick into bed with me.

Annoyance ripples through me.

Landry is difficult.

Sassy and prissy and kind of fucking rude.

A flash of blonde in the doorway steals my attention. It's her. Little Landry. This morning, though, her prickliness from before is gone. Beneath her heavily made-up face is a tight, tortured expression. Her eyes are bloodshot like she's been crying.

Irritation burns in my gut, this time, no longer toward her. Someone made her cry. I don't know why that bothers me—a girl I've literally only just met—but it does.

I sit up straight, clenching my jaw as I watch her make her way willingly toward me. She sets her bag down on the desk and sits down. After a huff that seems to be an effort to ward off more tears, she begins gnawing on her bottom lip, blue eyes searching mine like I have answers.

Just ask the right questions, baby.

"Laundry." I smirk at her. "Looking good."

"Chevy. And you look all right yourself."

All right.

The gall of this girl.

"I see someone woke up and took their bitchy pill this morning. Do you ever forget it?"

"Never." She makes a sour face but it doesn't hide the slight tremble of her chin. "You left our house in a hurry yesterday."

I blink at her in confusion for a moment until I remember that she's referring to Sully, not me. This acting gig is hard sometimes.

"Homework," I lie. "Why are you sad?"

"Sad?" Her head shakes and her upper lip curls slightly. "I'm not *sad*."

I lift a brow, waiting for her to elaborate. She doesn't. I swear to fuck she likes being difficult.

"You're going to make me beg for details, Laundry?"

"Can anyone really *make* you do anything? Didn't think you were the type." She studies me for a beat, something akin to respect gleaming in her eyes.

She really is going to make me drag this shit out of her.

"Come on. Let's go," I say as I push my chair back.

Her brows pinch together. "What? Class is about to start."

"Like either of us are in the mood to concentrate on class today. Something's up and you need to vent. We're leaving."

I reach for her hand, but she jerks it back, shaking her head almost violently. "I can't leave campus with you."

Ouch.

"I'm not going to kidnap you," I grit out. "I just want to buy you some fucking coffee." She doesn't move, so I throw my hands up on the air in exasperation. "*On* campus."

Her lips press together. She thinks about it all of three seconds and then she's rising to her feet. This time, when I reach for her hand, she lets me take it. I think it surprises the both of us because her eyes dart to mine, widening.

I don't give her a chance to back out and tug her along with me. A chick with a nice rack smiles at me as I pass, but I don't return it. If I'm going to derail Ty Constantine's efforts, I need to make sure Landry has someone she'd rather be with.

Me.

Checking out the tits of every hot girl I encounter isn't going to help me in my cause.

We pass our professor on the way out. He

shoots me an irritated scowl, but I don't give a fuck. I'm not actually trying to get a damn degree here. I give Landry's hand a comforting squeeze. She's quiet as we walk, never attempting to pull her hand from mine.

"Grab us a seat over there," I say when we reach the campus coffee shop.

She surprisingly obeys without a fuss. While she commandeers the loveseat nestled away from all the other tables and chairs, I order our coffees and a couple of muffins.

"What's this?" she asks when I approach with our tray.

"Caramel macchiato." I flash her a taunting grin. "Since you're salty all the time, I figure you might like something sweet."

She rolls her eyes, but she can't hide the cute smile tugging at her lips. Noted. This girl likes sweet treats and a little flirtatious teasing.

"Spill, woman." I settle on the cushion beside her. "I'm listening."

Taking her sweet ass time, she picks up her mug, inhales the scent coming from the steam, and gingerly takes a sip. I track the way her pink tongue darts out and chases a trail along her upper lip, cleaning off the steamed milk left behind. My mouth waters for my own taste—something I don't really like admitting to myself.

"What was your deal Monday?" she demands, rather than coming out with what's really bothering her. "You were…different."

I can only imagine what Sully's broody ass did or said. He's so fucking resentful of Bryant that he probably whined like a bitch to her.

"Not everyone is sunshine and roses all the time like you, Laundry," I deadpan. "You're goals as fuck, though."

"You're such an asshole." She scowls at me. "Why did I think coming here with you would be a good idea?"

So much for wooing the girl.

"Fine," I concede, letting out a sharp exhale of resignation. "I was tired. I get crabby when I'm stressed and tired."

It's the truth…about Sully. When we were kids, he required a nap or he was the absolute worst. I'm pretty sure we went through like sixteen nannies during our first few years of life because of him.

"You have a Bronco too," she says. "Why do you have two cars?"

"That piece of shit—" I bite off my words and scrub my palm over my face. "My car was getting detailed so I borrowed my neighbor's lame-ass car.

Any other questions, Detective?"

She turns from me and reaches for her bag. What the fuck. She's going to leave. Because I can't be a chill guy for three seconds. My dickish ways are going to ruin this long before Sully's whiny ways do.

"Hey," I grit out, gripping her wrist to keep her from standing. "Look at me."

Of course the salty, spoiled girl doesn't. I cup her cheek and guide her head until she's facing me. Her features pinch and she winces. Like I hurt her. Frowning, I run my thumb along her cheekbone. She does it again. Cringes as though it's painful.

"That's why you're all dolled up today?" I demand. "Covering a bruise?"

Her blue eyes sparkle with a variety of emotions, none of which I can pin down and figure out. "Dolled up? That sounds so sexist. Like putting on makeup is—"

"Your feminist rant can wait. Tell me how you got that bruise."

"I can't."

"Someone did this to you?"

"It was...nothing."

"It was obviously something," I spit back at her. "Let me guess. You ran into a door."

"Fuck off, Ford!"

Her efforts to leave are futile. Not with my tight grasp on her arm, locking her in place beside me. She's my temporary prisoner until I decide to free her. My dick jolts.

Not the time, prick.

I gently stroke her cheek as I peer into her blazing blues. There's a lot that goes on inside Landry's head. I wish I had access to her mind, so I could pick it all apart and discover what makes her tick. What upsets her. What excites her.

So I can exploit it, of course.

"It better have been a wall, Laundry." I brush my lips along the bruise. "Because if I find out it was a person, things will go very, very badly for them."

Her breath hitches and she stills. "You're not my boyfriend, Chevy."

"Yet." I pull back and wink at her. "Not your boyfriend *yet.*"

Heavily painted eyelashes flutter in front of me as she rolls her eyes. I don't miss the smile she's desperately trying to hide. The salty girl is sweet in the center.

Which makes me wonder why the fuck any-one would hurt her. Her non-answer is the only answer I need. Someone gave this bruise to her and she's too afraid to say anything. This is surprising considering her last name and financial status.

She's eighteen.

If it were her father, she could just leave. So who then? Friend or boyfriend? A different family member? Ty?

I have a hard time believing Ty Constantine would hit his date on their first dinner together. My gut points to the father, but I'm missing some pieces in this story—a story she's clearly dead-set on evading.

"Can we please talk about something else?" she croaks out. "Anything else. Please."

Sliding my hand from her wrist, I slip down to her hand, linking our fingers together. Her entire body relaxes, the tension from our conversation melting away.

And like the good wannabe boyfriend I am, I let it slide. We spend the entire class period keeping things light and discussing great restaurants, movies, and a whole lot of other shit. Not once do we circle back to the bruise on her face. But, I haven't forgotten about it. The second she excuses herself to go to the bathroom, I grab my phone and text my brothers.

Me: *Find out who the fuck hit Landry.*

Probably not the best idea involving Scout on this shit, but I want answers—answers Landry seems to be avoiding at all costs.

My job is to stick my nose into every corner of her business. To make a mess of her life, too, but it seems she's doing a damn fine job all on her own.

CHAPTER TWELVE

Sully

D ELLA DOES THE sign again—the one I clearly
don't know. Her eyes gleam with mischief
and an antagonizing grin turns her cute, girlish
expression into something far more sinister.

I swear, this kid is the devil.

Ignoring her taunting, I pull out my phone
and go on a hunt for insults in ASL. Not so
surprisingly—because that's how our world is—I
find a whole bunch of links with information and
a YouTube video. It takes about five minutes until
I learn she called me a dummy.

"Dummy?" I say, mimicking the sign back to
her.

Her smile is victorious, and she nods. Then
she signs, *You.*

I learn how to sign the word *brat* and make
sure to say it too, enunciating so she doesn't

misunderstand. Once again, I swear I got the most difficult job of the three of us. Sparrow gets to pretend to be a college student and Scout does whatever it is that Scout does.

Meanwhile, I'm over here having to learn a goddamn new language.

And babysit a monster.

Said monster beams at me and points toward something flashing by. Then she signs, *cat*.

If Della is the devil, then Heathen is her mascot. They're both rotten to the core. And my dumb ass somehow got roped into bringing this damn cat with me every time now because *the cat is good for the children*.

For fuck's sake.

"Focus, kid," I grind out. "You're supposed to be learning."

She giggles and shakes her head before giving me that sign again. This time I know what it means. *Dummy.*

"You're an asshole, you know that right?" I mumble under my breath.

Della's nose scrunches, confusion dancing over her features. It's a reminder why I'm here. To try and improve her lipreading skills. I really suck at this job. It's only a matter of time before this kid tattles to her daddy that I don't know what the hell I'm doing.

And that's only one part of this dumb job. I'm still supposed to somehow creep around and find information for Bryant. I don't know what he expects me to do. Sneak into the dude's office and peek at files? Good luck with that shit. No one is getting in there unless he allows it. Spy on his conversations? Pick locked doors to see what skeletons are hiding? I'm conveniently avoiding this whole super sleuth aspect. It's not like Bryant will ever really know for sure.

"Be serious," I say in a stern tone, making sure to make clear movements with my mouth. "Focus."

She stabs a finger at my forearm, nailing me right in one of the spots Heathen shredded this afternoon when I tried to get her into her travel kennel. I glare at the evil little girl. The delight on her face reminds me of Scout anytime he'd torment someone when we were younger.

Twisted psychos.

"Everything going okay in here?" a voice asks from the doorway.

I snap my head to find Landry slowly making her way into the room. There's a soft expression on her face that I haven't seen before. With the sun streaming in through the windows and blanketing her creamy features, she's almost angelic. Her hair shimmers, catching each ray of light and reflecting it back my way.

Find out who the fuck hit Landry.

Sparrow's text from earlier burns its way into my mind. What kind of dick hurts someone who looks like Landry does? Flawless and innocent. But they did and the slight bluish bruising hidden under layers of makeup proves it.

But who would do this?

I've researched and read all about her father. He's your typical arrogant rich guy, but I don't get child abuser vibes from him.

Child?

Landry is anything but a child.

Maybe this is the dirty secret Bryant wanted me to expose. I can try to get information from the girls. I'll have to be careful. I don't know if this guy has the rooms bugged or not. I'm probably being paranoid as fuck, but I suddenly have the heebie jeebies.

Landry signs something to Della. I miss their entire exchange, not able to keep up with the rapid conversation. Finally, Landry laughs, the sound almost surprised.

"What?" I grumble.

"Nothing." Landry's skin flushes. "I just

didn't expect that."

I frown at her. "Expect what?"

"For Della to, um, like you."

"Wow. Thanks, honey. Way to stroke my ego."

She cocks her head to the side, the golden strands of her hair sliding over her still-pink neck. I have the urge to push aside her hair and slide my thumb over the pulsing vein there.

"Sorry about earlier," she says, pausing to nibble on the inside corner of her lip. "I was being a bitch."

Sparrow didn't say anything about her being a bitch. In fact, he didn't say anything at all aside from the fact he wanted us to find out who hit her. It looks like it's up to me to get to the bottom of this since I can't rely on his shitty intel. At least my job has a little more purpose than before. This is something I can get behind, because, dammit, I don't want that fucker hitting her. I'm going to get her to confide in me through whatever means necessary.

My dick jumps at the thought of her whispering all her secrets to me. All I'd need to do is get my mouth on her pussy. I can guarantee I could get anything out of her at that point. My tongue is my best asset.

"Ford?"

"It's fine." I glance at Della. "Snack time?"

She nods and bolts from the room, clearly eager to leave our lesson. When I return my gaze to Landry, her eyes are probing and curious.

"What?"

"She really likes you." Her lips curl into a smile. "I'm just surprised is all."

"She only uses me for my cat."

Landry's smile grows and I find myself fixated on it. Her mouth is the most interesting thing in the room. Pink and luscious and lips made for kissing.

"Maybe," she says as she walks over to the window that overlooks the city, "but at least she's learning."

Learning?

How to be a brat, sure. But learning anything from me? Hardly. I smother a scoff at her words.

"She was watching you and trying." Landry looks over her shoulder at me. "That's new for her. She's so stubborn most of the time."

"I wonder where she gets that from," I deadpan.

"Family trait. Comes by it honestly." The humor in her voice fades as her shoulders tense. "I shouldn't be in here alone with you."

I prowl toward her, unable to help myself. Landry Croft is our mark—the girl we're supposed to mess with in order to make our uncle happy. This should feel like one of our usual jobs. Cold. Boring. Repetitive.

It's not.

Like the sun streaming in, blanketing her angelic form, I'm warmed. The heat seeps through my skin and into my bones, thawing chilly parts of me that've been ice cold for the past year. I'm grateful our job is to woo her and pull her off track with her "arranged marriage in the making" because I can give in to my selfish craving. I can do this…

Her breath hitches the second my hands find her hips. A tremble quakes through her body, but then she tightens every muscle and goes still.

"What are you doing?" she demands, her voice breathy and confused.

"Touching you."

"You shouldn't." Another shiver. "Seriously."

Her hands move to cover mine, but instead of yanking them off her hips, she rests them atop mine. Taking this as permission, I dip down, burying my nose in her hair at the side of her neck. She digs her nails into the flesh on my hands. Still, she doesn't slip out of my hold.

"Fate says otherwise." I murmur the words near her ear. "We're in the same classes and I've been hired to tutor your sister. Can we really ignore fate?"

"Ford…"

The name on her lips—the fake one—cools my blood. It's kind of fucked up that we're leading her on. And while Sparrow and Scout can ignore the guilt, I have a more difficult time.

"How long does snack time last?" I ask, letting my thumbs tease under the hem of her shirt, finding silky skin that needs touching.

"Forever if you'll let it. She looks for any excuse to leave this classroom."

"So we have time…"

"Time for what?"

I slide my hand beneath her shirt, gently caressing her stomach. "This."

"Ford, we can't."

The tortured way she says those words has me wanting to lock the classroom door and proving to her we absolutely can.

"Why not, honey?" I murmur, nuzzling her hair.

She melts against me, leaning her head against her shoulder and baring her neck to me. I use my free hand to sweep the hair away and then press my lips to her sun-warmed skin. Her breathing comes in quick, shallow pants as I slide the hand under her shirt, higher and higher and higher. I think her breathing stops altogether when my fingertips tease along the underside of one of her tits.

She's so responsive and fucking needy.

The things I could do to this girl. So many things.

"I want you," I admit. I kiss her neck, this time more than a peck, tasting the sweetness of her flesh. "I know you want me, too."

She doesn't argue. Not so innocently, she rubs her ass against my dick that's straining in my jeans. Landry craves for me to make her feel so damn good. And I will. When the opportunity arises, I'll strip her bare, spread her thighs, and feast on her pussy until she's on a high she'll never come down from.

"I like you, honey," I murmur, my breath hot on her neck. "And you like me too. This thing between us is inevitable. It was the second I laid eyes on you in class."

With those words out of me, I cup her breast over her bra and suck on her neck. A hot as fuck moan escapes her. It lights a fire inside me with the need to consume this woman—to pin her down, lick her sweet spots, and drive my dick into her over and over again until we're both sated.

I suck harder on her neck, the urge to mark her a stupid need I can't ignore. She whimpers and it sounds like a bit of a protest.

A door shuts nearby, making Landry freeze in my grip. She curses under her breath and then jerks out of my arms, spinning around to face me. I run my tongue along my bottom lip, eager to taste more of her. Her blue eyes track the moment, burning with the lust that's most definitely mirrored in my own eyes.

"My dad is home," she croaks out, nearly stumbling as she puts distance between us. "He's home and you can't be here."

I lift a brow, amused by her words. "I'm being paid to be here." Adjusting my chub in my jeans, I can't help but grin at how pink she turns. "Am I embarrassing you?"

Her features harden and her voice is shrill. "This isn't a joke, idiot. He's... You just don't understand." Panic ripples over her making her eyes dart toward the door and her body tremble.

I follow her stare to the doorway. As soon as a man enters the space, the warmth of the room is sucked out. A bone-deep chill creeps its way inside me. Based on the way Landry shudders, I'd say she feels it too.

He's the typical rich prick in an expensive suit. His arrogance is stifling. As though I'm supposed to take one look at him and bow at his feet. I can't stand assholes like this. They act like they're gods.

Reminds me of Winston Constantine.

The chill inside me is quickly doused in gasoline. I light the match, feeling the burn of hatred all the way down to my toes, and face the man, showing him I'm not afraid of him. I hope my expression implies I'd rather kick his ass.

"Landry, sweetheart. Who is this?" He's glaring at me, but speaking to his daughter in a cold, clipped tone. "I said—"

"Ford Mann. He's Della's tutor." Landry closes her eyes for a moment and then I watch her transform into someone else—someone regal and sure of herself. Someone brave and not at all timid. "She's already learned so much, Dad. I was just discussing her progress with Mr. Mann."

I have the urge to laugh, because my lips weren't discussing anything. I was tasting and exploring. My fingers still tingle with the way her lacy bra felt against my skin.

"Her tutor," Alexander parrots, his hard glare assessing me from head to toe. "Hmm."

Landry giggles—girlish and sweet. What the actual fuck?

"Della's a quick study," I say, turning on the charm I've seen Sparrow use on people countless times. "Surprised the hell out of me."

"Where *is* the studious child?" Alexander asks, cutting his eyes to his daughter.

Landry, to her credit, doesn't falter at his angry tone. Her smile broadens and she regards her father like he hangs the fucking moon. Again...what the actual fuck? Before she can answer, the child in question stomps into the room, scowling with Sandra pulling up the rear.

"Mr. Croft," Sandra says, a polite smile on her face. "Lovely to see you so early from the office. Can I fetch you a drink?"

This show these women are putting on for this man is nauseating.

"I can grab it for you," Landry says, taking hold of her father's elbow. "Plus, I wanted to run some party ideas by you. Come on. We'll leave them to finish up their lesson."

Alexander stares at me for a beat longer before allowing his daughter to whisk him from the room. Sandra scurries after, clearly eager to dump the kid back off on me. Della glowers after them.

I tap her shoulder and wait for her to look at

me before saying, "Dummy."

Her lips quirk into a small smile and then she signs back, *dummy*. At least Della and I have a common enemy. I know why I don't like the guy, but her? I'll get to the bottom of it. Pulling out my phone, I shoot my brothers a quick text.

> **Me:** There's something up with the dad. A real prick. The kid doesn't like him.
>
> **Sparrow:** You think he hit Landry?
>
> **Scout:** Seems obvious to me.
>
> **Me:** I don't know. We need to find out. She didn't tell him she knew me from school.
>
> **Sparrow:** Because she doesn't know YOU from school.
>
> **Me:** Fuck off. You know what I mean. Ford. She didn't mention knowing Ford from class.
>
> **Scout:** Daddy's girl has secrets.

Yeah, she does. And we're going to uncover each one of them. Because it's our job—to meddle in people's lives and fuck shit up. We're really good at it, too.

CHAPTER THIRTEEN

Landry

AWAY. AWAY. AWAY.

That's all that was going through my mind as I ushered Dad out of Della's classroom and over to the living room bar. By habit, I glance out the panoramic windows, my go-to escape, but his ominous reflection has me jerking my attention back down to the bar top. I don't want him seeing the desperation in my eyes. My mindless chatting seems fake and slightly shrill from nerves, but Dad doesn't appear to notice. He watches me intently as I pour him a glass of wine. I can't stop the trembling of my hands, nearly sloshing wine all over the place. Sucking in a deep breath, I attempt to slow my speeding heart and relax.

He reacted horribly to Ty's friendliness. I can only imagine what he'd do if he knew Della's tutor just had his hand up my shirt.

Heat races over my skin, scorching a crimson path. Quickly, I hand Dad his glass and then try to change the subject to anything but the man in the other room.

I can't believe I let him touch me. Kiss my neck. Play a dangerous game in my own house. So reckless and stupid. Ford Mann tears down my defenses so easily. It's both exhilarating and terrifying all at once.

"What do you think you'll be?" Dad asks, drawing my attention from thoughts of Ford to him. "Have you decided?"

"Della wants me to be Little Red Riding Hood and she wants to be the Big Bad Wolf."

"You do look lovely in red, sweetheart. And Della can be quite feral."

I laugh at his joke. Though it's true and probably said as an insult, he says it almost lovingly. I'll take that over his cruelty toward her any day.

"Are you inviting the entire city again?" I tease, earning a genuine smile from him. "Last time, I'm pretty sure you let anyone in."

Dad chuckles. "I learned from that mistake. I didn't get to enjoy myself because I had to make too many rounds. This time, I've asked my assistant to send invites to my birthday party to an exclusive, intimate list of names. All influential people, of course. Quite a few Constantines."

Tension snaps each one of my muscles taut. I can't help but think of the way he struck me. All because I was chatty with Ty. Will that happen again? I feel like he wants me to be two different people.

Two different people.

Kind of like Ford. I wonder how he turns it on and off because he was a completely different person this afternoon than at school.

Maybe his secrets are like mine. Painful. Hard to swallow. Frankly, humiliating.

It makes me want to sneak away with him, snuggle close, and beg for him to tell me all about what dark shadows are in his world. Then, I wouldn't feel so alone.

There's definitely more to Ford than meets the eye.

"Hey," Dad murmurs, setting his glass down on the bar top. "Walk with me."

His hand slides to the small of my back and he guides me through the living room to the sliding glass door that leads to the balcony. We step outside and the oppressive air that always suffocating me dissipates, momentarily getting carried away by the breeze. It's fairly windy today, but at least it's warm. I bask in the sunlight for a moment, closing my eyes and letting it wash over me to chase away the chill.

"I'm a terrible father." His voice cracks, showing rare vulnerability. "Last night…I was drunk."

Drunk.

I grab onto the railing to steady myself. My eyes snap open and I grit my teeth. The things he does when he's drunk are unforgiveable.

"Landry, I'm sorry. I didn't mean to hit you." He lets out a pained sound that cuts through me like a knife. "If your mother knew what a bastard I can be when I drink too much, she'd haunt me and push me off this balcony."

"It's fine," I lie.

"No. It's not fine." He grips my shoulders and turns me to face him. "You're my daughter. My beautiful, brilliant, perfect daughter. It was wrong. I hurt you and I'm sick about it."

"I didn't mean to make you mad."

Guilt shines in his eyes but he doesn't look away. I'm glad he's facing what he's done. He inspects my cheek, the bruising covered well under layers of makeup.

"You didn't make me mad," he murmurs, brows furling. "It's just…It's hard watching my little girl grow up into a woman. Seeing you with

Ty Constantine—so happy and carefree—felt like you were being taken from me. You've always been mine. And now…"

"I'm not going anywhere," I tell him vehemently. I'll never leave Della alone.

His expression softens. He kisses me on the forehead. "You will one day. Ty isn't a bad guy. I actually like him. With his family name, bright future ahead of him, and the way he was so enamored with you, I think he'd be worthy of dating you."

"But, Dad—"

"He's a good man, sweetheart. You deserve someone good."

I nod and smile at him.

"Am I forgiven?"

"Of course." I drop my stare to the tight knot of his tie. "I was upset, but I'll be all right."

"That's my good girl."

His phone rings, thankfully saving me from anymore of this conversation. He shoots me an apologetic smile before taking the call, leaving me on the balcony alone. My thoughts quickly escape those of my father and sneak back to the man teaching my sister.

Ford.

His lips were so hot on my neck. I'd nearly

melted into him when he sucked on my skin. A thrill shoots through me wondering if there will be a hickey left on my neck. Just one more bruise to hide with makeup. But this one, at least, is one I enjoyed receiving.

God, this is such a problem.

Ford is such a problem.

When he was being an arrogant prick, it was easy to keep him at arm's length. But, today at school, and then just now when we were alone, I didn't want to leave his arms at all. I wanted to throw myself into them and take solace in his strength.

This isn't one of Della's storybooks, though.

This is my life. There isn't a heroic prince to save me from my prison tower. I'm the hero, and I have to figure out a way to save the little princess before the villainous king has both our heads.

I slip back inside and follow the sound of Dad's voice. He's locked in conversation in his office. Sandra is in the kitchen, having a meeting with the kitchen staff. Knowing I can steal another minute with Ford, I pounce on the opportunity.

Della darts out of the classroom, nearly smacking into me. She grins—quite wolfishly I might add—and then skips down the hall to her room. I peek in the classroom to find Ford on one knee, wrangling his cat Della told me all about into a pet carrier. He curses at the creature a few times before managing to get it locked up.

"Heathen is a vicious bitch," Ford says, grinning up at me. "You can keep her if you want."

"Way to sell it," I tease.

He rises to his feet, leaving the carrier on the floor. Before I lose my nerve, I rush over to him. Standing on my toes, I tilt my head up and press a soft kiss to his cheek. I start to pull away, but his strong arm snakes around me, pulling me to his solid chest.

"What was that for?" he rumbles, hooded eyes searing into me.

"To thank you. For being so good to Della."

"What do I need to do in order to get your lips on mine?"

Is this how it feels to like a guy and be liked back? I'm so inexperienced in the dating department it's not even funny. The way he looks at me and touches me, like I'm already his, is distracting. It makes me want to forget about all my troubles and stress.

"It's not like that," I lie, my voice a needy whisper.

"It's not?" He smirks, clearly amused by my

lies. "So this thing between us is what? Just friends?"

Not only am I seriously lacking when it comes to boyfriends, I'm no better in the friend department either. Of course I'd become enamored with the first guy to push past my defenses and force his way inside.

"Yeah, just friends. We already established this on Monday." I swallow and shrug. "Do you even know how to be just friends with a woman?"

"Nope."

He chases the word out of his mouth toward me and then his lips are on mine. Soft and gentle at first. I sigh at the sweetness and surprise of it. A groan rumbles through him and he takes the opportunity to drive his tongue into my mouth. He tastes like caramel, which is fitting since his eyes are that rich light brown shade in this moment. I want to devour him. Clinging to his shirt, I tug him closer, needing to kiss him longer, deeper, harder.

His teeth find my bottom lip when we pull back just enough to catch our breath. I suck in a shocked breath and he follows it with a throaty chuckle. Then, his mouth is back on mine, owning my lips and tongue with his.

It feels good.

Really good.

To be tasted and explored.

His kisses are more than possessive. They're filled with such passion. Like I can hear his thoughts and feel his desire with each swipe of his expert tongue over mine.

Dad's voice, calling for Sandra down the hall, kills the mood. I jolt in Ford's grip and jerk away from him. Smoothing down my hair and licking my lips, I try to right myself after such a soul-stealing kiss.

It's nearly impossible.

Gone are the playful smirks and taunting grins.

Ford watches me, a frown transforming his features. As though he can't figure me out. The hunger in his caramel eyes makes it pretty easy to know what's going on in his head. He wants to take my mouth with his once more. The feeling is mutual.

But I can't.

Not with Dad on the prowl.

"We shouldn't have done that," I whisper, unable to look at him when I say it. "My dad—"

"We did do it, though. It's done, honey." He winks at me. "And it's going to happen again, too. Soon."

"Ford."

"Landry." He breaks into an impish grin. "I'm not sorry about it."

Me neither.

The fluttering in my chest and the silly smile tugging at my lips is all the proof I need. I'm not sorry and that's a problem.

Maybe he could help us.

Hope vines its way around my heart and gives it a squeeze. Maybe he could.

Chapter Fourteen

Sparrow

I CAN'T SIT still, wearing a hole in the rug in our living room as I pace back and forth in front of the window wall. Hell, I even scrubbed all three bathrooms earlier because I needed to expel some energy. I've been like this all damn day. Ever since seeing Landry. Cleaning and pacing. It boils my blood that she has a big-ass bruise on her face. Furthermore, it pisses me off that she's protecting someone.

All fingers point to her father.

She's eighteen, though. Why the hell does she put up with it? Is the family fortune really worth it to her?

If I could have my mom back with us, I'd give up the suits and cars no matter how much it would pain me. It's just money and stuff to me—something to entertain me while time slowly creeps by.

Landry obviously has her reasons, but what are they?

I'm missing part of the picture and it's driving me crazy. If Sully doesn't get more information from her this afternoon, I'll be forced to take on his job, too. His heart isn't in it.

It's not because I want to see *her* more. Nope.

"I can hear your thoughts," Scout says from where he's sprawled out on the sofa, the television remote resting on his bare chest. "Loud as fuck, little bro."

Little my ass.

We both know I can take him in a fist fight. It's been proven many times over the years. He's crazy as fuck, but I'm relentless and unstoppable.

"Just thinking," I growl. "Since when do you care?"

He laughs, cold and distant. "Since we started sharing the same real estate in Mom's womb."

Liar.

Scout doesn't care what I'm pissed about. He just likes to pretend he does.

"You got more tatts." I motion to his chest that's littered with scars and a lot more ink than I remember.

"Yup."

The sun is setting on the horizon and a few stray rays of light highlight a strip of dust across our dark gray wood floors. I itch to hunt down a broom and mop, but that'll only entertain Scout and I'm not in the mood for his shit.

"Fucking expensive," he says, drawing my attention back to him. "But worth it."

A giant bluish-gray serpent is hiding behind beautiful orange and red exotic-looking flowers of all sorts. Interesting.

"You know, if you're bored of walking back and forth, you could always clean my room," Scout offers, not at all helpfully. "I'm sure there's laundry you could do."

Laundry.

The only Laundry I wouldn't mind doing isn't here.

Scout goes back to flipping through the channels while I try my damnedest not to continue to pace the living room. Sully's not replying to my texts. I just want to know how this afternoon went for him and if he managed to pluck anything else from Landry.

I go back to brooding but only for a few more minutes before the front door opens. Heathen is making some demonic half-meow, half-growling sounds from her carrier while Sully bitches at her for being evil and useless. He releases her from her cage and she bolts across the room, a flash of black fur. She launches herself up onto the sofa and then prances over Scout's chest, curling herself on the snake tatt.

Fucking fitting if you ask me.

Match made in hell, those two.

Scout strokes Heathen's fur, not even bothering to gloat to Sully that the cat likes him more. Sully ambles into the living room and falls into one of our beloved recliners.

I study him intently, looking for any answers he might have regarding Landry.

He's smirking. In a pleased-as-fuck sort of way. It rankles me. I pop my knuckles on one hand one by one, the loud cracking sound echoing in the large room.

"What are you so happy about?" I demand, unable to keep the venom out of my tone.

Sully grins at me, wide and victorious. "I kissed Landry."

The blood running through my veins thickens like molten lava, scorching me from the inside out. Both my hands curl into fists.

Why am I so pissed off?

It's the damn job.

Because it's Ivy Anderson all over again. In the

ninth grade, we thought it'd be great for one of us to go out with Ivy and then see if she could tell us apart. We'd take turns pretending to be Sully. It wasn't until we all had our turn with her in bed—and a pregnancy scare—that we didn't want to pretend anymore. I didn't want to be Sully. I wanted to be Sparrow and I wanted to take her out on real dates—dates where she'd say my name, not his.

But Ivy didn't take too well to being duped.

Not only did she break up with Sully, but she also told her lawyer dad that we tricked her. Our teenage prank turned into restraining orders and police involvement. It took a lot of Mom's money and a free tummy tuck for Ivy's mom for it to finally go away. They dropped the charges after making us sweat it out for a few months and then Ivy went to live with her aunt in California.

I still think about that girl to this day.

She was one of the few people who actually had the ability to come between me and my brothers. There were a lot of fights between us once we all started sleeping with her. We're territorial and possessive. Ivy was mine, but she was also Sully's and Scout's. She was our toy and not one of us likes to share.

Now, we have Landry.

A job. A fucking job.

Except, I actually like her. She's sexy in a bitchy kind of way and a lot more interesting than the vapid chicks I hop into bed with on the regular. I didn't realize how monotonous my life had gotten until we started injecting ourselves into Landry's life.

"Sparrow," Sully barks. "Did you hear me?"

I cut my eyes to him, grinding my teeth together in an attempt to hold in the anger simmering beneath my surface. "I heard you."

Scout sits up and eases his bad leg off the couch. He stretches it out in front of him as he repositions Heathen into his lap. The cat's purring is practically vibrating the entire damn condo. I lift my stare to Scout's dark eyes to find him watching me.

"This is going to be easier than I thought," Sully continues. "We just have to work on getting her alone more."

"You guys remember Ivy Anderson?" Scout asks.

Me and Sully both flip him off.

"What?" Scout demands, grinning. "You two were obsessed. Got us into all kinds of trouble because of it too."

"Rich coming from you," Sully spits back.

"Your obsession with our stepsister nearly got us killed."

Scout's playful nature bleeds away and his expression goes blank. "Careful, little brother. You're poking a wound that's not quite healed yet."

"Maybe you deserve to bleed a bit for that bullshit you put us through." Sully jerks to his feet and storms toward his room. "I've got shit to do."

His bedroom door slams behind him hard enough to make the windows in the condo rattle. Heathen hisses toward the sound. Scout scratches under her chin until she snuggles against him, calming back down.

"You're going to fuck her now, aren't you?" Scout asks, a brow lifted in question. "Because it drives you crazy he's kissed her. So competitive."

"Screw off." I flip him off again. "I'm not going to fuck her. She's a job."

Scout laughs and shrugs, seeing right through my words. I'm absolutely going to fuck her. Hopefully soon, too, so I can get this burning need out of my system.

I *will* get her out of my system.

I fucking better.

✧ ✧ ✧

AFTER POUNDING OUT my stress at the gym in our building, I make my way back into the condo. Scout is cooking something in the kitchen and Sully is frowning hard at his laptop at the dining room table. ASL books are spread around him like *he's* the damn college student.

At first, I thought he wasn't, but he's really taking this shit seriously.

All the irritation I managed to beat into the punching bag swells up inside me once more. It's so annoying how Sully always gets the girl. They always want to date him because he's "boyfriend material." Little do they know, he's every bit the asshole Scout and I are. He just hides it better behind his broody persona that chicks seem to drool over.

Does Landry think he's "boyfriend material"?

It makes me want to out his ass right now. To tell her we're all just fucking playing her because we were told to. Because it's our position in this new "family" we found ourselves in when Winston Constantine broke ours apart.

But, if I tattle on our whole charade, not only will Landry refuse to speak to me or see me, Bryant will lose his mind. The guy is a weasel, but he's got fangs too. You don't do someone like him dirty unless you want to get shredded in return.

Hard pass. I'm not about to lose everything just because I'm pissed at my brother.

I need to get laid.

There are several past hookups that would jump at the possibility to blow me.

Ignoring both my brothers, I stalk into my bedroom and close the door. I take a quick shower and then wrap a towel around my waist, not bothering to get dressed. I sprawl out on my bed and pick up my phone, ready to hunt for a piece of ass to take the edge off. What's waiting for me is a text from Bryant.

> **Bryant:** *I need a guy who can wear a suit and command a room this weekend. And that's you. Your brother will fill in for you.*

Fill in for me?

It takes two seconds for me to realize he means at school.

> **Me:** *Sully can be your suit guy.*

> **Bryant:** *It has to be you. Head out Friday morning. Pack a bag and a couple of your nicest suits. I already texted Scout. He'll take your place.*

Fuck.

Fuck. Fuck. Fuck.

Me: *Scout? Seriously?*

The dots move and stop a couple of times. I know I've pissed him off. It's time to back off even though my mind is screaming at me to argue until I get my way.

Me: *I'll be ready.*

Bryant: *That's what I thought. You'll be rewarded for your compliance.*

Prick.

I consider throwing my phone across the room but opt for swiping the lamp off my nightstand instead. It crashes to the hardwood floor, making a loud clatter. Taking a deep breath, I exhale and then reply back to him.

Me: *I need Landry Croft's number.*

He immediately responds back with it. It bothers the fuck out of me that he has it and so ready to use it. Almost like he knew one of us would end up asking for it.

Once I've cooled off, I dial the number, not bothering to thank Bryant for the number. A sweet, feminine voice answers on the second ring.

"Dirty Laundry."

A beat of silence. "Chevy?"

My chest tightens and for a second, I'm no

longer agitated. Her familiar voice is breathier over the phone and speaks straight to my cock.

"'Sup?"

"You seriously have the audacity to ask what's up right now? How did you get my number?"

"Not hard to find when you're looking."

"Did you snoop while you were here?"

"Kind of difficult to snoop when you decided to put your tongue down my throat. I was a little distracted."

She goes silent again. "We can't do this, Ford."

"So it's a this now?"

"I can't..." She trails off and then huffs. "I have to stay focused, especially at home."

"Because of him?"

More silence.

"Laundry. Because of your dad?"

"You don't understand."

"No, I don't. Did he hit you?"

"I'm not answering that question."

"Answer it and I'll hang up."

"I guess we'll be on the phone all night then."

A smile tugs at my lips. I can almost imagine her sitting on top of a princess bed in silk pajamas and pouting. Fucking cute.

"What are you wearing?" I ask, chuckling

when she scoffs at the question.

"We're not doing that."

"What?"

"Phone sex! Your hand up my shirt was enough for one day."

The humor fades and a growl rumbles from me. "I touched your tits?"

"What's wrong with you, Ford? Why do you act like two different people? I don't understand you."

Fuck.

"I'm sorry. Okay? I'm just…shit is fucked up lately and you're the only part of my day that's not."

"See, when you're not being a total dick, I actually like you." She sighs as though this frustrates her, but I can sense her walls lowering a bit. "You're lucky my dad got called back to the office tonight. Otherwise there'd be no way I'd tell you anything. But since he's not here, I guess you can know that I'm wearing a nightgown."

"A nightgown? What are you? Eighty?"

"Oh my God. Dick!"

I untie the knot of my towel and stroke my cock. "You called for my dick and now he's wide awake. Does that mean you're going to play with him?"

"Your cock isn't a him. Is this really what people do when they have phone sex? It's corny."

A laugh barks out of me. "Corny? Babe, I have never once been told I'm corny when it comes to sex."

"Now you have. And don't call me babe."

"Fine, Laundry. Take your panties off and play with me."

Her breathing picks up and I lazily rub at my cock in tandem.

"Wanna FaceTime?"

"Are you insane?" she hisses.

Maybe I'm more like my brother than I'd like to admit.

"Just a bit. I want to see your lips part when you come."

"Because you're a pervert."

"Scared?"

"Of you? No."

"Then what's the big deal?"

"I'm not that kind of girl."

"Yet. Not that kind of girl yet."

She sighs heavily, seemingly annoyed. "Why are you this way?"

"Persistent?"

"I was going to say obnoxious."

"I'm used to getting what I want." I grin,

imagining her rolling her eyes. "When I want something, I'm relentless."

Like coming. I really want to come. With her. In her.

"You don't say…" she mutters.

"Smartass."

"Ford…"

"Hmm?"

She groans. "I just…I don't do this sort of thing, okay? With anyone. It's not you, it's me."

I nearly laugh at her words, but I realize she's being serious. She's nervous or insecure or some shit.

"You not doing this with anyone is what makes it all the more special." I pause, letting those words sink in. "Are you a phone sex virgin, Laundry?"

Based on how standoffish she's being, I'd say she's more than just a phone sex virgin. My dick practically weeps at the thought of being the first man to get inside her.

"God. You have to make everything sound so dramatic." Her irritation only serves to make my dick harder. "Maybe I just don't want you to watch me when it happens."

"When you come for me?"

"Ford."

"Laundry." I abandon my cock to reach into the nightstand drawer. After fetching a bottle of lube, I slick up my dick and then continue my stroking. "Since you don't want me to watch, will you let me listen instead?"

She goes quiet for a moment as she mulls this over. "And then you'll let me go to bed?"

The nerves are back in her voice, barely hidden beneath her feigned annoyance. This is special. It will be special because she's special.

"Yeah, babe. I'll let you go to bed after you come all over your fingers. I promise you'll enjoy yourself. And with how wound up you always are, you could stand to let off a little steam."

"Fine."

"Fine?"

"Do you need a definition of the word fine?"

"Your bitchiness is hot."

"I hate you," she grumbles, though I don't believe it at all.

"Nah, you love me. Time to play."

I close my eyes, trying to imagine her atop her bed with her small hand rubbing at her pussy. It's a tantalizing fantasy—one I'm going to make a reality soon.

"I bet your clit is throbbing," I purr. "Pulsating because it needs to be sucked and bitten."

She scoffs. "You would bite my clit?"

"Fuck yeah, babe. I'm a biter. Now pinch it. Right now."

"This is weird," she complains, breathless.

"No, it's hot. Pinch. Now."

She whimpers, which means she's obeying like a good girl, and I have to strangle the base of my cock to keep from coming right then.

"It'd feel just like that. But sharper. Use your fingernails."

"That'll hurt."

"In a good way, Laundry. I need to hear that sexy sound again."

I'm rewarded with a pained moan that's laced with pleasure. Fucking hell. Her innocence is intoxicating. I want to drown in it.

"Ford," she whines.

What I wouldn't give right now to have her saying my real name right now. Sparrow. All whimpers and mewls and moans making love to *my* name. Fuck, I want that.

"Keep going, pretty girl. I want to come all over my hand imagining it's my fingers touching you rather than your own."

It doesn't take much coaxing before she's crying out in pleasure. I follow on the heels of her orgasm, shooting hot semen all over my bare chest. Fuck, that felt good, but it was only a taste. I want more from this girl. A whole lot more.

"You okay?" I ask, my own chest heaving with ragged breaths.

"Mmhmm."

I grin at the thought of rendering her speechless. "It would have been so much more fun watching you."

"I think I've been your entertainment enough for one day."

"And, to think, we have the rest of our lives," I taunt. "Just me and you until the end, babe."

"You're lucky I feel…" She sighs. "Sleepy."

"Sleepy? Laundry, you wound me. I took your phone sex virginity and you're sleepy? My ego can't take any more bruises."

"Your ego is needy."

"It likes stroking—"

"Time to hang up now, Chevy," she mutters, unable to hold back a laugh which makes me crack up in response.

Our laughter fades away to silence, aside from her soft breathing. For once, I keep my mouth shut and just listen.

"And, yes," she whispers, so softly I almost don't hear, "it was my dad who hit me. I have my reasons for staying, but if I can allow you to walk me through an orgasm, I think I can trust you with the truth. *Can* I trust you?"

"You can." My words are icy and all a lie. "See you Friday."

I end the call before I do or say something stupid. All I can think about is some grown-ass man backhanding Landry. Sure, she's a frosty bitch a lot of the time, but she's also delicate and sweet. For her own father to hit her…it's inexcusable.

I swipe the come off me with my towel and then quickly dress in some black jeans and matching hoodie. Flinging open my bedroom door, I find Scout standing on the other side, his hands gripping the doorframe above his head. Evil glints in his dark gaze as he studies me. The sick fucker was listening in on…hell, probably all of it.

"Smells like sex and revenge," Scout says, flashing me a wild grin. "Who do we get to hurt?"

"You fucking know. Grab Sully. We're leaving in five."

It's time to pay a certain rich piece of shit a visit.

Chapter Fifteen

Scout

SOMEONE SHOULD TAKE Sparrow's license away.

"Jesus, Sparrow," Sully barks from the backseat. "I'd like to arrive in one piece."

Sparrow ignores him, choosing to crank up the volume, blasting us with "Kamikazee" by Missio. He's in a mood. Ever since Sully came home bragging about sucking face with this girl.

My phone buzzes with a text.

Ty: I have some bougie event I gotta attend this weekend. Kill me now.

No can do, Constantine. Big Morelli won't let me.

Me: You're a Constantine. Don't you come out of the womb with a cigar in one hand and a cognac in the other, bougie boy?

He sends me a bunch of middle finger emojis to which I reply back with crying laughing emojis. Sully didn't think I could do this shit, but it's easy. The guy is so damn needy to have a friend that he eats up every morsel I toss at him.

> **Me:** Have you seen that girl anymore? What was her name again? Lori?
>
> **Ty:** Landry. And no. I didn't get her number and I haven't had the balls to ask her dad for it.
>
> **Me:** I could probably find it for you.
>
> **Ty:** You know people?
>
> **Me:** Dude. I'm not the mafia. But I did fuck one of Croft's assistants. I could get it for you.

I really hope Croft's assistants are females, otherwise this lie will get awkward kind of fast.

> **Ty:** The hot redhead or the older lady? You totally nailed the cougar, didn't you?
>
> **Me:** A gentleman never kisses and tells.
>
> **Ty:** You're not a gentleman. You're a dick.

I'm distracted from my phone when we pass by the building Bryant tasked me with torching. It took some effort, but the end result was a fuck-ton of firetrucks and a total loss. They still can't tell it was arson, according to Bryant's intel, and they sure as hell haven't linked me or him to it. Arson isn't usually my gig, but he did get me information I needed.

Ash.

Winston keeps her safely at the Constantine Compound most of the time. They attend events that Morellis aren't invited to. Me and my brothers aren't invited to anything where Ash might show.

My phone buzzes again.

Ty: *You're such a prick for making me beg. Please get me Landry's number.*

I glance over at Sparrow who's pissed as hell over the fact Sully kissed her. And I could bet money that Sully would be more than pissed if he knew Sparrow got her off over the phone. I wonder how angry they'll be when they find out I've given Ty her number just to fuck with them.

They're obsessed with this girl just like they both were with Ivy Anderson. I didn't like Ivy all that much, but when you're fourteen, you don't turn down the chance to get laid by a cheerleader. I sure as hell didn't.

But Ash?

She was different for me.

I hated her and her father for joining our

family. They were an infection that got to my mother and ultimately got her severed from us.

I wanted Ash to pay.

I wanted to hurt her. I did hurt her.

Eventually, I would have broken her completely.

Winston Constantine ruined everything.

All I want is the opportunity to get Ash in my grasp once more. To stare down at her, watching her wither and wilt like a dying flower.

It won't be childish games like last time.

I shoot Ty the number. When I realized Sparrow had been talking to her earlier, I texted Bryant to also get her number. I felt like it was useful to have. You never know when you need information like that.

> **Ty:** You amaze me, man. Seriously. Thanks!
> **Me:** Good luck getting past Daddy Croft…
> **Ty:** Right?!

He sends me some dumb emojis of a bicep flexed. Idiot.

Sparrow mashes the button on his stereo, silencing the vehicle. The clink, clink, clink of his blinker is almost comical. Since when does he use a fucking blinker? Not to mention, he's been blowing through most red lights and going well over the speed limit whenever there are less traffic-congested areas.

We pull into a parking garage—one I know well now. It's Croft's office building. Sparrow pulls the ball cap lower over his brow and creeps into the parking garage. Since there are other businesses in the building—a couple restaurants, some shops, and even some residential units—it's hard as shit to find a parking spot. Eventually, we get lucky and find a spot that someone is exiting.

"What now?" Sully asks, leaning forward between the front seats.

"We wait." Sparrow goes to turn back on the music, but Sully smacks at his hand. "What the fuck?"

Sully growls right back. "What's the plan? How long do we have to wait here?"

"We're not going to wait here," I tell them. My brothers are not the mastermind. Their intentions are good but without me, they'd be waiting forever. "We're going to go find his car and hide nearby."

"And then what?" Sully demands.

I reach beneath the seat and pull out my Glock. "Then we teach him a lesson."

"Woah. Dude, no. We're not fucking killing him," Sparrow exclaims. "Fuck him up, yes, but

K WEBSTER

not shoot his ass. Put the gun away, psycho."

"Fine," I say with a smirk, shoving it back under the seat. "I guess those guns will have to do." Sparrow grunts when I flick his bicep. "Let's go."

We slip out of Sparrow's death machine and stick to the shadows. Our ball caps and hoodies, all in black, will make it impossible for the cameras to pick out who we are. Several flights of stairs later, we make it to the floor Alexander parks on. His midnight-blue Bugatti is parked at an angle, taking up two spots.

"I fucking hate this guy," Sparrow spits out.

"You and me both." Sully crouches into a shadowed area near the car.

Me and Sparrow find our own hiding spots. It reminds me of when we were toddlers. We'd hide and Mom would seek after us. I fucking miss her.

Mom's not coming this time.

We wait for over two hours for this workaholic prick to emerge from his office. I don't know what Sparrow and Sully do to pass the time, but I text back and forth with Ty because the guy just will not stop.

"Psst," one of my brothers hisses.

I shove my phone into my pocket and ready myself, waiting for this guy to approach his vehicle. I'm about to creep from the shadows to attack him, but Sparrow bursts forward all fiery rage and a guttural roar of fury. Sully pounces too, however, with a lot less noisemaking. I prowl after them, amused by how furious my brothers are.

This is personal.

That much is evident when Sparrow puts his hands on his throat and starts squeezing.

This just got more interesting.

Alexander is choking out startled cries and what sounds like pleas for us to just take his money. He has lots of it, apparently.

Sully kicks Alexander hard on the side. The man squirms, trying to fight the both of them off, but my brothers are too strong.

I'd assumed we'd just rough the dickhead up a little, but Sparrow is seconds from crushing this dude's windpipe. Sully must realize it at the same time I do because he shoves our brother off Alexander. Sparrow stumbles away, cursing under his breath. Sully swings his leg, nailing Alexander in the side again. If he didn't break any ribs, I'll be shocked. Patiently, I wait for my turn. Sparrow grunts and snarls like a goddamn bull, but lets Sully get his fill. Alexander is barely moving by the time he finishes with him.

"Let's go," Sully snaps, starting back toward

the stairwell.

I start for Alexander, walking slowly because my knees are hurting from being crouched for so long. I shove my hand into my pocket and push my fingers through the holes of my brass knuckles. He grunts when I reach him and straddle his chest. His throat is purple and blue, but other than that, he looks fine.

I slam my fist across his cheek.

Pop!

A laugh bursts out of me when blood rushes down over his cheek. *Doesn't feel so good to get hit in the face does it, old fucker?*

This time I slam my brass knuckles into his nose. The sickening crack and subsequent flood of blood is satisfying. I don't even personally know this Landry bitch, but if she's got my brothers all agitated enough to want to kick this guy's ass, then I'm there for moral support.

We're a triple threat. Always.

I go for his fucking teeth this time. Someone grabs me in a headlock, dragging me away before I can make impact. Snarling, I attempt to fight them off. I realize it's Sparrow, so I know I won't win. Going limp, I let him haul my ass away. Once he's certain I won't go finish what we started and land a death blow, he takes off toward the stairwell since we parked his car on a different level. It's not until we're inside the vehicle and peeling out of the parking garage do we even speak.

Naturally, it's me to break the silence.

"That was fun." I grin at Sparrow. "Too bad we left at the good part."

"Jesus, Scout? You always take things too far." Sparrow shoots me a nasty glare. "Don't fuck everything up on Friday."

"Friday?" Sully asks.

"Bryant needs me at some meeting or something," Sparrow bites out. "He wants Psycho over there to fill in for me. Seriously, Scout, don't fuck this up. She's already suspicious. You have to play it cool."

She? Ahhh. *Her.* Landry. I apparently have a date with his little girlfriend on Friday.

"I'll behave," I promise, my voice angelic and quite convincing, though everyone in this car knows it's a lie. I don't behave. Ever.

"Fuck," Sparrow spits out. "Whatever. Just don't turn this into another Ash situation."

This piques my interest. This Landry must be pretty fucking intriguing if they think I'll get my panties in wad over her like the both of them apparently have.

I can't wait to see what the big fuss is all about.

CHAPTER SIXTEEN

Landry

D AD WAS JUMPED after work on Wednesday night. Not mugged or robbed or whatever. No, several guys came up to him and beat the crap out of him. He took a trip to the ER via an ambulance when he finally came to and called 911. I didn't even know what happened to him until he came into my room early yesterday morning after being released from the ER looking like a train hit him.

Though I was secretly happy to see him on the receiving end of someone's fists, I couldn't shake the uneasy feeling that it had something to do with me. The timing was too perfect.

This morning, my driver was escorted to campus by two police cars. Dad thinks he was targeted on purpose and he's not taking any chances with my safety, so naturally he has his cop buddies to follow me.

I'm afraid of what they'll find, especially if they happen to see Ford.

This is bad.

So bad.

What is it about Ford Mann that makes me lose my mind and forget my purpose? He's a distraction I absolutely cannot afford.

Dad will connect these dots. He will. Just as soon as he's healed and not laid up in bed in pain.

My stomach twists and my vision darkens. I'm going to faint. Or be sick.

Ford did this. I know he did.

The walk to class is difficult because my knees keep buckling. Why would he hurt my dad? He doesn't know him. He barely knows me. Yet, I'm not an idiot. I told him on Wednesday that my father hit me, and coincidentally, Dad gets jumped later that night.

I could have called Ford and confronted him over the phone. But every time I picked up my phone, I couldn't bring myself to call him. It doesn't make sense. This thing with him is too fast. For him to beat my dad up as badly as he did feels over the top—an extreme reaction to a comment made by someone he barely knows.

You had phone sex with him. He knows you

enough.

This isn't right. His infatuation—bordering on obsession—is too much, too soon. I'd thought he could help me, but I'm thinking I'll just be jumping from one possessive monster into the arms of another.

I'm supposed to be saving me and Della, not causing more problems for us.

God, I trusted him. I really trusted him. And look where that got me. I can't afford any slipups and Ford is becoming my biggest slipup yet.

My ears ring as I near the classroom door. What will I even say to him? Should I just ignore him and hope he goes away? This thing is spiraling and the moment my dad comes out of his painkiller-induced haze, he's going to want retribution. He'll exhaust all his resources to find out who did this to him. And when he finds out Della's tutor—my classmate—did this, he'll blame me somehow. The timing is too suspect not to.

And then what?

I can't even begin to imagine.

As I enter the room, my gaze automatically snaps over to our spot. Relief floods through me when I don't see him. Maybe he's ashamed of what he did. Maybe he doesn't want to face me.

My heart rate slows and the churning in my stomach settles. I'll still have to see him later when he comes over for Della, but at least, for now, I'll have a reprieve. It gives me more time to plan what I'll say to him.

All thoughts come screeching to a halt when my skin feels as though it's crawling. That creepy feeling you get when someone is watching you, peeling you apart layer by layer. I snap my head to the right, my stare landing on a muscular guy dressed all in black who's sprawled out in a desk that seems too small for him.

Ford?

I freeze mid-step, unable to look away. His eyes aren't maple syrup or smooth caramel today. No, they're fathomless like melted dark chocolate, hot and swirling with some unknown emotion. With just one burning stare, he drags me into unknown depths where I can't breathe or move or speak.

Terror.

It's the only emotion I can describe that's setting my nerves alight and my hairs standing on end. The urge to flee is overwhelming, but fear has me paralyzed, rooted in place.

He has a personality disorder.

I know it. I can see it now.

It's the only explanation. I read once about dissociative identity disorder. The different alters that live within one person and varying personality traits, but also medical conditions. It was a fascinating subject to read, but it's not so fascinating when the villainous alter is watching you like you're a snack he's about to eat.

And not in a sexy way.

Like he will tear the meat from my bones and spit the leftovers in a heap after.

Ford needs help. I'm absolutely certain that this version of him is the one who hurt my dad. The empty deadness in his dark eyes is terrifying.

Move, girl.

Just move your legs and sit far, far away from him.

I can't move, though.

I'm a little rabbit with her foot caught in a trap. The predator is salivating over me, toying with me.

There's no way in hell I'm confronting him. Not now. Not with him dressed like he's ready for a funeral—my funeral. Not with the way he cuts me open and dissects me with his eyes.

He sits up in his seat, slowly raking his gaze over my form. I feel exposed and naked. Heat burns over my flesh. His stare alone is almost painful. A tremble quakes through me.

And still, I can't move.

"You okay?" a guy asks, stopping beside me. "You look like you've seen a ghost."

Yeah, mine.

I feel like this shadowy, monstrous version of the man I had freaking phone sex with and kissed will be the one to end my life.

Not my father.

Him.

"I…" I trail off, clearing my throat. "I'm, um, fine."

The guy remains beside me, his concern boring into me. I can't look at him. I have to keep my eyes on the threat in front of me.

"Are you afraid of that guy?" he asks, his voice low. "Do you need help?"

Help?

I need help, but this guy isn't going to be able to help me. No one can. I need to figure out a way out of my mess in a way that doesn't result in Ford or my father destroying what little life I have.

Ford rises to his feet, his features darkening. He glowers at the guy at my side and squares his shoulders. A vein pops out on Ford's neck. His jaw tightens and his hands curl into fists.

Oh crap.

Run!

I want to scream at this guy who's only trying to be nice, but I can't find my voice. He says something to me. It's muffled by the roaring in my ears.

A storm is coming.

It's barreling my way.

We're about to be decimated.

The guy gently grips my arm, trying to get my attention. I squeak in surprise, jerking away from him.

"I'm okay. I'm fine. I promise. Just leave me alone," I hiss, my fear sounding more like venom toward the one person in this room full of people willing to help me.

"Okaaaaay."

The guy walks away, honoring my wish—my *death* wish.

Ford limps slightly, yet it doesn't diminish the raw power rippling from him. He's dangerous in this moment. Starved for me. As he nears, I try not to cower. Just another monster like my father.

I can handle him.

Lifting my chin, I meet his dark eyes that flicker with intensity. He doesn't stop until he's towering over me. His scent is different today.

Not buttery sweet or like the sea with a hint of spice.

He smells decadent. Heady. Like an expensive mocha latte sprinkled with cinnamon. His scent is anything but dangerous. It's intoxicating.

"Landry." He says it like a question. As though he's confirming it. "Hmm."

The rumble of his voice vibrates through me making me shiver. A lot of eyes are on us. Class hasn't started, but we're standing in front of everyone and giving them a show. I can't do this with an audience. The idea of being alone with this man is terrifying, though. I'm out of options.

"Ford."

He cocks his head to the side, amusement making his hard expression transform into something more familiar. It's a trap I fall easily into. My muscles slightly relax.

"You're scared of me." His apathetic words are almost said with a yawn.

Am I that transparent?

Straightening my spine, I affix him with a hard glare. "I need you to leave me alone." *Because I know you beat my dad up and if this gets back to him, he's going to completely lose it.*

"Leave you alone?" His eyes narrow. "Yeah, that's not going to happen."

"What you did to my dad—" I start and snap my mouth shut when several students glance over at us.

"Go on," Ford urges, his voice low and lethal sounding. "I'm listening."

His taunting is both confusing and maddening at once. My mind scatters in a thousand different directions. I don't understand him, especially now, but this nagging curiosity says I want to. If only to better know how to deal with my newest opponent.

"Can we talk?" I mutter, unable to find my voice. "Alone?"

A dark brow arches and he smirks. "Alone?"

"I'm not doing it in front of the whole damn class," I snap, my fear quickly morphing into anger.

How dare him inject himself into my life and shake things up.

My life is already a mess. I don't need him adding to it.

"Saucy." He chuckles, dark and devious. "Let's go somewhere private then, prickly princess."

Prickly princess.

I prefer Laundry or honey over that stupid name.

When I don't move my feet, he reaches down

and takes my hand. It feels clammy inside his large, powerful one. He tugs, guiding me to the door.

This feels like a death march.

Suicide.

And yet, I don't run.

I let him pull me away from the safety of other people.

A chill numbs me to my bones the second we exit the classroom. He slowly limps along, taking me through a series of hallways until I don't know where we're going. The amount of people grows more and more sparse.

"Did you get hurt when you beat up my dad?"

He stops mid-step, cutting his eyes my way. "I did what now?"

"Beat my dad up."

"All by myself?"

I frown at him, confused at his words. Dad just said he'd been jumped. There wasn't a mention of more than one attacker.

My dad isn't exactly a small guy, but Ford is young and built. He could easily take my dad on in a fight. By himself. But everything in his expression tells me there were more than just him.

I don't have time to consider it any longer because he pulls me into a handicapped bathroom. As soon as the door closes, he snaps the lock on it.

Oh God.

I'm alone with him.

His hand jerks toward my face and I flinch out of habit. But, rather than striking me, he grips my jaw, angling my face in different directions as though he's studying every detail. All I can do is stare back, hating how attractive I find him even when he's being like this.

"You're nothing like her." His words are spat at me almost cruelly. "Nothing."

"W-Who?"

He rubs his thumb over my bottom lip, dragging the flesh almost painfully to the side. Then, he slips his thumb between my lips. I bite down on his thumb because I don't want it in my mouth. I don't want him touching me at all. He hisses in pain and his lip curls up.

Oh God.

I've enraged him.

No turning back now. I'm already here, trapped in his grasp. And since there will be no flight, all that's left is to fight.

I bite harder, feeling my teeth pierce his flesh. A metallic taste washes over my tongue. I've drawn blood. Good.

"Feisty little thing," he growls. "So you want to play, huh? Let's play."

CHAPTER SEVENTEEN

Scout

OH, I LIKE her.

I can see why my brothers are so enamored.

She's a fiery, devilish temptation all dolled up to look like an angel. The thing with angels, though, is they're easy to drag to the dark side. You just give them a taste of sin or a gift of pleasure. Breaking their wings is a treat. Crushing their halo is like a taste of heaven itself.

Welcome to the dark side, princess.

My thumb hurts like a sonofabitch, but it's not like she can bite it off. She'd have to go through bone and she's not a fucking dog. Eventually, she'll let go. I'll make her let go.

With my free hand, I grip her tit over her shirt. She cries out in surprise. Her death grip on my thumb doesn't relent. Stubborn as fuck.

I grab her tit roughly before releasing it. She sucks in a sharp breath around my thumb as my other hand finds the button of her jeans. Without much effort, I undo her button and work the zipper down.

"Let go," I warn, my voice like shards of glass stabbing at her.

Her answer is to bite harder.

Fuck.

I shove my hand down into the front of her jeans, the silk of her panties the only barrier keeping my fingers from pushing inside her. I'm not interested in fingerfucking her, but I have an idea to make her turn my thumb loose that's still held hostage between her vicious teeth.

"Wednesday night, you came like a good girl over the phone. I know you've been fantasizing ever since. For this moment." I grin wolfishly at her. "Tell me I'm wrong."

Fuck. Maybe she *will* bite my goddamn thumb off.

I rub my middle finger over her panties, working it between the lips of her pussy. The second it pushes against her clit, she whimpers. My brow lifts as I watch her pretty face turn a lovely shade of red.

"When you moan and finally release me, I'm

going to shove my fingers somewhere else. Somewhere where you can't hurt me."

Her blue eyes flash with a mixture of fear and desire. Dirty little girl. She's warring between hating this moment and wanting more.

"You can't stop me, either," I taunt. "Your pleas will fall on deaf ears."

Each breath she takes is ragged. Almost needy. I rub at her clit, enjoying the way her lashes flutter and the grip she has on my thumb loosens.

"In fact, I'll get off on your begging," I continue with a sneer. "I'll come all over your face as you cry."

Her eyes close and her nostrils flare. With each rub against her sensitive spot, her hips jerk. She likes my touch. Filthy falling angel.

Come down a little more so I can break your wings, beautiful.

Lips close around my thumb and I can almost imagine how they'd look around my dick instead. Her teeth no longer ravage my skin because her tongue has taken over, needily laving over my flesh.

Shouldn't have let go, angel.

I yank my hand from her mouth and the other from her pants before she can orgasm. The shriek of surprise and disappointment make my cock thicken. Too easily, I could fuck her. She could scream no all she wants but her wet pussy would be arguing with her all the way.

She wants, no needs, for me to release her.

Break her because you can.

Grabbing hold of her hair, I twist her around so she's facing the mirror. I push her forehead against it so she can see the need burning in her eyes. She doesn't even fight me as I jerk her jeans and panties down past her ass.

"F-Ford," she whispers. "I'm sorry for hurting you."

"No, you're not."

"We can't do this. Not here. Not like this."

"Such a romantic, prickly princess. But don't worry. I'm not going to fuck you."

She frowns, confusion written all over her soft features. It's not because I don't want to fuck her. I do. Shockingly, I absolutely do. I'm just not going to do it right now. She secretly wants it. Until I find out all her secret wants, I'll enjoy making her wait.

"Get them wet," I order, bending her body with the force of my own as I lean against her. "And don't bite this time. You won't like where I bite back."

Fear shimmers in her eyes in the mirror. With

my grip still in her hair, I ignore the throbbing in my thumb and once bring my fingers within chomping distance. Not gently, I push my fingers into her mouth deep enough she gags. My dick jumps at the thought of making her do this while shoved all the way down her throat. I use my fingers to fuck her mouth—four of them, all but my aching thumb. Slobber runs down over her chin and tears race down her cheeks.

"Good girl. Your mouth is trainable."

Fury flashes in her gaze, but I yank my fingers out of her mouth before she can do any damage. I twist my fingers tighter in her hair and then slip my wet ones down over her ass crack. She moans—the sound fearful and horrified—and she goes completely still. I find the slick opening of her pussy and tease it with my longest finger.

"You want this, hmm?"

She tries to shake her head no, but my grip on her hair is too tight. I force her to nod. More tears. A sob. Pleading.

"If you want it so bad," I growl, "then fucking beg for it."

"Y-You're a monster."

"You have no idea."

Our stares lock. She sees right through me. Straight to the beast that lives at the very root of my soul. Glowers at him, unafraid of the consequence of her bravery.

"Beg."

"Fuck you, Ford."

I push a finger deep inside, loving the moan that tumbles out of her. Before she can enjoy it too much, I pull it back out. Her panting fogs up the mirror in front of her face. That won't do. I need to see every expression on her pretty face.

I yank her upright and bring my teeth to the side of her neck, seeking out flesh through the mess of golden-blonde hair. She whimpers when my teeth press into her neck but don't bite down. I breathe heavily over her flesh, letting the fire inside me burn her, warning her of the hell that's to come.

"Are you afraid?" I murmur, letting my finger dip inside her cunt again. "Hmm?"

"Always."

Her angrily spat out word has me pausing. She's always afraid and it pisses her off. Poor princess is weak and she hates herself for it.

"You don't have to be afraid," I taunt. "It's a choice. You choose it. That's on you."

"You make it sound easy. Like I should be okay with the fact you have me at your mercy, free to do whatever you want."

"I *can* do whatever I want. You can't stop me either. You're trapped."

"I'm not weak," she snaps. "You're weak. Preying on a little girl. A fucking monster!"

Her blue eyes are wild, enraged beyond belief. She's not talking to this demon. She's talking to the ones that live inside her head—the ones who always torment her. The ones responsible for her continuous fear.

"If you're not weak, then by all means, take control."

She blinks several times, chasing away the haunting thoughts possessing her. Her tearstained cheeks are bright red and my blood is smeared over her lip and chin. Wrecked and in such a feral state, she's fucking mesmerizing.

"Make me come." Her nostrils flare. "I want you to make me come and then I want you to leave me the fuck alone."

I shove my finger deep inside her, pull it out and then shove two inside. She cries out but doesn't back down. Her boldness has hardened her into stone. Beautiful granite.

"Harder," she demands. "Make it feel good. *If* you can."

My dick is straining against the zipper of my jeans. I want to fuck this mouthy brat until she's boneless and can't remember her own name.

"If," I parrot, grinning at her reflection. "You have no fucking idea who you're taunting."

"The snake." She pushes her ass against my hand. "You're a snake but I'm not afraid of you."

Her trembling could argue that fact, but I let her win this round she's so bravely fought. I squeeze another finger into her tight pussy, fucking her like I would if it were my dick. Rough and relentless. So hard she cries. Such a beautiful sound.

I finally release her hair because I need my free hand. Sliding it around to her front, I squeeze her tit, drawing out a delicious moan, before diving south. My fingers push between her pussy lips, seeking out her sensitive clit. She lets loose a surprised shriek and grips my wrist as though to stop me from making her come.

Nothing can stop me now.

I won't stop until her cunt is leaking with pleasure, running down her thighs and soaking her clothes.

"That's it," I rumble, my mouth finding her ear. "Give it to me."

Her pussy squeezes around my fingers, her desire evident in the way it slicks up my hand. I fuck her hard with my fingers, making sure to graze her g-spot each time. She claws at my wrist but not because she wants me to stop.

She wants this.

Needs this.

I pinch her clit and tug at it while fingering the spot inside her that's the button to straight ecstasy. Her body responds, like I knew it would, and she detonates. Like a nuclear bomb, obliterating everything around us.

She screams.

So loud I'm forced to abandon her clit to cover her mouth. She shakes uncontrollably in my grip, fresh tears running down her cheeks and soaking my hand. I expect her to run the second she comes down from her high, but she surprises me by relaxing in my arms.

Safe with a monster.

It's a laughable thought.

My humor is muted, though. I'm too transfixed on the way her cunt continues to spasm around my fingers that are still wedged inside her. How her hot breath tickles my hand with every strangled surge of air she attempts to suck into her lungs.

She groans against my hand that covers her mouth as my other fingers slide out of her. I step back, leaving her trembling form, wrecked and used and sated by the sink. Her blue eyes sear into mine in the reflection. Bringing my wet fingers to my nose, I inhale her scent—lavender and mandevilla. So delicate and sweet.

I flick my tongue out and run it along the glistening remnants of her orgasm on my fingers. She sucks in a sharp breath, watching my every movement like I'm the most fascinating creature she's ever encountered.

Her taste is foreign to me.

Sugar laced with something addictive, like heroin.

A sweet shot of obsession.

"Now I understand the pissing match Wednesday night," I say, flashing her a knowing grin. "I understand quite well."

She cries out when I pounce on her. I easily twist her body around and push her bare ass against edge of the sink. I dip my mouth to hers, trying to memorize her scent for later when I jack off to this memory in the shower. A barely audible whimper from her has me wanting to chase it and taste it and suck it from her lips.

My mouth crashes against hers. I can taste the twang of my blood still smeared on her lips. I wonder if she can taste the blissful high of herself. The kiss ends sooner than I'd like, but if I don't escape the confines of this bathroom, there's no telling what I'll do.

I can't let myself go there with her.

She's just a substitution for what I really want.

The one I will have one day.

"See you later, prickly princess."

With a wink, I leave the trembling girl alone. I wonder how long until she realizes her wings are gone. She'll remember this moment—the moment I ate them while she rode my fingers into oblivion.

Sorry, beautiful, but you're not an angel anymore.

CHAPTER EIGHTEEN

Landry

I NEED HELP.

Not help to escape this hell, but real psychological help. After what I allowed—what I actually enjoyed—today at school, I'm positive I'm losing my mind.

This isn't normal.

Certainly not healthy.

Oh, God.

Tears sting my eyes but I refuse to let them fall. Not here in his room. Not now. Not while my father lies in his bed just a few feet away, softly snoring, while I watch. If he woke up and saw me so wrecked, I wouldn't be able to blame it on worrying over him. No, he'd see right through that.

And he can't see that.

Ever.

As much as I don't want to be in his room, I need to feel him out when he wakes from his nap. To see what he knows and if any of it leads back to me or Ford. I'm getting pretty good at reading him, so if he knows anything, I'm sure I would be able to tell.

From somewhere within the condo, Sandra yells at someone. Probably Noel. She holds her position of power over them all, reaming them constantly when they don't measure up to her standards.

I just hope that it's not Della. It's the most frustrating thing when someone yells at a completely deaf person. She isn't affected by it. It only punishes everyone around her.

Thoughts of Della make my mind drift back to Ford. I tighten my thighs, clenching my sex. It's sore. Aches from the abuse.

I nearly laugh.

Abuse?

Then why did my body freaking sing at his cruel touch?

Truth is, there were many parts about this morning, while locked in that bathroom, that I secretly enjoyed. A dirty little secret that I share with Ford's evil alter ego.

He'll be here soon.

I can't face him. Not now. Not ever.

Glancing over at my father, I make sure he's still sleeping before picking up my phone and texting Ford.

> **Me:** *I would appreciate it if you don't speak to me ever again.*

His response is immediate.

> **Ford:** *What??? Why?*

Is he even for real?

He's sick. Suffering from a mental illness. And my idiotic self got swept up in the darkness that is Ford Mann. Because I'm apparently a magnet for monsters.

> **Ford:** *Laundry, what happened?*
>
> **Me:** *YOU. You happened, Ford. I was an idiot for trusting you.*

He starts ringing my phone. Thankfully, it's on silent. It buzzes and buzzes and buzzes. Psycho. He's a stalker. Without a moment's hesitation, I block his number. That will buy me some time. At least until he shows up to tutor my freaking sister.

I can't escape him.

Not him or my father.

This life is a prison. I'm going to have to grab Della and disappear. Even if that means living a life on the run, always trying to outrun my father's limitless resources. It's better than waiting around for a plan. My plans keep getting derailed.

My phone buzzes again and a burst of anger flashes through me. He won't leave me alone. I'm ready to call him every name in the book, but it's not him.

Unknown Number: *Hey, you. It's me. Ty.*

I blink at the phone, unable to form thoughts. Ty Constantine is texting me. How? Why? What the hell is going on right now?

Unknown Number: *Okay, so this is probably creepy. I'm sorry. It's just I had to leave in such a rush the other day when your dad got mad. And then I heard he got attacked. Just worried is all. Are you okay?*

I change the contact to Ty Constantine before replying back.

Me: *I'm fine. How did you get my number?*

Ty: *Let's just say it was work to get it. How's Alexander?*

Me: *Asleep. Lots of pain meds. Broken nose and cracked rib. Cheek is stitched up. Looks* *like he's been in a car accident. But, he'll be okay.*

Unfortunately.

I know my father. He'll come out of this, hunt down the man who did this to him, and ruin his life. He will ruin Ford's life.

Ty: *Ouch. Tell him I'll hold down the fort while he's gone. ;)*

A smile tugs at my lips. I can almost imagine his handsome face in front of me, winking in a teasing manner. Ty trying to fill Dad's shoes at his company is laughable.

"Who's making you smile like that?" a voice rasps out.

Jerking my stare from my phone to my father, I attempt to quell the rising surge of panic. Even in his battered, sleepy state, he's powerful and very much still the person who has his thumb on me.

"Uh…" I chew on my lip and then shrug. "Ty. I don't know how he got my number."

Dad blinks at me slowly, his lids heavy thanks to the drugs. "Hmm. Interesting."

"He wants to know how you're doing. How are you doing?"

"Been better."

My phone buzzes again, but I don't look down at it. I'm trapped in my dad's penetrating stare. I squeeze my phone so hard I wonder if it'll crack. Swallowing hard, I motion toward the end table.

"Want some water?"

"I'm fine. Aren't you going to answer that?"

I nod and look down at my phone. It's a picture of Ty dressed in a suit. He's in a limo, looking quite relaxed and happy. Must be nice not to be wound up so tight all the time.

> **Me:** What do you want?
>
> **Ty:** Thanks. You look nice too.
>
> **Me:** Sorry. I'm stressed. You look nice. And you have no idea what I look like right now.

I look like I was fingerfucked by a monster at school and being stared down by one as we speak. Not sexy at all.

> **Ty:** I can't imagine a scenario where you'd ever look less than beautiful.
>
> **Me:** Thanks. Is that all? I need to go.
>
> **Ty:** No. I wanted to see if I could take you out on a real date. Just the two of us.

My heart stutters in my chest. Is that why he's dressed so nice? Is he coming here? That can't

K WEBSTER

happen. Dad won't let me go anywhere alone with him. Hell no. And if he shows up while Ford is here… I can't even visualize what kind of situation that would turn into.

"Well," Dad grunts. "What does the kid want?"

Peeling my stare from my phone, I meet my dad's hard glare. "He, uh, wants to go on a date. Just the two of us."

Dad studies me for a long beat. Sweat dampens the back of my neck. I try to remain calm and steady. Then, he nods. Barely perceptible.

"What?" I whisper, frowning at him.

"It's fine. You can go out on a date with Mr. Constantine."

"Dad, I don't understand."

"What's there to understand? The answer is yes." He groans in pain when he tries to sit up. "Of course, I'll send a security detail because I can't rule out that what happened wasn't a calculated attack by people who wanted to hurt me personally."

"You think it was someone you know?"

"Or sent by someone I know."

"You didn't get a look at the guy?"

"There were three of them, I think. Maybe more. It's a blur."

220

My phone buzzes again.

Ty: *I'll take that as a no. Is it creepy if I try again tomorrow?*

I'm still reeling at Dad's words. Did Ford bring a bunch of friends? His brother? He's mentioned a brother before. The truth of the matter is, I don't know much about Ford. I don't know what kind of people he hangs out with or his motives for befriending me.

This morning was more than what friends do.

His fingers were inside you, girl.

He made you come.

"Are you going to answer the poor guy?" Dad asks, gesturing at my phone. "Don't keep him waiting."

I nod slowly and then tap out a reply.

Me: *Fine.*

Ty: *Fine…what? Try again tomorrow?*

Me: *Fine. As in, we'll make it a date.*

He sends me a bunch of smiling emojis, clearly happy with that answer. I'd smile back except I can't shake the way Dad looks at me. Like he's setting me up to fail. If he only knew. I failed spectacularly this morning. Any minute, that failure is going to show up at my home and who knows what sort of catastrophe will ensue.

> **Ty:** *I'm on my way to an event my family is making me attend, but when I get back in town, I'll text you about our date. Tell your dad I hope he feels better soon.*
>
> **Me:** *K. Bye.*

I lift my chin and meet Dad's probing stare. "He's excited and hopes you feel better soon."

Silence befalls the room. Sandra is no longer shouting at the help. It's quiet aside from the booming of my heart that seems to be echoed in my ears. I fidget in my seat, hating how exposed I feel right now.

Can he see it written all over my face?

What I did today with Ford?

The doorbell rings and I jump. Anxiety claws its way up my chest, gripping my throat and rendering me unable to breathe. My face heats, giving me away. It's so damn obvious. Dad, who never misses a thing, watches me with narrowed eyes.

"It's just a date with a boy from a powerful family, sweetheart. Not a marriage proposal. You'll always be my little girl. No one else's. Just mine."

The possessive, threatening tone has me withering.

There is no escape.

I was stupid to even hope.

CHAPTER NINETEEN

Sully

SOMEONE IS BLOWING up my phone and it's pissing me off. As if dealing with Heathen, who's acting like a beast from hell in her carrier, isn't enough, I have someone calling my phone over and over again.

For fuck's sake.

Exiting the elevator, I set the hissing cat in her carrier down, and fish my phone out of my pocket. It's Sparrow. He can be such a goddamn woman sometimes.

"What?" I demand, irritation dripping from the word. "I'm kind of busy."

"Yeah," he snaps. "I can tell. I only called you fifteen times."

"What's wrong? Is Mom okay?"

He sighs. "I'm sure. She's in prison, not dead. No, this is worse. It's Scout."

My blood runs cold. Scout went to school in place of Sparrow today. Since Scout isn't answering his phone, I've been on edge wondering how it went. I mean, he was on a college campus, so surely he couldn't have gotten into too much trouble.

"He did something. I don't know what, but it's bad." Sparrow curses and breathes heavily into the phone. "She told me never to speak to her again."

"Fuck," I grumble. "Did she say why?"

"I asked her what happened and she said, '*You* happened.'"

"Did you talk to Scout?"

"Not answering his phone."

"I'm sure he was just being a dick. It's fine."

"Dude, she blocked me."

"Could she have found out it was us Wednesday night? Would he have told her?"

"Knowing Scout, anything's possible. Do you think he could have hurt her?"

Flashes of the past burn behind my eyes in rapid succession. I'm not going to let him go down this path again. Last time, we were collateral damage. This is a pattern for him—obsess over someone he can't have, take it too fucking far, and then get destroyed by the ones who love her. In this case, Alexander Croft has the ability to crush us like Winston Constantine did.

"I'll find out," I assure him, "and I'll make it right."

He lets loose a long, relived sigh. "Thanks."

"I have a question, though."

A beat of silence and then a bit of hesitancy in his voice. "Okay."

"Why were you talking to Landry?"

"What do you mean? It's our job."

"Texting or talking on the phone. Your job was to deal with her at school. Nothing more. You didn't tell me you were talking to her on the phone, too."

"It's not a big deal, man."

"It is because I have to make sure my part of the story adds up. It's fucking embarrassing when I say shit or do shit that contradicts what you've done. Why are you keeping your interactions with her to yourself? I told you what happened when I was at her house. I just don't understand why you aren't sharing what happens when you're with her."

"I gotta go."

"No. Fuck. Just answer the question, Sparrow."

"Nothing," he growls, a bit too defensively I

might add. "Nothing of importance."

"Have you fucked her?"

"Seriously? When? At school? Fuck off, Sully."

"Stop being a pussy and tell me what the hell's been going on."

"What? You want to know that I had phone sex with her? Huh? The night after you fucking kissed her?"

He's jealous.

This is Ivy Anderson all over again.

Or, worse, Ash Elliott.

At least with Ivy, we got in a little bit of trouble. With Ash, our lives blew up in our faces. We barely survived that shit.

And Landry?

Her dad is evil and connected with the Constantines. The potential of this going nuclear is a real possibility.

Scout is acting crazy.

Sparrow is turning possessive as fuck.

And me?

I want to throttle Sparrow for carrying on a secret phone sex rendezvous behind my back and to punch Scout for hurting her or doing whatever the fuck he did.

This means I'm in just as deep as them.

"I think you need to take a step back," I state,

voice cool. "I think we all need to."

"We can't," he bites back. "It's our job. *She's* our job."

"We'll quit. Bryant can get over it."

Sparrow laughs, cold and cruel. "We're Morellis now, Sull. We don't get to just quit. You know this. It's why you've been such a pissy bitch lately. We're stuck and there's nowhere for us to go."

"I'm not a fucking Morelli. I'm a Mannford."

"Just find out what he did and fix it. I'll do damage control on Monday at school."

Heathen snarls from her carrier, reminding me that she's an unhappy bitch in that cage.

"Fine. I'll text you later."

Not bothering to wait for him to reply, I walk over to the Croft's door. I ring the doorbell, ignoring the hideous sounds my cat is making.

Not my cat.

Scout's cat since she likes him more.

I'm just borrowing her at this point to keep the charade up.

A few minutes later, the door opens. It's not Sandra or one of the other staff or even Della. No, it's her.

Landry.

The root of this growing problem between me

and my brothers. I know why, too. When I'm in her presence, I sort of forget she's a job. I grow fixated on how her bottom pink lip is slightly swollen and how it tasted when I kissed her. I'm entranced by the way golden-blonde hair dances with her movement, framing her pretty face and drawing your attention there always. Even dressed in just jeans and a T-shirt, she's elegant and lovely and tempting.

I know how her tit feels beneath my palm. Full but not too full. Enough to grab onto and claim.

Her blue eyes are hard as she assesses me. Accusation gleams in her stare. Maybe even a little hurt, too. A glimmer of fear.

What did you do to her, Scout?

"Hey, honey."

She visibly relaxes at my words. The fierce stance she'd been in fades and she grabs onto the doorframe as if to steady herself. Her nose turns pink and tears well in her eyes.

Fuck.

Scout did hurt her.

How do I explain this? She thinks I'm him. I have to fix what it is he did to her. Somehow. Some way.

"May I come in?" I ask, keeping my voice soft.

"Please?"

"I shouldn't let you within fifty feet of me."

A tear grows too heavy for her eyelid and races down her cheek. Despite her words, she wants me to make it all better. I can see it in her eyes. Reaching a hand up to bridge the distance between us, I cup her cheek and swipe away the wet streak with my thumb.

"I'm sorry," I murmur.

It's the truth. I am. I'm sorry that my psychopath brother has somehow gotten his claws in her. He's rough and brutal and fucking scary when he wants to be.

She steps back, but it's not to escape me. It's an invitation. Della peeks around the corner and sticks her tongue out at me. I stick mine out at her and then offer the cage.

"Take Heathen," I say, making sure she sees the movements of my lips. "I'll be in the classroom in a minute."

Della grabs Heathen's carrier from me and disappears. Once I close the door behind me, I grab onto Landry's hand, tugging her into the bathroom just off the foyer.

"I can't be alone in here with you," she whispers, but she doesn't fight me. "If Dad saw…"

We whipped his ass pretty good. I doubt he'll

be prowling the house right now looking for his daughter. I bet he'll be down for a few days at least.

I lock the bathroom door behind me and pin her against the countertop with my hips. She sucks in a breath and her blue eyes search mine.

"Listen," I start, but she cuts me off.

"Your eyes are the color of caramel."

"And yours are blue like the sky on a hot summer day."

She smirks. "That's not what I meant, lover boy. I meant that when your eyes are like this, you're different." Her brows furl. "A lot different than this morning."

"I'm sorry," I say again. "There are things about me you don't understand. Things I can't exactly tell you."

"You're sick." She taps at my head. "Here."

You have no fucking idea, honey.

"Yeah. A little, I guess. What can I do to make it better?" I stroke my fingers through her hair, making sure to be gentle and caring. "Let me kiss you."

"It's not like I have a choice."

"You do right now. With me. In this moment. Can I kiss you?"

Her brows scrunch as she studies me with

intensity. "You've lost your mind."

"Look at me, honey. Today...*that* won't happen again. You can trust me."

"Trust you?" She barks out a disgusted laugh. "No, Ford, I can't trust you. You're hiding so much from me."

I rest my forehead against hers for a moment, closing my eyes. "I know I'm a complicated man, Landry. I really hope one day you'll fully understand...my layers. Until then, trust that I care a lot about you and would never do anything to intentionally hurt you. I truly am sorry for what happened to you." I reopen my eyes and pull back so she can see the sincerity in my stare. "Now, please, can I kiss you?"

She makes me wait an eternity, but eventually she nods. I tangle my fingers in her hair, tug until her mouth parts and is primed for a kiss, and then press my lips to hers. At first, she's tense, but as my tongue teases along hers, she turns to putty in my arms.

I kiss her deeply, but I make sure to infuse my apology into it. Soft swipes. Gentle caresses. Sweetly murmured things to her whenever we pull apart enough to breathe. I could continue kissing her all afternoon. I wonder how much it would take to fix what Scout did to her.

"You hurt me," she whispers, her fingertips finding the center of my chest and pushing. "I was scared."

"Where did I hurt you?"

She scowls and turns her head from mine. "You know where."

Taking a chance, I slide my hand between us, finding the warmth between her legs over her jeans. "Here?"

"Y-Yes."

"I can make it better." I tug at the button and then lower the zipper. "I'll kiss it all better."

"Ford," she murmurs. "We...I...You..."

I leave her to her mindless stammering as I kneel. With as much tenderness as I can muster, I ease her jeans and panties down her thighs. Her pussy—waxed smooth—makes my mouth water for a taste. I run my thumb over her slit and then pull aside one lip, exposing her pink bud. With a grin, I lick the small nub, loving the way she whimpers in return.

Her fingers tangle in my hair and she gasps when I suck her clit into my mouth. I want to rip off her jeans completely so I can spread her thighs. I'm starved and want to feast on her sweet-tasting pussy. To get my face all up in her slickness, sucking off all the juices of her pleasure I can find.

I ache to tongue her tight hole, licking away the soreness of the hurt Scout inflicted.

A growl rumbles from me, loud and needy. I'm about to start ripping away her clothes completely when she stops me with a smack to the head.

"Oh God. No. Quit. We can't do this here." Her voice raises an octave, panic laced in her tone. "My dad."

Though I'd love nothing more than to keep going, I know she's right. He's a bastard who hits his own daughter for fucking nothing. I can't image what he'd do if he found out we were doing this.

"I really, really want to apologize to your perfect pussy," I rumble, running my nose along her slit. "But, you're right. The things I want to do to you will take hours." Glancing up, I wink at her. "One orgasm just isn't enough. It's gotta be all or nothing, honey."

Her smile, though she tries to hide it, peeks out. Maybe I've been forgiven for my brother's sins. I'll make it up to her over and over again when we have the time and privacy, that's for damn sure.

"I have to go check on my father," she says with a slightly disappointed sigh. "I'll see you

Monday."

She jerks her clothes back on and slips out of the bathroom, leaving me unsated and with a raging erection. I stand back up, wash off the scent of her pussy, and manage to cool the blood that was making my dick hard.

Maybe I fixed shit with her.

I find Della in the classroom trying to con Heathen to come out from beneath a table. Heathen hisses at her but she doesn't hear. Walking over to Della, I playfully thump her on the head.

She signs something vicious to me, but I don't know what the fuck it means. Lifting a brow, I point to our usual spot where we work.

"Playtime's over."

She cocks her head, frowning. I say it again and gesture at the cat. With a huff of understanding, she abandons her efforts and walks over to the desk. Once she's seated, she signs slowly to me. We don't discuss the fact that I don't know ASL, but she's not stupid. For some reason, she plays along. Probably using me for the damn cat.

It takes me a minute to decipher what she's saying.

Dad got beat up.

Playing innocent, I say back to her, "He did?

How terrible."

She grins and shrugs before signing something I don't know. Then, she takes the time to spell it out for me, *k-a-r-m-a.*

"Karma?"

Yes. She folds her hands in her lap and waits patiently for our lesson to start as though she's a sweet little cherub and not the little devil herself.

I like this kid.

And Alexander definitely had that shit coming.

A sudden realization hits me right in the gut. The smile I'd returned to Della fades. If Alexander hits Landry, I wonder if he does the same to Della.

Karma.

I've seen the way she looks at him—with barely hidden hatred. It's on the tip of my tongue to ask her if he hits her too. In the end, I keep my mouth shut. Deep down, I know the answer. He does.

It makes me want to beat his ass all over again.

CHAPTER TWENTY

Sparrow

NORMALLY, I'D BE completely fine with attending an event where I'm required to wear a nice suit and flash my charming smile. I'm good at it. I actually like it, unlike my brothers.

Not tonight.

Tonight, I'm buzzing with anger and frustration. I am stuck in fucking Boston of all places. Bryant wants me to attend some real estate dinner and bid on some properties. Basically, he wants me to rub elbows with people in the biz, learn a thing or two, and then somehow use it against his enemies.

Maybe Sully was right. This is bullshit. Our lives. How we're chained to the Morellis, specifically Bryant, and have no hope of doing anything else.

Rather than sulk like my brother would over

what I can't do anything about right now, I focus on my task at hand.

Schmooze.

Sully will smooth out things with Landry, hopefully, and what he doesn't fix, I'll manage myself.

After dropping my car off with a valet driver, I make my way into the building that's bustling with well-dressed people. This is my element. I was born to party with the elite. I'd like to think I get that from Mom. I clean up the best of the three of us and can fake a smile that gets me damn near whatever I want. It doesn't hurt that I'm wearing one of my most expensive bespoke Tom Ford charcoal suits. Sully says these pants give me a David Beckham ass. I think he's just being a dick when he says it, but I take it as a compliment. The only thing I'm missing is something lovely hanging off my arm. A few women try to catch my gaze, as though in tune with my thoughts, but I'm not interested. I'm too distracted to flirt. Besides, the only arm candy I want is her. I try not to imagine Landry in a sexy, fitted dress because these David Beckham pants don't have room for a ten-inch boner.

"Ford?"

A tall, broad guy with fuckboy blond hair and

a goofy-ass grin saunters my way. I stare at him blankly because I don't know this asshole. He's certainly not anyone I'd willingly associate with. But he knows our alias, though.

"Yeah?"

"You didn't tell me you'd be going to this shit." He laughs and smacks the side of my arm. "Dude, you were right about Landry."

I quickly connect the dots.

Landry?

This has to be Ty fucking Constantine.

"I'm always right," I grunt, playing along. "What happened?"

"I texted her. We're going out on a date next week. *Without* her daddy."

"Her dad's a real asshole, yeah?"

"Shit, yeah." He leans in and whispers conspiratorially. "He still didn't come into the office today. When he got jumped, they really must have fucked him up."

"Hmph."

He smacks my arm again and I swear to fuck I'm going to smack him back if he does it again. "What crawled up your ass and died today? Usually you're not so grumpy."

I blink at him in confusion. What kind of act has Scout of all people been putting on?

"Is it the girl you were telling me about?" he asks, frowning. "She still avoiding you?"

Did he really tell her about Ash?

"Always," I grunt out.

"You're just going to have to get her alone. Make her hear you out."

"I don't think it'll be that easy. She's married."

His eyes bug out of his head. "No shit? Man, you didn't tell me she was married. You really do have it bad if you're pining over a married woman."

"We have history." I shrug and cast my gaze into the crowd, my mind on other people who aren't Ash. "Kind of hard to forget what we had."

"You'll get her back if it's meant to be." He squeezes my shoulder. "I can help. Just tell me what to do."

Ask your cousin if my brother can have his wife so he can torture her some more. Can you do that, Ty boy?

"Thanks, man," I say instead. "I need a drink."

Ty winks at me. "Follow me. I've already scoped out the bar."

He saunters away, weaving through the crowd. I follow after him, growing more and more irritated as the seconds tick by. When he reaches the line, he turns to regard me, studying me intently.

"You're not limping. Knees feeling better today?"

Dammit.

"Comes and goes," I lie. "I can hide it if I have enough oxy."

"Oxy?" His eyes widen. "Seriously? That shit'll fuck you up."

How does Scout put up with this guy? He's chatty and too damn friendly. Everything I say he has to inspect it under a microscope.

"So," I mumble, changing the subject, "where will you take Croft's daughter for your date?"

He frowns like he doesn't like me steering the conversation away from my non-existent drug problem, but indulges me anyway because, apparently, he's a golden boy in need of a friend.

Hell, you have to be damn near desperate to befriend Scout.

"At first," he says, leaning in, "I was thinking some place romantic. Five-star restaurant or whatever. Carriage ride. I don't know. Something fancy."

"You decided against that?" I lift a brow in question.

"I don't know…I thought maybe I'd just take her somewhere low-key. A movie. Maybe the arcade. Fill up on junk food. The girl seems like she could unwind a little."

No shit.

Landry is wound tight with a frozen stick up her ass. She'd probably really enjoy the movies. But with someone like me. Not this fuckboy. I could get her to relax.

"I think the movie's a good idea," I admit, though it pains me to do so.

I have to play nice with this guy. Part of the gig. It's just better when Scout's dealing with this part and I'm dealing with Landry.

He continues to ramble about all his date ideas. A bunch of shit to make her swoon. By the time it's our turn in line, I'm ready to smack my hand over his mouth so he'll shut the hell up.

Ty orders our drinks and pays. I take the dark liquid, knocking it back eagerly. The burn scalds my throat, but it feels good.

"You straight chugged that whiskey, man." He shakes his head. "You sure that's a good idea with the oxy?"

I'm about to answer him when I notice a familiar face in the crowd. Another goddamn Constantine. Thankfully, it's not Winston, but it is one of his mini-me brothers. Perry. If he sees me chatting it up with his cousin, our cover will be blown. I have to get the fuck out of here. Bryant can kiss my ass.

"You're right," I mutter, turning my back to Perry as not to be seen and blow my cover with Ty. "I'm not feeling so hot. I'm going to head to my hotel."

"You'll be here tomorrow night too, right? This event is two days. Please say I won't be doing this shit alone." He gives me the puppy dog eyes. "Dude, please."

"Yeah, whatever. I'll see you tomorrow."

"I'll text you later!"

Ignoring him, I stalk out of the building. I made an appearance. It's time to get the fuck out of here.

✧　✧　✧

I'M BUZZED.

Not from the one drink I had at the event, but the three or four or seven more I've had since I arrived at my hotel. The bar is dark and swanky. I've been able to drink away my frustrations in relative peace.

The walk back to my room is a blur. It takes a few times to get the keycard into the slot.

Eventually, I make it inside. I strip out of my suit and climb onto the bed in just my boxers.

I want to talk to her.

It's not fair that Scout somehow fucked this up for me.

There's a missed text on my phone from Sully that says he thinks he fixed things. I'm not convinced. I need to hear it with my own ears. But she blocked me.

It takes intense focus, but I find her number on my cell and then use the hotel phone to dial her. I'm not even sure if she's awake this late, well after midnight now.

"Hello?"

The breathiness of her voice speaks straight to my cock. I close my eyes, imagining her sexy little mouth.

"Hello?" she says again. "Who is this?"

"Sparrow."

"What? I can't hear you. You're mumbling. Who is this?"

"Laundry, it's me."

She lets out a heavy sigh. "Chevy?"

I grin, imagining her shock. "Yep."

"I blocked you from calling me."

"And I'm calling you to tell you to un-block me."

"Are you drunk?"

"Little bit." I scrub my palm over my face. "I miss you."

"Miss me? Ford, I just saw you. You literally stole a kiss before you left."

Fucking Sully.

"That wasn't me," I slur. "That was my loser alter-ego."

"Are you jealous…of yourself?"

"Yep. I also hate parts of myself."

"You have problems, Chevy."

"And you have answers to my problems, Laundry."

"You confuse me. You're never the same person."

"Can you un-block me?"

"Fine."

"FaceTime me."

"Okay."

I don't want to hang up, but I have to. She makes me wait a long five minutes before she calls me back. I answer on the first ring. Her pretty face is lit by a bedside lamp. The only light I have is coming into the room from the bathroom.

"Hey."

She smirks. "Hey."

"I wish you were in this bed with me right

now."

"Ford…"

"Don't call me that." I close my eyes. "Call me Chevy or…" Sparrow.

"Or what?"

"If you weren't so stressed about life or whatever it is that has you wound up all the time, what would you do? You're about as interested in college as I am. It won't take them long to figure out we suck and never do our assignments."

She scoffs. "I do my assignments."

"Liar."

"I *need* to do my assignments. I've just been distracted. I'll catch up."

"Maybe we should have a study date." I grin at her. "Naked study date."

"You're a brat."

"Seriously, babe. What would you do?"

She gnaws on her bottom lip so hard it's a wonder she doesn't draw blood. "I try not to think about it."

What kind of answer is that?

"Why not?"

"Because I don't have a future." The bitterness in her tone can't be hidden. "I'll end up marrying some rich, successful guy and popping out a bunch of babies. The end."

"Sounds like a lot of sex, though."

She smiles even though I can tell she doesn't want to. "I'd do something with my hands."

"Hand jobs?"

"Oh my God. I'm hanging up."

I laugh and then laugh harder when she sticks her tongue out. It's so cute. If I were there, I'd suck it into my mouth and make her forget she was mad.

"When my mom was alive, she used to do all the floral arrangements for Dad's parties. I loved helping her. We'd spend hours working with exotic flowers. It's when we'd have our best talks." She smiles wistfully. "I miss her."

"I miss my mom, too."

"She's gone?"

"Yeah." I close my eyes and then sigh. "So, a florist, huh? I could see you in a cute little shop cutting flowers."

"It's not exactly dreaming big," she mutters. "What about you?"

I shrug. "I don't have choices either. I'm my uncle's bitch."

"His bitch?"

"I run errands and shit for him."

"He's in the mafia?"

We both laugh.

"I wish. That shit would be entertaining. But, nah. I just go to parties and do odd jobs. It's boring and pointless. My brother hates him for it."

"Are you and your brother close? What's his name?"

"Sullivan. And we're close as brothers can be. Still, he's a fucking prick most of the time."

"My little sister can be a monster, but I'd never admit that to anyone but you."

God, I wish I could kiss her right now.

"So?" she says. "What would you do if you didn't have this uncle of yours?"

"Honestly, I don't know. I haven't allowed myself to think that far ahead. At one time I thought I'd follow in my mom's footsteps. Become a doctor. But…shit happened. I just don't think about it now."

"Maybe you'll figure it out."

"Maybe."

"I should go to bed now," she whispers. "It's late and your eyes keep drooping."

"Send me a picture and I'll get off the phone."

She rolls her eyes but nods. "Fine. I'll send it after you hang up."

"I'll call you tomorrow, Laundry."

"Bye, Chevy."

She hangs up. I stare at the screen until a picture comes through text. In the photo, she's smiling at me. It's sweet and adorable. Rolling onto my side, I take a selfie and send it back to her. She sends me some sleeping emojis and I take the hint.

I fall asleep staring at her face and then I have dreams about her sassy mouth.

CHAPTER TWENTY-ONE

Landry

IS FORD NICE to you?

Della makes a sour face before signing, *He's a dummy.*

I bite back a laugh and then probe some more. *He isn't a good teacher?*

He's a good teacher, she signs, and then shrugs. *Just a dummy. Even Heathen knows it.*

"You're a brat," I tease, signing and saying the words. "You know that?"

She nods happily, grinning. Then, she makes an evil face at me before signing, *Is he your boyfriend?*

My blood runs cold. Is it that obvious that me and Ford have something going on? If it's apparent to my sister who doesn't pay much attention to everyone around her, I can only imagine what my dad thinks, since he watches my every move.

"No," I say in a harsh tone, making sure to enunciate so there's no mistaking what I'm saying to her.

She signs, *Liar.*

"Enough." She's so brazen sometimes and if she gets too comfortable, it could be bad for her. "Apologize."

Sorry. She snaps her hands in a jerky way, not looking at all sorry, but it's better than nothing.

I need for her to stay on her toes because the weekends are always the worst for us. Two whole days stuck at home with Dad. Our chances of pissing him off are greater, which means she can't afford to behave this way. Not even with me.

"I'm going to check on Dad." I make sure to also sign the words.

Her playfulness fades and she scowls. *Why?*

"Della," I admonish. "Don't be rude."

Don't be mad at me. She swallows hard and then signs, *I just don't want to live with Dad anymore. I want us to move far away. Can we, Landry? Please?* She signs the word please like five more times in a row, her eyes glossing over with tears.

My heart cracks right down the center. I know she hates him as much as I do. Sometimes, when curled up in bed together whenever Dad's out of town, she expresses these types of wishes. They all seem like far away fantasies. This plea, though, isn't some fantasy. It's desperation—a desperation I feel echoing in my soul.

One day soon, I sign to her, *but no more talk of that right now. It's not safe.*

Her shoulders slump, dropping her gaze to her lap. The defeat written all over her kills me. I wish I could give her what she wants right now, but I can't. And talking about this stuff is reckless and dangerous. Neither of us can afford to slip up. Especially when he's at home, forced to rest. It'll give him too much time to think—too much time to notice what his daughter is up to.

He'll notice Ford.

Start asking questions.

Then, the accusations will fly.

I can't allow that.

Since my sister is done talking to me, I get up and leave her room. Sandra is off for the weekend. One of the cooks, Gloria, comes in early on Saturday mornings to prepare meals for the weekends, but is usually gone by noon. Then, it's just the three of us.

Suppressing a shudder, I make my way to Dad's room. At one time, I loved running in there on Saturday mornings. I'd wriggle between Mom and Dad, begging for them to turn on cartoons. They'd indulge me and Dad would have Gloria bring us all breakfast in bed. Chocolate chip pancakes with extra whipped topping for me.

I haven't touched one since Mom died.

I haven't done a lot of things since she died.

That innocent kid died right along with her. That kid was forced to grow into an adult who has to protect her little sister. I'd be bitter that I've lost the easy parts of my life, but I don't regret the relationship I have with Della. I love her and know Mom would be proud that I look after her, making sure her life is as normal as possible.

God, I miss Mom, though. So much.

Dad is sitting up in bed on his usual side, a laptop perched on his thighs over the sheet. His hair is messy and dark blond scruff is growing in on his cheeks. The bruising on his face is worse today, swollen and dark purple.

"Hi, Dad," I greet, my voice cheery. "Doing okay today?"

He looks up from his laptop, cutting his icy blue eyes my way. "Feel like hell, but I'll heal. Work never stops. Missing two days while in the middle of this Tokyo deal has really been an inconvenience."

"I'm sorry."

He frowns. "It's not your fault."

That's debatable.

"If you need anything, just—"

"Come sit," he says, his tone stern. "Like old times. You used to love to watch me work."

Used to.

Back when I was naïve and thought my dad hung the moon. Before I saw he was a man of shadows hidden behind a sunbeam smile.

"I don't want to disturb you," I utter, fidgeting in the doorway.

"Never." He pats the bed beside him. "Come cuddle, sweetheart."

My hands tremble, but fisting them helps keep the shaking at bay. I make my way over to the bed and climb on. He lifts the sheet, inviting me to get under them with him.

Della was right.

I shouldn't have checked on him.

But I need to feel him out. To see what he knows, if anything. If he suspects I had anything to do with it, I'll need a strategy to talk my way out of it.

His smile is warm, but he's guarded. It puts me on edge too. Maybe he can sense the whirl of emotions inside me. Usually, I'm much better at hiding the fear and hatred I have toward him. Ford, though, distracts me and makes things difficult for me.

Last night, before I went to sleep, I deleted any trace of conversations between me and Ford. I even went as far as to change the contact to "Study Partner Girl Whose Name I Can't Remember" in case he asks about the number. I'm hoping he's been too busy with the attack to dig that far into what I'm doing. Still, I can't be too careful.

I settle into bed next to Dad. His computer is open to a spreadsheet and he has a chat window up where he's talking to Gareth about one of their game acquisitions. I'm thankful that it's nothing about me or Ford or Della.

"Did you sleep well last night?" Dad asks, taking hold of my hand. He runs his thumb over my pulse point.

Knowing him, he can probably tell if I'm lying just by seeing if my blood pumps faster. I keep my breathing even and nod. He squeezes my hand.

"Good." He brings my hand up and kisses the back of it. "I know school has been a lot for you."

"It's fun," I assure him. "Thank you for getting me in. I didn't know how much I wanted to go to college until I got there."

"I know you better than yourself. You know that."

The room fills with silence. I don't like his insinuation, but I could totally be reading into it, too. I'm on edge, so everything that comes out of his mouth feels like foreshadowing of what's to come.

He doesn't let go of my hand, keeping it locked tight in his grip. I feign tiredness and lean my head against his shoulder. The quiet may as well be an entire drumline banging in my ears. It's deafening and maddening. Every word on the tip of my tongue feels like a trap. The silence, though, feels like I'm being exposed.

A sound from the doorway draws my attention. There, standing like an angry and powerful little god, my sister glowers at my father.

Not now, Della.

Read me a story, Landry. Her signed movements are sharp and demanding.

I lock eyes with my sister and give her a slight shake of my head. What is she doing? We both know it's best if she avoids Dad at all costs.

"Della, come here," Dad barks at her, making me jump in response.

Della flinches, not because she can hear his

words, but more like she can feel the impact of them. The swat before the painful blow.

I start to get up, my heart in my throat, but Dad squeezes my hand until the bones feel like they'll snap. A pained cry leaps from my throat. Della can't hear it, but she must see the agony on my face because she obeys our father immediately, rushing to his side.

"Dad," I plead, my voice more of a sob than anything.

He grabs Della by the front of her shirt the second she gets close and yanks her forward. Her green eyes are wide with terror.

I have to stop this.

"Daddy, please," I croak. "She just needs a nap."

He ignores me to lean into Della's face. His laptop sits on his legs undisturbed like grabbing both his daughters is barely an interruption of his precious work.

"You will not be a disrespectful shit in my home," Dad snarls at her. "Do you hear me?"

Her eyes have left his and are locked on mine, filled with tears and fear. Of course she doesn't hear him since she's not even looking at him. He releases my hand to grab hold of her chin, forcibly making her look at him and not me.

"I'm sick of your attitude problem," he snaps. "Blatant disrespect and ignoring me when the situation suits you."

She squirms in his hold, clearly hurting at the way he's gripping her face. I tug at his arm, muttering pleading words, but to no avail.

"Dad, stop—"

He swings his elbow back. It hits me right in the mouth. The sharp, sudden pain has me falling back onto the bed. Dad curses and then little footsteps thud away.

She's gone.

She got away.

I bring my throbbing hand up to touch my bottom lip that stings. Bright red crimson stains my fingertips. I'm bleeding.

Dad grunts in pain and then he's positioned on his side. I can tell it hurts his ribs, but the concern in his stare is winning the battle. He fixates on my bloody mouth and his expression twists into one of horror.

"My God, sweetheart. What happened?"

You. You happened, Dad. You always happen.

He moves away briefly and then returns with a tissue. Gently and with the care of a loving father, he dabs at my lip, attempting to clean away the blood. I squeeze my eyes shut, refusing to let the tears come. He's stolen enough of those.

I can't look at him.

Right now, all I can think about is hearing Ford's voice. If he knew Dad hit me—albeit accidentally—he'd be pissed.

This is the problem with friends or liking a guy...you start to rely on them when times are tough. Someone to lean on or confide in. An escape.

"I'm so sorry," Dad chokes out. "I keep screwing up with you. Ever since your Mom..."

Mom dying was the catalyst for my life turning upside down and turning into...this. Hell. Literal hell.

I can feel Dad's fingers on my face, stroking and caressing, as he croons sweet, apologetic words. I hate this. I hate him. He kisses my bruised cheek.

Yeah, Dad, you did that too.

All the hurts, both inside and out, are from you.

Always you.

He's too close—too heavy—too much. His soft kisses are just as abusive as his cruel back-handed smacks. I don't want them. I don't like the breathiness of them or the quantity. Anytime it gets to this point, I want to crawl into a hole and die. Horrible flashes of other times, worse than this, steal my breath and have bile creeping up my throat.

It never gets easier.

I can't do this.

Everything feels worse right now. Maybe because I've had a sample of normalcy recently with Ford, every harsh reminder of my reality is a brutal stab to the chest.

I can't breathe.

I can't breathe.

Go away. Go see her.

Thoughts of Mom are always an escape. My memories of her are such happy ones and easy to snatch up when I can't take this stupid life a second longer. Since I'm too overwhelmed by this moment, I slip to a happier time. Me and Mom sipping hot cocoa while we fuss over poinsettias to decorate the house with for a family Christmas party. It smells like cinnamon and apples, the pies in the oven a delicious aroma that makes my mouth water. Oh, it's snowing outside. How beautiful—

A shrill ringing shreds my happy memory, thrusting me into the now. The cold, hard present that reeks of my father's cologne. His mouth leaves my neck and he rolls away to grab the phone. Based on the sharp, angry words, something happened with work. He starts yelling at Gareth.

I'm awake.

Here.

Shaking so hard my teeth are chattering. I right my shirt and run out of the bed. Tripping over my own feet, I nearly faceplant. Dad ignores me, too busy barking out orders to Gareth, which is fine by me.

I can escape.

The rush to my bedroom is a disgusted blur. I lock my bedroom door behind me and then strip out of my clothes. The scalding water burning my flesh does nothing to erase the lips and roaming touches that don't belong on my body. I scrub and scrub and scrub until my skin feels like it's on fire.

I'm reminded of a time, years ago, where I curled up on the floor of this very shower in such severe pain I thought I was going to die. I'd watched blood color the water and slip down the drain wondering if I could disappear so easily. I don't remember much about that day aside from Sandra scolding me for nearly freezing to death from staying under the icy spray for so long.

When the water grows cold, I shut it off, wrap up in a warm towel. I can't shake the oily feeling and continue to tremble almost violently. Other times, I do my best to block it out and think of something else, but my efforts aren't working this time.

What happened?

Am I broken?

I thought I was strong to endure such horrors, yet here I am losing my shit.

Because I deserve more than this. Being with Ford, I've begun to feel not only desired and wanted, but truly cared for. He's what's different.

God, I need Ford.

Scrambling from the bathroom, I locate my phone and then go to my dark closet. I crawl to the very back, sitting on some shoes and pressing my back against the wall. I dial his number and try to keep my teeth from chattering.

"Hey," Ford greets, his voice warm and happy.

The strength I'd been harnessing melts away and I cling to his voice. I need him to hold me up. I'm so tired of holding myself up. I can't do it anymore.

Tears burst out of me, an ugly sound of despair clawing out of my throat. No words come out. All I can hear are his reassuring words over and over again. I know he's asking me questions, but I can't answer them. His voice is enough. I just need his voice.

Until…

"I'm coming over. Give me fifteen minutes or so."

I sniffle and pop open my eyes. "Y-You're coming over?"

"You're upset," he growls. "I need to make sure you're okay."

Selfishly and probably stupidly, I choke out, "Hurry."

Relief floods through me, though this probably isn't the best idea. I don't care. In this moment, I care about one thing. Ford. I need him to hold me and make me feel like I have someone besides a little kid on my side.

Someone strong.

Someone who cares.

Someone like Ford.

CHAPTER TWENTY-TWO

Scout

SHE'S SO HAPPY.

Smiling and carefree.

I would smile too if I conned the richest man in New York to put a ring on my finger and put babies in me.

What does Ash have to worry about these days?

Certainly not me.

I'm no longer a threat in her world. Winston made sure of that. My fucked-up knees remind me daily.

She's safe.

Except now. Not right now. She's leaving their condo in the city, alone, heading to the baby shower Bryant told me about.

My car is parked on the street not fifty feet from the entrance of the building, giving me a prime view of when she exits. This almost seems too easy.

I've already scoped out the location of the restaurant. They don't have a valet service, but they do have an alleyway that's used for dropping off affluent clients. It's private and quiet, however, not at all secure. I'll make sure to haul ass over there so I can beat her there.

Then, when she's not expecting it.

Surprise, sis.

I'm back.

Come to claim what's mine…you.

She stalls, chatting with the doorman. My phone buzzes in my pocket. I tug it out and discover messages from Sparrow and Scout in our group text.

Sparrow: *She's bawling her eyes out!*

Sully: *What happened?*

Sparrow: *I don't know. Trying to figure that out now.*

Sparrow: *She wants to see me. Fuck.*

Sully: *I'm on my way there.*

I stare at their exchange, pissed that I wasn't included on this rescue mission. It's because they're obsessed with her. They don't want to fucking share.

Glancing up, I take one long look at Ash, trying to decide what I'm going to do. This is the best opportunity I've had in the past year. Am I really going to give it up to see what's going on with Landry? To make sure I'm not being squeezed out?

"Fuck," I growl, putting the vehicle in drive.

I peel away from the curb and slowly drive past where Ash is standing. She turns just as I'm driving by and sees me staring at her. The color bleeds from her face. Her entire body tenses.

With two fingers to my brow, I give her a salute and keep driving. My heart is pounding like a drum in my chest. Everything screams in me to pull a U-turn in the middle of the road to go back for her. To drag her into my car and strap her to the seat beside me.

Mine.

Mine.

Mine.

But Landry is also mine. She made that abundantly clear when she came all over my fingers. When she liked the brutality of my touch and whimpered so prettily. Knowing Sparrow and Sully are trying to keep her all for themselves is infuriating. Stingy pricks.

The entire drive to the Croft residential building I replay the tightness of Landry's cunt, the taste of her juices, the sound of her moans. By the time I arrive, my dick is obscenely hard in my black jeans. I rub at my erection over the denim, trying to ease the need to come.

Out of time.

I can either rub one out with the valet watching, or I can see what Sully is getting up to with our girl. The valet man does a double take, frowning in confusion at me. Pulling out a wad of cash, I shove it in his hand.

"You're not seeing double. You're just tired. Keep it close by for me."

He nods, eyes widening at the money. "Sure thing, man."

I leave him to it and prowl inside the building. Keeping my head low, I avoid any people on the way to the elevator. My phone buzzes again.

> **Sully:** *She's a wreck, man. Her lip is split. She went to grab her shoes and then we're going to the gym here in the building so I can talk to her about what happened. I'll keep you posted.*

I quickly Google this building to learn which floor the gym is on. Once I locate it, I exit on that floor and make my way to the gym. There are a couple of people on the elliptical machines and stationary bikes, but the weight area, in a separate room, is empty. I slink past the people working and into the weight area to find a darkened corner behind a giant orange ball.

Now, all I need to do is wait.

Seconds later, Sully rounds the corner, Landry at his side, their hands linked together. Seeing them together like that lights a match inside me. It burns hot and fast, torching all thoughts but one.

Mine.

He sits down on a bench, straddling it, and urges her to sit in front of him, mirroring his position. Once she's settled, he takes both her hands in his.

"Talk, honey. Tell me what happened."

Her head is bowed, her hair hidden beneath the hood on her hoodie. I wish he'd push it back so I could see her face. I'm tempted to reveal myself just so I can see the shock in her pretty blue eyes reflected back at me.

"I'm just having a bad day." Her bottom lip quivers. "A really bad day."

"I can see that." His voice is soft. So soft. I don't think I've ever heard Sully speak to anyone that way. Interesting. "Talk to me."

"I can't," she whispers, her voice shaking.

"Honey," Sully says, lifting her chin so she's looking up at him, "you can. You're hurt. You can trust me, remember?"

Rather than explaining to him what has her so upset, she cups his cheeks, drawing him to her. His lips are gentle as he kisses her supple mouth. It's as though he has to handle her with kid gloves or she'll break. I know for a fact she can take rough handling and barely crack.

She's much tougher than she lets on.

His hunger for her wins out. Grabbing her ass, he pulls her up into his lap so her legs wrap around his middle. A needy moan escapes her, singing straight to my cock. As quietly as I can, I pull down my zipper and unbutton my jeans. I pull my throbbing dick into my hand, eager for some sort of release.

Sully's massive hands squeeze her ass as he moves her against his lap. They're dry humping like there aren't people just around the corner. So dangerous, but so hot.

"We have to talk about this," Sully murmurs. "As good as this feels, it's only putting a bandage on the problem."

For fuck's sake.

Don't be a pussy, man.

She ignores him, kissing him with all the fiery

passion she possesses. Sully shoves one hand down into the back of her yoga pants, his palm splayed out over her ass cheek. This must feel good because she starts panting harder. I stroke my dick in tandem with the sounds she's making. I'd kill for some lube right now, but since I don't have any, I make do with licking my hand a couple of times to get it nice and slick.

"Ford," she hisses, breaking from their kiss so she can look at him.

With his free hand, he yanks down her hood, revealing her messy, damp hair. He stares at her like she's the most beautiful thing he's ever seen.

These fuckers are obsessed.

I know obsession when I see it.

"I'm going to come." Her whispered words sound surprised. "Ford, oh my…" She tilts her head back, baring her pretty neck.

I want to bite it and suck it and wrap my hand around it.

Mine.

Mine.

My breathing comes out quick and harsh. If they weren't so consumed in one another, they'd hear me. I know the second she comes because her body tenses before trembling. She swallows down the cry of her orgasm as not to alert anyone.

He starts to lift her hoodie, giving me a flash of her small bra-less tits, but she stops him, dragging it back down.

"Ford," she says, breathing heavily. "We can't do this right now."

Right now. Not never.

Images of her trussed up and captive in my bed are too much. I come silently, my semen hitting the orange ball with a barely audible patter. While I tuck my dripping dick back into my jeans, I keep my stare fixated on them from my hiding spot.

They're so enamored in each other.

Which means she's just as enamored with me.

My turn. My fucking turn.

I'm about to stand up and demand my turn when some doofus walks into the weight area. As soon as he noticed the two of them, his face blanches and he stumbles back.

"Oh, I'm so sorry, I, uh, I'll leave."

The dumb shit hurries to leave them to their dry fucking, but the moment is lost. Landry is already pulling from my brother and standing. He thrums with need, his dick trying to tear through his jeans as he reaches for her.

"I shouldn't be here," she mutters to herself. "This was a mistake. I was upset but if he finds me gone." Panic flashes over her features making her reddened skin pale to a ghastly white. "I have to go back home."

"Honey," Sully growls. "Let me go with you. To make sure it's safe."

"No, lover boy." She smacks his hand that's still reaching for her. "I appreciate…"

Appreciate what, prickly princess? Making you come in your little panties and giving your lover boy *blue balls in the process?*

He rises to his feet, capturing her waist and pulling her to his chest. "Did he hit you again?"

"That was an accident, I think." She frowns. "It's other stuff. I just…never mind. You've calmed me down, but I really need to get back. I'll call you later."

They share another long, passionate kiss until she peels away from him. She runs off, leaving Sully alone with his nine-inch boner. I stand up, ignoring the searing in my bad knee. Slowly, I hobble toward him. He hears the sound of my feet on the mats and whips around to face me.

Shock turns into brief fear and finally into fury.

"What the actual fuck, Scout?" he snarls, shoving my chest. "You were spying on me?"

I reach down, rubbing at my knee, and scowl

at him. "She's my job, too."

His brown eyes flicker with a multitude of emotions, but the one that's most prevalent is possessiveness. He doesn't believe she's a job like he's supposed to, and he certainly doesn't believe she's mine too.

"What did you do yesterday?" His cold tone cuts straight to the bone. "To Landry?"

"I got a lot further than almost second base." I smirk at him. "I know what her pussy feels like."

His jaw clenches. "You fucking raped her?"

"Fuck off," I growl. "I'm not the only bad guy here. You're lying to her while you try to get into her pants!"

He shoves me so hard my head hits the mirror wall behind me. Thunk. Glass splinters from the impact and my head throbs from the force of it.

"I should kill you."

At this, I laugh. "Kill me for fingering her in the bathroom when she fucking begged for it? Come on. Look at yourself. You're obsessed. She's the new Ash."

Sully grabs the front of my shirt, his nose coming inches from mine. Thank fuck his boner is gone or this would be uncomfortable. "Ash was yours. Landry is ours."

Wrong.

So fucking wrong.

Ash was mine. Landry is mine.

"She's not yours," I clip out. "Just like Ivy was never yours."

"So help me," Sully bites. "If you fuck our lives up again—"

I shove him away from me. "Stop acting blameless, you fuck. We're all wired the same way, which is why we always want the same girl."

"I am *not* wired like you."

Before we can unpack that and I can remind him we're goddamn triplets, a different guy peeks his head around the corner. Unlike the dweeb from earlier, this dude is stacked and could probably take both me and Sully at once.

"I think you two should go," the guy says, darting his attention back and forth between us. "Haven't seen you around the building before. If you don't leave, I'm calling security."

"We're leaving," Sully snaps at the guy. Then, to me, he hisses, "Stay away from her. Deal with your job and we'll deal with ours."

I shoot him the bird. "Okay, little brother. Whatever you say."

He storms off, cursing under his breath. Sully knows better than anyone he can't tell me what to do.

I do what I want.
I always do what I want.
And right now…I want her.
Landry Croft.

CHAPTER TWENTY-THREE

Landry

I SCREWED UP.

Calling Ford and involving him more was a mistake. He'd seen right through my lies. Deduced that my father was the cause of my pain. Again.

But, in my desperate need for comfort and escape, I left Della alone with him. Bile creeps up my throat as I sneak back into our condo. It's nearly silent, which means he's no longer on his phone call. Sometimes his calls last for hours, but not this one.

Oh, God.

Rushing to Della's room, I pray that she's okay. That he hasn't hurt her in any way. When I peek in, she's watching cartoons. She can read some, having picked up on it earlier than most because of her knowledge of ASL, but mostly, she watches her shows when she wants to zone out.

I start to go inside, but Dad's voice calls to me.

From my room.

Slowly, I turn and walk toward the sound. He's sitting on my bed when I enter my room. His face doesn't look any better, and probably won't for weeks, but he's showered and shaved what he could.

Shame makes his blue eyes shimmer with pain.

I don't understand his hurt since he's the one always inflicting it.

"Sweetheart," he starts, frowning at me. "I'm…"

Sorry?

You're always sorry, Dad. Always.

The sorriest dad on the planet.

I want to scream at him. To accuse him of being a disgusting monster, but I don't. I can't make the words leave the prison of my mouth. They're trapped, just like me and Della are in this condo.

"You know I'm sorry," he rushes out. "You know this isn't me. *That* isn't me."

Elaborate on that, Dad. What exactly is that?

I may not be able to say the words, but I

know my pain and hatred for him can't be masked. Not right now when my nerves are so raw and I can still feel his mouth on my neck. No amount of kissing Ford could erase it.

"I know you're disappointed in me." He swallows hard, lowering his stare. "Let me make it right. You can have anything you want. Just name it."

Freedom.

It's on the tip of my tongue.

"I don't want anything," I grit out.

I'm not a transaction. He thinks he can erase his wrongdoings with gifts. That the bruises and cuts on my flesh will magically disappear during the exchange. That the emotional torment and abuse I've endured will fade with the appearance of a shiny new bracelet.

"Money? A trip? Spa day with your sister?"

He's reaching now if he's trying to use Della to get into my good graces.

He stands up, wincing only slightly at the pain in his ribs. Slowly, he prowls toward me. My entire body thrums with the urge to flee. Bravely, or stupidly, I keep my feet rooted and stare up at him with a rare flash of defiance.

"You have exactly thirty seconds to figure it out while I'm in a generous mood," he bites out, nostrils flaring. "If you can't come up with something, I'll have to take Della shopping with me. Maybe I can get it out of her what you want."

I gasp, like he's punched me in the stomach, and gape at him. He's not going anywhere alone with my sister. I don't trust him not to irrevocably ruin her. At least I'm older and stronger. I can bounce back better than she can. She's little and fragile and mine to protect.

An idea forms in my head so suddenly, and absolutely perfect, I almost cry in relief.

"A car," I say, meeting his stare. "A really, really expensive car."

His brow lifts, clearly amused at my show of bitchiness. I guess it's better than being angry. "A car, huh?"

"A classic car. Something restored to original perfection," I continue, letting the idea really transform in my mind. "I don't know much about cars, but I know the sixties were a good era. I want it black, too."

Old. Untraceable. An unassuming color. And fast.

In a vehicle like that, I wouldn't need much of a plan. Just a head start. He wouldn't be able to track me like he could a new Tesla or Range Rover. We could get out of his crosshairs.

Suddenly, I'm overwhelmed by excitement.

"Of course, sweetheart," Dad says, dipping down to kiss my forehead. "Anything to make you happy." He steps back, studying me with narrowed eyes. "Now, if you'll excuse me, I have to call Gareth back. I love you."

I can't say the words back. The smile I give him is wobbly and forced but he accepts it. As soon as he's gone, I lock the door behind him and go into my closet to look for my phone. It's still shoved under a heap of clothes where I'd left it.

Ford left a few texts, but I need to hear his voice again. To apologize for running out on him when he was only trying to help. He answers immediately. There are voices in the background—people talking and laughing—and it makes me wonder if he's in our building lobby, though it usually isn't so busy.

"Laundry."

My heart does a twist inside my chest. I close my eyes, imagining his dark, maple syrup eyes and his scent that reminds me of spices and the salty sea.

"Hey, Chevy."

"Everything okay?" He must go someplace a little quieter because the background noise is muted. Maybe he's in his car now.

"I'm sorry for doing that to you," I blurt out. "You were only trying to help. It felt good, but…"

"It felt good," he parrots, his voice carrying a slight, angry edge.

"Great. It felt great," I assure him so his precious ego won't take a beating. "I wish I could have made you feel good too. Like that. It's just…my life is a mess. You've come into my life at exactly the wrong time."

"What every guy wants to hear," he deadpans.

I smile, imagining him pout. "It was nice to have someone to turn to, though. Even when you're being all crazy or confusing me, you bring me comfort and make me feel safe."

"Are you friend-zoning me, Laundry?"

"Ha. Like you'd allow that."

"You're beginning to learn what sort of man you're dealing with."

Am I though? He's still such a mystery.

He lets out a deep sigh. "I miss you, babe."

"You literally just had your hand in my pants."

"You know what I mean," he growls, sounding pissed. "I didn't get enough time with you."

"I think you're toxic for me," I admit in a whisper. "See you Monday."

We hang up and I go to my pictures to look for the one I saved into a folder called "Files for English Class." Hidden in another folder called "Citations" is a picture of Ford.

Lazy, arrogant smile.

Dark messy hair.

Hooded maple eyes.

I miss you too, Chevy.

CHAPTER TWENTY-FOUR

Sparrow

THE BLACK MERCEDES pulls up to the curb, deposits Landry like she's trash, and then zooms off. She stares after it, a frown marring her pretty face. Goddamn, I like looking at her.

I whistle from the inside of my car. My window is down so I have an unobstructed view of this girl. "Get in, Laundry."

Her grin is brilliant and wide for me. Dazzling like the sun. I almost have the urge to rip off my sunglasses in order to see every detail, even if it blinds me in the process.

She opens the door and tosses her bag into the backseat. Then, she slides into the passenger seat, closing herself in with me. I roll up the window to give us privacy before leaning over the console to grab hold of her. My hand slides into her silky golden tresses and I tighten my hold on her, drawing her to me.

"Kiss me, babe."

She smiles wider and then her lips are on mine—eager and desperate. I groan against her mouth. Fuck, she tastes so good. Like vanilla and mine. To drive home that last thought, I nip at her bottom lip. She moans, though it sounds a little pained. Pulling back, I note the small scab on her lip.

My blood fucking boils.

This is a job. This is a job. This is a job.

Try telling my raging heart that.

"I want to kill him," I tell her, my words dripping with pure honesty. "Fucking kill him."

"We can't do this here." She frowns, no longer smiling. "I missed you, but this is too open."

I take her hand, threading my fingers with hers and kiss the knuckles before releasing her. "Buckle in, Laundry."

She squeals when I peel out of the parking lot. I take the turn out of the lot practically on two wheels before gunning it down the straightaway. I smirk at her which, earns me a scowl. So cute.

There's a building nearby that's under construction. I'll hide out there with her for a bit. We pull up and aren't stopped by anyone. I pull off my sunglasses and toss them on the dash. There are several work trucks parked on the first level, so I make it to the second level before finding a dark spot to tuck my car into away from prying eyes.

Once I shut off the car and we're bathed in silence, I unbuckle and angle my body toward her. If I didn't know any better, I'd think she was being a bitch. She's giving off icy vibes and is tense as fuck.

But I do know her.

It's her defense mechanism.

She's protecting herself.

"Do you know how to delete search history?" she asks, her brows furling.

Strange question.

"I'm sure I could figure it out." I cock my head to the side and run my finger along her jaw. "Why?"

She swallows hard but leans into my touch. "What about texts? How do I erase their existence? Deleting them won't be good enough."

"You're afraid your dad is going to find out you have a boyfriend?"

Her lip curls up. "You're not my boyfriend."

Winking at her, I flash her a smug grin. "Keep telling yourself that. I claimed you first. Don't forget that."

Her features darken like she's in on the secret—which she's absolutely not. Then, she just lets the comment slide. Sometimes I wish I knew what she was thinking about. Like now.

"He can't know about what we've been doing," she says with a ragged sigh. "He can't know about my plans."

"Plans?"

"Put it this way," she huffs. "One time, months ago, I researched NYU a little bit. He surprised me with enrolling me in school. Who does that?"

Okay, so yeah, that's fucking creepy and controlling.

"I'll call my uncle. If anyone can get information on scrubbing a phone or hiding tracks, it'd be him. You trust me?"

"Yeah, I trust you," she says with a smile. "Plus, I know your uncle is the mafia daddy or something. His connections are solid."

"Mouthy brat."

"You like it." Her lips curl into something flirty and delicious. I want to taste the sinful smile. "Can I use your phone?"

Her words chill all the heat coursing through me.

"What? Why?"

She looks down at my phone in my cupholder. "The Internet. I need to look something up."

And chance Sully or Scout texting about her during that moment?

Hell no.

Her hand reaches for it and I grab her wrist.

"Come here," I demand, tugging her toward me. "I need to hold you."

I can tell she's pissed based on the gleam in her eyes, but she allows me to pull her over the console and into my lap. She straddles me, settling herself comfortably between my body and the steering wheel.

Snagging her by her neck, I pull her to me, eager to taste her mouth for the second time today and distract her from using my phone. She moans, the sound needy and raw. I wonder what other sounds I can draw out of her.

"I need to see you," I murmur against her mouth as I rub my palms under her shirt, caressing her back.

She nods, lifting her arms. I pull her shirt off and then admire her sexy little tits in her pink bra. Leaning forward, I bite one of them over the lace. So fucking hot. She groans, her fingers messing up my hair as she clutches on.

I hook my fingers into the bra straps, pulling them down her arms. She grinds against my cock, seeking the friction we both need.

"When I get you in my bed, babe, I'm going to take my time sucking on every little freckle on your body." I grab hold of the cups of her bra, jerking them down roughly. "Right now, I don't have a lot of time."

She cries out the second I latch my teeth to one of her nipples. I pull back until I know it hurts and then release her so I can dive back in. Tonguing the reddened nipple, I suck and tease away the pain.

She's no longer seated on my lap but up on her knees, eagerly feeding me her tit, clearly aching for the abuse followed by the sweetness. I take the opportunity to undo her jeans. These quarters are too cramped. I'm not sure how in the hell we're going to do this, but I'm game to try.

"Fuck," I groan as I kiss between her breasts. "Why are you so goddamn sweet?"

She laughs. "I thought I was salty."

"Changed my mind, Dirty Laundry. You're sweet and it's going to give me a damn cavity." I jerk on her jeans, drawing them to her midthighs before they meet resistance from being parted. "Too many clothes, woman. I need you naked."

Her breath hitches when my fingers tease her pussy. So wet and dripping with sweet need. I'm dying of a thirst only she can quench.

"L-Let me see your eyes," she breathes.

I angle my head up to look at her as my finger enters her body. She gasps and a tremble quakes through her.

"You like it when I fuck you with my fingers?" I ask, lifting a brow. "Need more?"

"Y-Yes."

Another finger easily slides inside her. And then a third. If she's going to take my cock, her cunt needs to be able to take more than three fingers. Slowly, I gently fuck her tight-as-sin hole, stretching her so she'll accommodate my cock. I'm hung and her probably-virgin pussy needs working up to it.

I suck on her tit, my eyes still on hers. She bites on her split bottom lip, hooded gaze boring into me. My mouth isn't gentle as I bruise her tits, but I'm careful with her pussy. I want it to feel good for her. I want to make her come before I even get the condom on my dick.

"That's my girl," I croon against her wet nipple. "Come all over my fingers."

With each deep dive of my fingers, I rub my thumb over her clit. Her breaths come out sharp and fast until I don't think she's breathing at all.

"Ford!"

Sparrow. I'm Sparrow. Not fucking Ford.

Her slick juices run down over my fingers as her body spasms. She's so fucking hot coming on my fingers. I can't even begin to imagine what she'd look like stretched around my cock. She rides out her orgasm until she's spent and boneless. I slip my fingers from her body. Grabbing onto her hips, I twist her around and press her chest against the steering wheel.

She's quiet, aside from her heavy breathing, waiting for me to get us into position. I fumble with my jeans until I've pulled my cock out.

Condom.

I need a condom.

But I just want to feel her slick pussy against my flesh before I pull a rubber on.

Hooking my arm around her stomach, I pull her back into my lap. My cock slides between her thighs, rubbing at her wetness. We both groan at the sensation of how it feels. Her hips rock back and forth. Fuck, it feels amazing.

Her body angles forward, like she's begging for me to penetrate her. I grip my cock and obey her. She cries out as my fat cock presses into her impossibly tight body.

"Oh my God," she hisses.

We're both drenched in sweat. This car sex is

fucking annoying, but I want her too badly to figure out better arrangements. Pressing my palm on her lower stomach, I lift my hips. I can feel my cock inside her, pushing against my hand.

I fill her to the brim.

Stretch her to the max.

I manage a hard thrust that has her crying out when we hear it.

Ringing. Over and over.

Her whole body freezes, turning ice cold.

It's her phone.

"Don't answer it," I mumble, biting her shoulder and then neck. "We're busy."

She moans when she reaches to grab it from the seat and I chase her ass with a hard thrust. I'm undeterred, picking up my pace, trying to remind myself to pull out since I skipped right over the condom like a dumbass.

"Ford, stop," she hisses. "Oh my God."

"What?"

"It's my dad!"

The ringing stops and then a text pops up.

Dad: *Pick up your phone. I know you're not at school.*

It starts ringing again. She completely shuts down. Stares at the phone in shock, no longer present in our fucking. Jesus Christ.

Sliding her off my throbbing dick, I twist her toward me so I can hold her. Her skin, which was just hot and sweaty, feels cold to the touch.

"I have to answer. I have to answer. I have to answer."

Her chants are almost robotic sounding.

"*Don't* answer it," I tell her firmly. "You can call him back."

But, with each furious text and incessant call, she starts losing her shit. She scrambles away from me, hurrying to throw her clothes on as quickly as she can. I look like a horny douchebag with my wet dick practically crying to get back to fucking.

That's not happening.

Ignoring the painful blue balls, I manage to put my dick back in my jeans while she does the one thing I told her not to.

She answers the damn phone.

CHAPTER TWENTY-FIVE

Landry

"**O**H, HEY, DAD."

Be calm. Be calm. Be freaking calm.

His silence may as well be screaming. I can feel the unspoken wrath battering against me like the force of a hurricane. What makes it worse is Ford is watching me, his face twisted in concern. I'm standing between two sides of my life, unsure what to do or how to behave. The fear of my father wins out and I attempt to smooth things over with him.

"This coffee shop on campus doesn't have a good signal. I think you're cutting out."

"You're not on campus," Dad says, voice dripping with fury. "Are you?"

"I am," I croak out. "Promise."

Lies. And he knows. I don't know how, but he does. It's probably my phone. He's a tech genius, so I bet he has a locator on my phone.

I'm so stupid.

"We'll see. If you're not waiting outside the front of that school by the time the driver pulls up, so help me Landry, there will be hell to pay."

He hangs up on me. I stare at my phone in horror, shock rendering me immobile for a few long seconds. My ears ring loudly and my heart pounds out of control. It's not until Ford squeezes my thigh do I realize he's speaking to me.

"What are we doing, Laundry?"

"School," I rasp out. "I have to get back to school or…"

He doesn't wait for me to elaborate and fires up the engine. The trip here was terrible because he drives like a maniac, but right now I'm thankful because it means I might make Dad's frightful deadline.

"Belt on," Ford barks. "And tell me why the fuck I don't stick around and beat his ass when we get back."

Shuddering, I buckle my belt and shoot him a glare. "Don't even joke about it. He'd bury you, Ford. It's what he does."

"Who's in the mob family now?" he jokes, but it falls flat because neither of us are feeling very playful.

I close my eyes and gnaw on my bottom lip that's still sore from this weekend. I'm all out of sorts. My nerves are eating me alive from the inside out. Parts of my body, though, still throb from Ford's expert touch.

We had sex.

Well, we started to. It would have been better had we finished. For those few minutes, it felt so raw and real and ridiculously hot. I was someone else. Not Landry Croft. If I could have frozen the moment, I would absolutely have.

That's not my reality, though.

This is. My reality is my father controlling my every move and punishing me the second I step out of line. The older I get, the harder it is to play by his rules. I don't want to be here with that monster. I want to be far, far away with Della.

What would a life without pain and fear even look like?

"I don't want to take you back to him," Ford grumbles. "I want to take you back to my place. Keep you safe."

I nearly burst into tears at the earnest, sweet way he says that. I'd love that. Then I could keep pretending we were in our own little world.

But where does that leave Della?

All alone with the monster.

"You can't call me anymore, Chevy. Don't text me or anything." My bottom lip wobbles. "I'll see you at school on Wednesday and later that day when you tutor Della. I can't risk him knowing I have a...you. I don't want him to know."

"Seriously?"

"Seriously. I'm deleting your number. Please don't make me block you."

His jaw clenches and he glares at the road. I feel like a bitch, but I don't know what Dad will do. I've had my fun and lived a little. Look where it's gotten me. I'm crushed at losing this thing with Ford. I have no choice, though.

"Pull in the back," I instruct when we make it back to campus. "I'll go through the building. He can't see me pull up with you."

"Your dirty little secret."

He's hurt and I get it. It doesn't change anything. My dirty little secret has to go to the grave now. I have to figure out how to convince my dad that I'm not sneaking around doing bad stuff. If I can't, I dread to think what he'll do.

To me. To Della. To Ford.

Ford pulls up to the curb and throws it in park. Before I can escape, he curls his palm around the back of my head and pulls me to him.

His lips crash to mine, possessive and comforting. I want to sink into his kiss and forget my life. Just live here in this blissful moment.

"We'll talk on Wednesday," he assures me against my mouth. "Tell me everything."

I can't make him any promises, so I don't. Not that he lets it deter him. He steals another soul-warming kiss before I physically wrench myself from him. I hurry out of the car and when I turn back around, he has my backpack in hand. I go to take it, but he doesn't let go.

"We're going to finish what we started, babe." He winks at me. "Next time, I'm going to take my time with you. Enjoy being deep inside you."

Heat floods my cheeks, but a silly grin finds its way on my face which is quite a feat considering the amount of stress I'm currently under. "Bye, Chevy."

"Later, Laundry."

He peels out the second I close the door. I don't waste time and rush into the building. Passing by the coffee shop on campus, I swipe an empty coffee cup with a lid from the trash can. The walk through the building toward the front makes my stomach cramp. Anxiety eats at my insides. I'm about to puke by the time I exit the building.

A shiny black Mercedes pulls into the lot and I make my way toward it. I'm hoping it's just one of our drivers and not Dad. When the car stops, the back door opens and Dad climbs out. He's suited like usual and wearing black sunglasses. From afar, you'd never be able to tell he got his ass beat last week.

I toss the empty cup into the trash can near the curb and force a smile. "Hi, Dad."

"Get in, young lady. You're not going to sweet talk yourself out of this one." He holds his phone up and I take note of a tracker app blinking my location. "You must think I'm incredibly stupid."

Dread claws at my throat. The smile falters on my lips. I try and fail to suck in adequate air as I climb into the stifling car that reeks of his cologne.

Breathe, Landry.

He doesn't know where you were, just that you were gone. Deny, deny, deny.

Dad gets back in the car, closes the door, and whistles at the driver. I sit beside him, trying like hell not to visibly shake.

The drive back home feels too long.

A prison sentence carried out silently.

Each quiet second that ticks by feels like another lead weight pushed down my throat and settling in my stomach.

"Thank you, Eric," Dad says to the driver when we arrive at our building. "Let's go, Landry."

Dad carries my backpack, holding it out beside him like it contains all the evidence he needs to prove crimes against me. I follow behind him, my eyes downcast.

What's going to happen?

Maybe he'll just accuse me of disobeying him and ground me.

That thought is almost laughable. He's too furious for that. I slipped out of his carefully cast net. Swam around in the dark abyss without him. He's going to want to know exactly what or whom I was exposed to.

We enter the elevator and the air is stifling. I'm suffocating on the cloying scent of his cologne. Swallowing down the bile, I attempt to get a handle on my breathing so I don't pass out. The elevator spins which tells me I'm not doing such a good job.

"I'm missing work because of you," he spits out, words burning me like acid as we step out of the elevator onto our floor. "I can't let this go unpunished."

Oh God.

"Dad," I whisper, trailing behind him. "It's not what you think. I was working on a project with a girl named Melody—"

He whirls around, pointing a finger just inches from my nose. "Do not fucking lie to me, child."

Child.

This is bad.

Really bad.

Tears burst free of their dam, streaking down my cheeks. He turns on his heel, ignoring my emotions, and stalks to our door. Once he's unlocked it, he holds it open for me.

"Go to your room," he growls. "Now."

I scurry away from him, hightailing it to my room. He follows me inside and closes the door. His lips purse as he sets my bag down on the bed. I stand awkwardly watching him as he unzips each zipper, pulling out item after item. Books. Laptop. Notebooks. Nothing of interest.

Which means he knows what's on my computer, just like I feared. It's a good thing I only used it for school. Once he's done emptying the bag, he holds out his hand.

"Phone," he barks. "Sit your ass down."

I avoid the bed because I don't want to be

near it with him, choosing to sit on my chaise lounge chair instead. He's quiet as he unlocks my phone and starts his hunt. The panic swelling up inside me is too much.

The room darkens and spins.

I'm going to pass out.

He pockets the phone and crosses his arms over his chest. Slowly, he makes his way over to me, staring down at me. I hate that he's within hitting distance.

"You're out of control lately," he spits out, furious. "I knew college was a bad idea. Too many unknowns."

His words are a punch to the gut.

"That ends today." He uncrosses his arms, fisting his hands at his sides. "You know a car is absolutely out of the question now. And your phone? Mine. Apparently, you're not responsible enough to even leave the penthouse or to have...*friends*."

Each word out of his mouth feels like another shackle, trapping me in this nightmare.

My phone buzzes with a text, making all the blood drain from my face. He pauses mid-rant and pulls it out of his pocket. The unreadable expression on his face is more terrifying than an angry one.

"Your boyfriend says hi." His tone is cold. "So sweet of him to check in on you."

Boyfriend.

Oh God.

I told Ford not to message me. Why would he message me?

"Dad," I whimper. "I'm sorry."

He shuts me up when he starts replying to the text. I have no idea what he's saying or what'll happen now. My life feels over. Collapsing in on my head. I want to die.

"Mr. Constantine will be here around six tomorrow to pick you up for your date."

I gape at him in a mixture of relief and confusion. "What?"

"This stunt you pulled today will never happen again. I will not have my daughter's reputation on the line because she likes sneaking off, but this arrangement with the Constantine family needs to happen. You'll see the young man and charm him like I know you're perfectly capable of doing. That will be your only focus. No more distractions."

"Yes, sir."

He pockets the phone again before cupping my cheek. I wait for a strike but nothing comes. Somehow that feels worse.

"I'm going to find out what you were up to. Your lies are transparent, sweetheart. When I discover what you're hiding, we'll determine your punishment from there. Until then, you're to stay in this room until your date with Mr. Constantine."

Not fully trapped.

I have Ty.

My last hope.

If I can get him to help me, I'll be able to leave this hellhole once and for all. At least now, being banished to my room, it gives me time to come up with a solid plan.

I have to.

The alternative is too terrifying.

CHAPTER TWENTY-SIX

Sully

T HE FRONT DOOR of our apartment slams hard enough a picture slides off my wall. There's only one asshole who flings doors shut like he's trying to break them. But that doesn't make sense because Sparrow should be at school. With a groan of irritation, I climb off my bed, throw on a pair of sweats, and make my way into the living room to see what has his panties in a wad.

Scout and the devil cat are sitting together in one of the recliners like a king and his favorite pet planning world domination. Sparrow is standing at the front door looking like a man with his dick in a vise.

"What the hell is your problem?" I ask Sparrow as he tosses his book bag into the floor.

His hair is mussed up like someone's been

running their fingers through it. If he weren't so unhappy, I'd be pissed thinking about how he got his hair like that.

Sparrow storms over to the other recliner and falls into it. His features are twisted into a scowl that reminds me of when we were younger and he didn't get his way. He's fucking pouting.

"Dude," I grind out. "Are you going to tell us what's up or make us guess?"

He rubs his palm over his face, sniffs, and then flashes me a smug smile. I clench my jaw, glancing over at Scout. Scout's watching Sparrow with an unreadable expression. Something brews in his dark eyes—anger, violence, jealousy.

I feel all three of those like a punch to the gut.

"So I was with Landry," Sparrow says, his smile fading. "I took her for a ride and parked somewhere private. Things got hot and heavy. I was trying to make up for what *you* did." He glowers at Scout. "One thing led to another and then we were fucking."

The room goes completely silent. Even Heathen stops purring.

He fucked her? He fucked Landry? Seriously?

"You fucked her?" I hiss, fisting my hands at my sides. "Why?"

Sparrow sneers at me. "She's our job."

Scout makes a derisive snort. Though he's apathetic about a lot of things, his attempt at boredom doesn't work. Not with this. I can tell he's just as mad as me.

Sparrow then goes into detail of everything that happened this morning from him picking her up to dropping her back off at campus. The smiles, the moments they shared, the hot sex. By the end of it, I want to ram my fist through his nose.

"Now, I don't know what's going to happen with her dad," Sparrow complains. "I don't know when I'll see her again."

"I'll see her tonight." I smirk when he shoots me a nasty glare. "Maybe if you'd have kept your dick in your pants and stayed at school like the *job* required, you wouldn't be in this situation." Crossing my arms, I look down at him, watching the vein in his neck pulsate with fury. "I'll make sure she comes this time."

"She fucking came," Sparrow growls. "And if you touch her—"

"You'll what?" I snap, throwing my arms in the air. "Tell her you've been lying to her? That you're just one third of the person she likes? Didn't think so."

Sparrow flies to his feet, bringing his nose to

mine. "If you touch her or speak of that shit, I'm going to beat your ass, Sull. You know I can."

Probably.

Do I care?

Nope.

I swing at him, managing to sucker punch him in the jaw and catching him off guard for all of three seconds. As soon as he recovers from the hit, he's on me, tackling me hard to the floor. His fist slams into my ribs just as I bring my knee up between his legs. We both howl in pain followed by a string of cursing.

Somewhere in the fog of our scuffle, I hear voices. I'm too fired up to care who it might be. Sparrow somehow gets his hand around my throat, his grip a crushing vise that has me struggling to suck in air.

"Boys!"

The older man's voice, sharp and furious, cuts right through our bullshit. Both me and Sparrow freeze, panting and sweating. I still want to kill him, but not with Bryant fucking Morelli standing over us.

Seriously?

Scout let him in?

Why the hell is he even here?

"What's going on?" Bryant demands.

Sparrow shoves away from me and stands. He doesn't offer me a hand, not that I expect him to. I rub at my sore neck and shoot daggers at him with my eyes.

"Sit, boys," Bryant instructs. "Now."

I drop onto one end of the sofa while Sparrow takes a seat in one of the recliners. Scout darts his eyes back and forth between the two of us, clearly fucking amused based on the way his dark eyes flash.

Bryant, immaculately dressed in a black suit, straightens his black tie and then sits on the arm of the sofa farthest from me. He may be getting up there in years, but right now, he's every bit the powerful patriarch of this family. I imagine had we known our biological father growing up—his brother—we'd have been raised to respect the suit and the whole boss-man vibe. But we weren't raised by a Morelli. Mom raised us to be self-confident, to take what we want, and to never take no for an answer.

"What were you two fighting about?" Bryant asks, his eyes darting between us.

"A girl," Scout tattles. "Every year we grow wiser and older, but some things stay the same."

For fuck's sake.

I discreetly flip Scout the bird. He shrugs,

cuddling Heathen against his chest. Sparrow won't look at me, obviously still super pissed. Well, fuck him. At least he got laid.

"Which girl?" Bryant asks, his tone clipped. "It wouldn't be the Croft girl would it?"

My turn to tattle. "He fucked her. Ruined everything."

"You're an asshole," Sparrow growls. "No wonder she wouldn't fuck you, Sour Patch Kid. At least I can be sweet once in a fucking while."

"It's not about you fucking her," I bite back, "it's about you fucking up the job!"

"Enough," Bryant snarls. "Scout, what happened?"

Scout chuckles, the sound dark and demonic. "Landry."

Bryant's nostrils flare. He's losing patience with us. I don't blame him. Not many people have gotten a front row seat to one of our fights. It's three times more obnoxious than the normal fight because not one of us will ever back down and Mom's no longer around to diffuse the situation.

"What's the status on the jobs I've asked you all to do?" Bryant asks, his voice icy. "Or have you all forgotten Landry Croft is a job?"

"Sparrow got Landry in trouble with her dad,"

Scout says, unhelpfully. "They'd been texting before, but she told him not to text her anymore."

"I'm going to try and smooth shit over when I go there this afternoon," I explain with a heavy sigh. "It'll be fine."

"And you?" Bryant asks Scout. "Your efforts with Ty Constantine?"

"He's my bestie now," Scout deadpans.

Bryant's jaw clenches and he pinches the bridge of his nose. The silence stretches on. Finally, he looks at Sparrow, brows pinched and lips pursed.

"Did you three have anything to do with Alexander Croft getting jumped last week?" Bryant's stare bores into Sparrow though he's asking all three of us.

"He hit her," Sparrow spits out. "That couldn't go unpunished."

Bryant rises to his feet and his face turns a grotesque shade of purple. Okay, so he's pissed. Really pissed. "You're done."

Sparrow cracks his knuckles and shakes his head. "It's a setback. We're not done."

"You. Are. Done." He jabs a finger at each one of us in rapid succession. "All of you. I'm taking you off this job."

"Why?" I demand, rising anger burning its

way up my esophagus. "Aside from today, things have been going well. She trusts us and isn't interested in Constantine."

"Going well?" Bryant sneers. "You attacked a very prominent man in New York who just so happens to be in an alliance with our enemy."

"He didn't see our faces," Sparrow offers.

"It doesn't matter," Bryant barks back at him. "It won't be long until he figures out who did this to him. It'll come back on me. My sons will…" He shakes his head. "This ends now. No more Ford Mann. Starting now, you're back to biting when I tell you to like the good little dogs you are."

Dogs?

Fuck. Him.

"I have another location," Bryant says to Scout. "Torch this one too, and for fuck's sake, don't screw this up."

"Arson?" Sparrow scoffs. "Really? That's a little more involved than a simple ass whooping, Bryant."

Bryant steps closer to Sparrow. "In case you forgot, it's my money that puts a roof over your head and food in your mouth. This apartment is mine. The cars you all drive are mine. I have the ability to take it all away. I'm not your fucking mommy."

Sparrow glowers at him, his jaw muscle flexing as he attempts to hold in his wrath. "Remind me again why we don't just up and leave this goddamn family? Start over fresh?"

Bryant pats him on the head. "Because I have something you want."

"We don't give a shit about Ash anymore," Scout barks out, shocking the hell out of me and Sparrow both. "Try again."

"Ahhh." Bryant bounces his gaze to Scout, to me, and then lands on Sparrow. "But you do care about your mother, don't you?"

"What the hell does that even mean?" Sparrow demands.

"One phone call," Bryant states, a smug expression on his severe face. "I can make it all go away with one phone call."

"Make what go away?" I start popping my knuckles as my nerves get the best of me. "What is it you think you have that we want so much? And what does this have to do with Mom?"

"I know you three haven't forgotten that your precious mother is in prison." Bryant smiles, cold and calculating. "I can make it all go away. You'd have your mother back."

What the actual fuck?

"You've had the ability to get her out of that hellhole and you haven't yet?" I growl, jumping to my feet. "You've been waiting for what? The perfect opportunity to make us do something for you? This is some sick shit, man. Really sick."

"I'll text Scout the location. He'll know what to do." He ignores me entirely, his attention on Sparrow. "Losing this building, in addition to the last one, will cripple our adversary's hold on the district he's trying to reform and revamp. They'll understand that they can't encroach on Morelli territory in the end. I'm simply giving them a reminder."

"A reminder that you're a piece of shit?" I spit out, unable to bite my tongue.

Bryant sneers. "A reminder that my family is in charge. Morellis don't play by the rules...we make them."

Me and my brothers watch him leave our apartment in silence. I've always hated Bryant, but now I really want to beat the living shit out of him. How dare he have a way to get our mother out of prison and keep it from us. He waited for the perfect opportunity when he needed to use that card and flung it in our faces with no remorse.

"I'm going to check on Landry," I tell my

brothers. "Don't try to stop me, either."

Sparrow glares at me, but doesn't say shit. Scout sits up straight and nods.

"Me and Sparrow will deal with the property," Scout says. "See what the fallout is from this morning."

"We're going to keep seeing her?" Sparrow asks, frowning. "That'll jeopardize us getting Mom out of prison."

"What Bryant doesn't know won't hurt him," Scout replies with a shrug. "Besides, if he can get our mother out of prison with a phone call, who's to say someone else can't do the same? There are two other families more powerful than his. The Constantines and the Crofts. Lucky for us, we have a connection with both."

"Ty?" I lift a brow at Scout. "You think he'd actually help us get Mom out of there?"

"I think rolling over and letting Bryant dictate our every move gives him all the power," Scout grinds out. "I'm done with him pulling our strings."

SANDRA ANSWERS THE door, her lips puckered in distaste. I know she doesn't like me but I don't give a damn. I'm not leaving until I make sure

Landry is okay. I have to talk to her.

"'Sup."

Her lip curls up. "Perhaps we should cancel this afternoon's lesson. Della is being quite precocious."

"I can deal with her," I assure the old hag. "Plus, you know how much she loves this cat."

Sandra glances down at the carrier and briefly closes her eyes. "Fine. As soon as the two of you get settled, I'll take a break. I could use one today."

She's always kind of cold and witchy, but today she appears to be on edge. Like she's waiting for something bad to happen. I don't like it. Especially after everything Sparrow told me this morning.

Sandra leads me through the quiet condo to the classroom. Della is waiting inside, coloring all over the desk. Sandra gives me a nod and smirk that says, "Told you so." I wave her off before setting down the carrier.

Della notices me first, scowls, and then sees Heathen, and grins. Brat. I kneel to let Heathen out. The devil cat hisses at me and then bolts. Della abandons her art and chases after her. Good. This'll buy me some time. While Della attempts to coax the cat out of hiding, I slip out of the classroom and tiptoe through the house. I pass a few open doors, but there's one near the end that remains closed. My guess is Landry is in there. Quickly, I turn the knob and peek inside.

I don't know what I'm expecting from her room, but it's not this. Landry is so interesting. There are layers and layers when it comes to this girl. I'd half expected her room to be filled with pictures or décor that reflects her personality. But it doesn't. It's sleek and fancy as fuck to go along with the aesthetic of the rest of the penthouse, but it's missing her...charm. It makes me sad because she doesn't belong here.

Lying curled up on the bed, wrapped up in a soft chenille blanket with only her blonde head poking out, is Landry. She seems so small and shattered. Her cheeks are tearstained, and her lips are puffy. I wonder if she cried herself to sleep. As quietly as possible, I close the door behind me and then approach the bed.

"Hey, honey."

Her eyes flutter open. They're bloodshot from crying and unfocused from sleep. I take her hand in mine, bringing it to my lips for a kiss.

"Ford," she whispers, her bottom lip wobbling. "You can't be in here."

"Come here," I instruct as I tug on her and

pull her closer. "We're not going to worry about that right now. I want to know how you're doing."

She allows me to drag her into my lap. Her face nuzzles against my neck. Hot breath tickles my flesh. For a moment, neither of us say anything. I hold her close and stroke her back.

"Talk to me," I murmur. "Tell me what he said."

Her body trembles. "I'm done with school. He, uh, took away my phone, too."

Bastard.

"He knows something's up with me," she continues. "He won't stop until he finds out what it is." She tilts her head up, frowning at me. "You're not safe. Us doing this isn't safe. He'll find out I'm seeing you and..." Tears well in her eyes. "He's going to ruin you because of me."

"He can try," I growl. "Don't worry about me."

"That's the thing, though," she whispers. "I do worry about you. I like you, Ford. And after this morning..." She chews on her bottom lip. "It felt so good being with you."

A spike of jealousy stabs me in the gut.

"Next time will be better," I vow. "You didn't even get to come."

Her brows pinch. "You got me off with your fingers first. I came, lover boy."

Imagining Sparrow fingerfucking her on top of everything else he's done with her is like icing on a shit cake. It pisses me off. I don't want to think about it.

"Come here," I growl, cupping the back of her head and drawing her closer. "I need to kiss you."

She moans, soft and sweet, as my lips press against hers. I kiss her deeply and with each stroke, I make promises to her. Promises that I've never made to anyone.

I'll make you happy.

You'll see.

"You have to go before he discovers you here," she murmurs breathily against my lips. "Please go. I'll see you again Wednesday."

I kiss her once more before resting my forehead to hers. "Wednesday. I can't wait."

Though I'm annoyed Sparrow got her in this situation, I'm not at all bothered by the fact I'll be the only one with access to her now. He can go back to finding Tinder pussy and Scout can continue stalking Ash for all I care.

As for me, I'll be the only one to see Landry.

Finally, I can have her all to myself.

"Ford?"

"Hmm?"

"What are you hiding?"

I go still at her question. "Nothing. Why?"

"You wouldn't let me use your phone this morning. It was shady. I don't care what it is, just tell me."

She doesn't care?

I don't believe that for a second.

If she ever learns me and my brothers played her, I feel like she's going to care a whole helluva lot.

"I'm not hiding anything, honey. I just…" I trail off before sticking with my original statement. "I'm not hiding anything."

"You *are* hiding something," she says, studying me. "I feel like I have it figured out, but it's just beyond reach. Whatever it is, it's fine. I'm not going anywhere."

Liar. Liar. Liar.

"But," she murmurs.

"But."

"But, if it's bad, he's going to find out. At least give me some sort of warning."

I look away, wondering if I could even tell her the truth ever. No, I can't. Because once she finds out I'm a triplet—one of three who she's been intimate with—she's going to lose her shit. This thing between us will end as abruptly as it began. I'm far too greedy to let that happen.

"Ford…"

Sully. My name is Sully. Just once I'd like to hear it on your lips, honey.

"What?"

"Do you have multiple personalities?"

She's dead fucking serious. I almost laugh. Almost.

"What? No."

"Then why are you so different every time I see you?" She tries to scoot out of my lap, but my hold tightens around her, trapping her in my arms. "Ford, tell me. What's going on with you? I need to be prepared for whatever it is. It's only a matter of time before my dad realizes you're my secret. Don't leave me blindsided."

I could tell her everything.

Right here. Right now.

But that sure as hell means I won't get to see her again. She'll feel betrayed. Might even tell her dad about how we imbedded ourselves into their lives. Right now, she's concerned he'll find out.

Which he hasn't.

But if I tell her the truth, he'll most certainly find out. The repercussions of that truth are much worse than continuing this charade with her.

We kicked a rich dude's ass. Defiled his

daughter. Committed fraud by lying about our identity. And the list goes on. He's connected to the Constantines, our mortal enemy. All it takes is for Alexander to find out our real names and who we are to the Constantines. Hell will absolutely break loose.

Scout blew up our lives last time. I'll be damned if I'm responsible for it this time.

"I told you," I hedge. "I have layers."

My answer earns me a glare and her tone is filled with warning. "Ford…"

"Know that I'll do everything I can to help you," I rush out, hoping my earnest words reassure her. "Just let me."

"I can't even trust you." She recoils, disgust written all over her face. "I think you should go."

"Honey—"

"Go!" she hisses, pointing at the door.

Grabbing her jaw, I pull her to me for one more kiss that leaves us both panting after. "You *can* trust me."

"I really want to," she whispers, defeated, "but until you stop hiding parts of yourself from me, we'll never get there."

I want to promise her we'll get there eventually. However, if she ever got the real truth about who I am—who we are—she'd lose *all* trust in me, even what little bit I've earned.

CHAPTER TWENTY-SEVEN

Landry

*C*AN I COME *with you?*
    Della's signed question physically hurts me, especially coupled with the pleading expression she gives me.

"No," Dad answers for me. "She's doing her part for this family. You, child, will behave and do your part."

Della isn't even looking at him, so she doesn't catch a word. Anxiety knots my stomach. Ever since yesterday, when Dad picked me up from school and grounded me from every aspect of my life, he's been distant and cold. Not that I mind the distance, but it just means he's up to something.

It makes me sick and uneasy.

Leaving Della with him for a few hours worries me, but luckily Sandra is staying late tonight, having decided to inventory the silver and polish it. She'll spend the entire time sucking up to him and praising his exquisite taste in cutlery. I may not like the witch, but Dad is less likely to do anything horrible, like smack her around, if Sandra is nearby feeding his narcissism with her endless compliments.

I'll bring you back some candy, I sign and smile at her. *Promise.*

The doorbell rings causing my nerves to rattle in response. This "date" with Ty is a means to an end. He's my key to this door I'm locked behind. Where Ford distracts me and complicates every situation we're in, Ty doesn't have that hold over me. He was nice and his texts, before Dad took my phone, were funny. He will help me. He has to.

"Della. Room," Dad barks. "Sandra, answer the door."

Della doesn't see Dad's mouth, so I quickly sign for her to go to her room. She's not happy but obeys. Dad is too volatile lately. Neither she, nor I, are going to do anything to set him off.

Ty enters the living room a moment later with Sandra on his heels. He's handsome in a pair of dark jeans, black boots, and a fitted red T-shirt that stretches over his nicely defined muscles. His blond hair is styled in a pompadour. It looks good on him. With his sharp jawline, piercing blue eyes, and height, he looks good enough to model. He smiles when he sees me, taking a second to appreciate my form as well.

Though I'm not as casual as him, I'm by no means overdressed. I'm wearing a Samantha Sung cotton stretch shirtdress with Bali boats printed on the fabric and my favorite pair of Jimmy Choo latte-colored leather espadrille wedge sandals that give me an extra four and a half inches in height. I left my natural waves in my hair today rather than straightening it so it's bouncier than usual.

"Wow," Ty says, his grin growing wider. "You look great."

His praise makes me uncomfortable, especially with my father present. I force out a smile and am overly polite back to him. "You look nice too."

He winks at me and then saunters over to Dad. They shake hands. Dad gives him a stern lecture about keeping his daughter safe. Ty promises to not let anything happen to me. With Dad's security detail attending this date with us tonight, I don't think neither Dad nor Ty need to worry. I'll be under constant scrutiny.

But I have a plan.

"Enjoy your evening, sweetheart," Dad says,

his tone cool. "See you before midnight." He walks over to me, snakes his arm around my waist, and kisses my forehead.

I try not to cringe or squirm out of his hold. It takes everything in me to hold still and endure it. Finally, he releases me. A shiver works its way down my spine, but I ignore it.

We bid Dad goodbye and Ty's hand finds the small of my back. He guides me out of the condo where four men are standing sentry outside our door. They're all dressed in black and wearing the same earpieces. If I had to guess, they're ex-military or something. Only the best for Daddy's little girl.

I'm not escaping with these watchdogs breathing down my neck.

The escape won't happen tonight, though. Soon, but not tonight. I just have to work out the details first. That means having a private word with Ty.

Right now, he's my only option. As much as I wish I could get Ford's help, until he gives me more about himself, I can't trust him. Not with something as important as me and Della's freedom. It's a sucker punch to the chest, but I can't risk it. I can't risk Ford's secrets blowing up in my face.

At least with Ty, what you see is what you get. He's transparent and real. I don't feel like he has some horrible truth he's hiding from me. Ty is my only hope.

Ty chatters about the movie and the last time he's been to see one. He moves easily from topic to topic, letting me brood in silence. We climb into one of Dad's Mercedes SUVs in order to fit everyone. I let Ty take my hand, though one of the security guys narrows his gaze at the action.

"So this isn't creepy or anything," Ty says under his breath. "I feel like we're on a reality show or something."

"Two out of five stars," I grumble.

"Only two?" He shoots me a silly grin. "That dude's neck tat alone gets a star. Seriously, man, did that shit hurt or what?"

Neck tat dude ignores him.

Rude.

"Anyway, so how've you been?" Ty asks, dropping his voice again. "School going okay?"

I bite on my bottom lip, trying not to burst into tears. "School's fine."

He frowns, glances at our entourage, and then presses his lips together. There's so much more to that statement. We both know it. Fortunately, he's smart enough to realize it and doesn't probe.

I relax when he starts babbling about this new car he wants. I'm able to smile and nod without fear of crying.

Eventually we make it to the theater. Our group of sentries surround us—one up ahead checking for only God knows what and the other three walking behind. If Ty is weirded out by the stares we're getting, he doesn't let it show. He chatters the entire time we wait in line to pay, then again on the way to the concessions, only pausing long enough to have me tell him what I want. I order a bag of Skittles for Della.

Once in the actual theater where our movie will be playing, we find a spot at the very top. A guy sits on either side of us, leaving only a chair in between. The other two guys sit closer to the exits.

It feels like an eternity until the movie begins. I sit patiently through the previews at the beginning and also through the slow start of the movie. When the action starts blasting through the speakers, I nudge Ty with my elbow and lean in. He notices my movement and holds the bag of popcorn toward me while bringing his ear close to my mouth. I point at the screen, pretending to ask him about the movie.

"Help me."

His eyes cut my way, wide and concerned. "Okay."

Just like that. Okay. I want to cry, but I can't afford to break down right now. My time is limited. This opportunity for escape is razor thin.

"I need money. A few thousand. As soon as possible."

"Your dad?"

"I am getting us away from him," I whisper. "He's a bad man. He hurts us, Ty."

His frown deepens. "I can get you money, but I'll have to access my trust fund. That means going through my parents. It'll take me at least until tomorrow. Maybe even the next day. Is it safe to wait that long?"

No.

But I don't have a choice.

"Do you want me to text you when I get it?" he asks.

"Dad has my phone." I swallow hard. "You've been texting with him the past couple of days."

He blinks at me in shock. "Glad I didn't send him a dick pic."

A smile tugs at my lips even though I'm scared as hell right now. "Probably best if you keep those pictures to yourself."

"I'm wounded," he teases. "And to think, I

actually thought you liked me."

I do like him. As a friend.

Maybe, in another life, I'd even like him like he likes me. *As more than a friend.*

This one is too complicated. Plus, my heart is a mess for someone else right now.

"You're one of the only friends I have," I admit. "I need your help. I'll figure out a way to repay you."

"I don't want you to pay me back. I just want to make sure you're okay." He glances over at one of the men watching us intently and then lowers his voice. "I'll leave a discreet note when I have the money. We can meet up and go from there."

Now all I have to do is find a way to leave again.

"If I don't surface at the meeting place because he has me trapped, then I'll need you to create a distraction so we can slip out of there unnoticed."

"Want me to wait twenty-four hours and then make my move?"

"Yes. Thank you."

He leans closer and kisses my cheek. "Everything's going to be okay."

I can't even allow myself to hope.

✧　✧　✧

"WE'LL WALK YOU inside, miss," the neck tattooed guy grunts. "You're dismissed."

Ty ignores the rudeness and presses a goodbye kiss to my cheek. I can tell he wants to say and ask a lot of things, but wisely doesn't with our audience. Despite the stress I'm under, I did enjoy Ty's company. He's light and funny and caring. Dread fills me to my brim and spills over the second I walk into my quiet home.

"I'll go speak with Mr. Croft," one of the guys says while the other three wait outside the condo.

I skirt past him and head to Della's room. The door is locked. Softly, I knock on the wood, not that she will hear me anyway. Panic clutches my throat as a thousand what-ifs play in my mind.

What if he's in there with her?

What if he hit her while I was gone?

What if he did much worse?

I start slapping the door and putting my weight against, trying to either get her to unlock it or bust through it.

"Miss Croft," Sandra hisses, hurrying down the hall toward me. "Have you lost your ever-loving mind?"

I wriggle the handle. "I need to make sure she's okay."

"Throwing a tantrum isn't the way to do it."

She scowls at me and then produces a key from her pocket. "Go see your sister. And be quiet before you upset your father."

She unlocks the door. I don't wait to be told twice. Rushing into Della's room, I find her sitting in the corner surrounded by all her stuffed animals. Her head is bowed as she strokes the pink cat's fur. When I kneel in front of her, she jumps. Wild, panicked eyes meet mine and then relief has her leaping at me. I hug her to me, unable to keep the tears at bay. Her small hands clutch onto the fabric of my dress like I might leave her again.

Never again.

The next time we leave, it'll be for good.

She pulls away from me and starts signing rapidly. *He spanked me with his belt. I wasn't listening. But I didn't hear him, Landry. I didn't. He doesn't use sign language.* Fat tears roll down her cheeks and she trembles. *I hope he dies.*

Me too.

God, I feel the same.

I just hate that a child her age has to feel that way. It's wrong. The way he treats us is wrong. We're not his daughters. We're his trophies to display however he pleases and if he's tired of looking at us, he banishes us to our rooms.

Look at me, I sign with my back to Sandra who's still in the doorway. *Can you read my lips?*

She nods, focusing hard on my mouth.

I'm going to get us out of here. I mouth the words, but don't let any sound come out for fear of Sandra overhearing.

Again, Della's head nods. Tears continue to fall down her pink cheeks. She signs, *Forever?*

Forever, I sign back.

Can we get a real cat? She smiles hopefully at me.

We can do whatever we want, Della.

All we have to do is wait for Ty to make good on his promise. We're almost out of here. Almost. I can hardly wait.

Chapter Twenty-Eight

Scout

I STARE AT the text I received this morning and shake my head. Not exactly what I had planned for the day, but I'm also not ready to give this up. Bryant told us to cease this "job" but he'll soon learn he doesn't control me. I only play along when it suits me.

> **Ty:** Meet me at that sandwich shop near work for lunch. I need to talk to someone.

While I wait on Ty to get to the restaurant, I read the text again. I'm curious to see what has him all flustered. I know he's flustered because usually when he texts me, he throws in stupid emojis and a lot of LOLs. This text is curt and to the point.

My phone buzzes. This time, it's in the group text with my brothers.

> **Sparrow:** *I could wait until her old man leaves to go to the office and then pop in to visit her. Make sure she's okay.*

> **Sully:** *I'll see her tomorrow afternoon. I'll check then.*

Sparrow sends a bunch of angry emojis and even more middle finger emojis. I should give Ty Sparrow's number and then they can talk in emojis until the end of time. Dumbasses.

The bell chimes on the door and Ty strides in. Gone is his usual smile. Something about the seriousness in his expression puts me on edge. Without the cheesy look on his face, he reminds me too much of Winston. I tighten my grip around my phone until it makes a cracking sound. Only then do I ease up.

"'Sup?" I nod my head in greeting. "You on the rag or something?"

He smirks. "Fuck off. No, I am slightly freaking the hell out though."

"About?"

"My date last night. If you even want to call it that."

"With the Croft girl?"

"Yes, idiot. Landry. I'm not exactly pining over any other women at the moment."

"Did she put out?"

"I wish."

I bristle at his words, but then find relief in them. "Spill, man."

He launches into the entire recap of his date. Apparently, according to him, Landry is trying to escape. I pretend to be shocked by the news, but I'm not. Her dad's an asshole. An abusive one at that. He's lucky my brothers didn't let me crush his entire skull in when we beat his ass last week.

"So, he hits her?"

Ty leans in, lowering his voice. "Or worse. She's fucking terrified. So terrified she's going to run away."

"And you're going to help her?"

"I've got to come up with the money first." He scowls. "My dad is being a dick about it. Wants to know why I need five grand. I'm spoiled. Blah, blah, blah. Then, once I have the money, I'm going to somehow get a message to her and have her come to my apartment."

The thought of Landry in his apartment angers me, but I don't lash out. Instead, I keep a tight leash on that shit. I'm smarter now. Especially when dealing with Constantines.

"You need a loan?"

He groans. "No, I mean, that's not why I wanted to meet up. But, yeah, man, if you're offering. The sooner I can get her out of there, the better."

"I can spot you the cash," I assure him. "Why'd you want to meet up then?"

"To vent. Catch up. Ask for advice. I don't fucking know." He rubs at the back of his neck, frowning. "I really, really like her. But, I'm basically helping her leave. Kind of stupid of me to hope for her to date me once she's free from her father, right?"

"Completely stupid," I agree.

"Thanks." He sighs heavily. "No, you're right. The best thing is to help her. If something comes of it, then that's great."

It won't.

Guys like Ty Constantine don't get girls like Landry Croft.

He's a golden prince and she's a prickly princess. He'll never appeal to her because her life is too fucked up. She's more of a villain girl. I'm sure of it.

"She looked so damn hot last night," he mutters. "Damn, I've got it bad for this girl."

Join the club, moron.

He meets my gaze and cocks his head to the side. "Enough about me and my drama. What's up with you and your girl? Did you talk to her?"

"Actually," I say, leaning forward, "I had a revelation."

"A revelation? Let's hear it."

"I like the idea of my girl, but when push came to shove, I didn't choose her."

Ty squints his eyes as though trying to make sense of my words. "Okay…who did you choose?"

"Someone new. I didn't realize my feelings for her until I needed to be in two places at once." I close my eyes remembering the fear on Ash's face and how I chose to leave her standing there so I could get to Landry. "I chose to leave her. The girl I've been obsessing over for this new girl."

He gapes at me. "No shit? For the record, I don't think this is a bad thing. Your old girl is married. Kind of a tough situation. What about the new girl?"

"Not married."

A grin transforms his face. "Tell me about her."

She let me finger her in the bathroom and came like a good little princess.

"Pretty. Innocent. Sweet." I smile at the thought of tasting her. "*So* sweet."

"Good for you, man. I'm glad at least someone is having luck in the female department. Maybe if I can get Landry to trust me a little, she'll let me take her on a real date. Then, who knows, maybe by then you'll be with this new chick. We can double date."

That won't be happening.

"What happens when her dad finds out it was you who helped her escape?" I ask, sitting back and popping my knuckles. "You think he'll let you continue on being his intern?"

The stupid smile on his face is wiped away.

"He can't find out," Ty grumbles. "Which, you loaning me the cash, actually works better. Less chance of him tracing anything back to me."

Ty eventually stops yapping long enough to go grab us a couple of sandwiches. While he's gone, I think about Landry.

Her breathy moans.

The way her body clenched around my fingers.

How pretty her mouth looked and tasted.

My brothers are just as captivated by her. There's something different about Landry. Something addictive and tantalizing. She lives with a monster, so it's only natural for more monsters to gravitate to her.

Obviously it's not the first time we've fixated on the same woman. It's a habit we can't seem to shake. But, unlike in the past, where we ended up fighting over the woman, this time I have a plan.

Ty returns and passes me my sandwich. It's a shame he's a Constantine. I don't completely hate the guy. Because of his last name, though, I'll always dislike him.

"Want to go clubbin' this weekend?" Ty asks around a mouthful of bread. "While I wait for Landry, I may as well have a little fun."

"Yeah, man. It's a date."

Ty says a whole lot of nothing. It doesn't require much engagement aside from the occasional laugh, head nod, or exclamation. Mostly, I think he talks to hear himself speak.

I pity the guy.

I really do.

He thinks he's going to save the girl from her monster. People like him aren't heroes. They're not ruthless enough. The ones who ever make it ahead are the ones who aren't afraid to cut their competition off at the knees.

His cousin Winston is that type.

Like me.

Willing to do whatever it takes to get what he wants. Ty is nothing but a dreamer. A watcher, not a doer.

I watch until the time is right.

And then I do absolutely everything in my

power to get exactly what I want.

Ivy and Ash and countless others slipped through my fingers. When I get my hands back on Landry, she won't be going anywhere.

"Sorry about your luck, bro," I say, grinning at Ty, though I have no idea what the fuck I interrupted him saying.

He gives me a strange look and then laughs. "You're so fucking weird, man."

"And you're desperate as fuck if you chose me, of all people, as your friend."

We both laugh, but one of us isn't joking.

CHAPTER TWENTY-NINE

Landry

T HIS IS HAPPENING.

It's really happening.

I take the entertainment magazine from Sandra and try to play it cool. The sticky note on the front does a good job of masking the real reason for it.

Landry,

Seeing a movie with you was fun.

I want to take you out again.

Let me know if anything interests you and we'll make a date.

-Ty-

"He wants to go on another date," I say, smiling at her. "I wonder if Dad will let me."

She stares at me for a long, penetrating beat,

but finally gives a shake of her head. "That'll be between you and him. I'll need to make sure I'm available whichever day because I know he prefers I stay to care for Della in your absence."

I don't let her guilt trip me. She signed up for this job. There'd be no way in hell I'd ever willingly work for that man.

"I'm going back to my room now," I tell her, feigning disappointment.

"For the best. Your dad won't be pleased to see you out and about when he expressed his wishes you stay in your room."

"Grounded for life." I shudder. If only she knew this was so much more than a simple grounding. He's ripped my life completely out of my hands and I don't think he's ever planning on giving it back.

I try not to hurry to my room as not to garner any unnecessary attention. Once the door is closed and I'm seated on my bed, I flip open the magazine, looking for my true hidden message. I find it on a Starbucks advertisement written along the inside edge of the page in neat, precise writing that could almost pass for a typewritten font.

It's an address and another note that says, ***plus 5k and a getaway car***. He even draws a winky face which makes me smile. Even though I'll probably have the address memorized by the end of the night, I still tuck away the entire magazine into my school backpack. Since Dad never found anything of interest in my bag and ended up confiscating my computer later, he won't be digging through my bag. I also fill it with a couple changes of clothes, a framed picture of Mom, and a few toiletries.

My purse, ID, and anything else that ties me to this life stays here when the time comes.

I'll need to make sure I pack Della a bag we can grab and go with too. She loves her stuffed animals, so making her choose just one is going to be difficult. I know, at first, she'll be confused, but once we're out from under Dad's thumb, she'll be so much happier. I'll find a way to buy her lots more stuffed animals.

We'll be safe.

Freedom is so close I can nearly taste it.

I wish there were a way I could thank Ty for doing this for me. There has to be a way. Maybe, once me and Della are settled someplace, I can find a way to pay him back. It's the least I can do for giving us this opportunity.

I'm so ready to leave this life behind.

To start fresh, happy and unafraid.

You won't see Ford again.

Thoughts of Ford enter my brain against my will. I don't want to think about him right now. As much as we're attracted to one another and have this undeniable connection—even when he's being Mr. Crazy Pants—I can't go there with him. He's a distraction away from my purpose.

Save Della.

Save both of us.

Because if we stay here much longer, I wonder how many more lines Dad will cross. How it might irrevocably change us somehow.

All that matters now is that we have a way out.

The second we can make a break for it, we absolutely will.

✧　✧　✧

I'M STARTLED FROM the book I'm reading when I hear shouts. Dad's shouts specifically. I abandon my book to creep over to my bedroom door. Since he's still yelling, I sneak out of my room unnoticed, even when my door creaks.

In the hallway, Della's pink stuffed cat lies in the middle of the floor, discarded and forgotten. I step around it and peek into her room. Empty. My heart leaps into my throat because I could bet money he's yelling at her.

Hang in there, little sis.

I'm getting us out of here soon.

I follow the sound of his voice to the living room. Dad stands over Della, towering over her like an angry giant. She defiantly glares up at him like she could take him.

She can't.

He's too big and cruel and ruthless.

"You fucking ruined it, you dumb piece of shit!" he bellows, gesturing at his computer on the coffee table.

The room reeks of his expensive liquor. An entire bottle of it has been knocked over and spilled onto the laptop. It drips to the floor making a pattering sound that can be heard between the echoes of Dad's shouting.

"You were meant to die, not her," he growls. "You took my wife because you're a fucking parasite. Now you're trying to suck the life out of me too!"

I'm thankful she can't hear a word he's saying to her.

She's no longer looking at him either, but instead notices me approaching. The relief at seeing me is a punch to the throat. All her bravery is gone and she looks to me to help her out of this mess.

"Look at me when I'm talking to you!" Dad screams, grabbing hold of her face.

With a rough shove, he sends her careening to the floor. She bumps her head on the end table.

"Dad! Stop!" I cry out, rushing forward to put myself between the two of them.

His hand swings out, hitting me on the side of the face. I stumble, tripping backwards over the coffee table and fall between the table and sofa. Pain shoots from my tailbone up my spine on impact.

Della is back on her feet, tears running down her face as her eyes search mine, looking to make sure I'm okay.

I start to get up, ignoring the literal pain in my ass, when Dad is on the prowl again after her. She scurries backward until she's trapped against a wall.

"I could snap your neck and no one would even notice or care," he threatens. "You're nothing but a fucking nuisance!"

He reaches for her neck, his large hand closing in on her tiny, delicate throat. If he gets a hold of her, he'll kill her. I feel it in my bones.

I'll never let that happen.

Grabbing the empty bottle, I charge for him. Swinging it as hard as I can, I nail him in the back of the head. He goes down hard, with a pained groan, taking Della down with him.

I stare down in shock as blood seeps from the back of his head.

What did I do?

Did I kill him?

He makes another pained sound.

Not dead, which means we have to go. Now's our opportunity.

"Della!" I grab her arm and drag her out from beneath Dad's unmoving form.

Though she's getting bigger, I can still carry her. Since she's shuddering so hard her teeth are chattering, I don't even try to make her walk. I carry her down the hallway to my room to grab my bag. Earlier, when I could, I slipped into her room to grab some of her clothes to add to my bag. I decided one bag was easier to deal with in a hurry than two.

I'm glad I planned it out because I didn't think about how I might have to carry Della.

On the way back out, I scoop up her pink stuffed cat, hurrying to the door. Dad is still on the floor in the living room. I'm not going to stick around to see if he's okay or not.

I have to get out of here.

It's now or never.

Miraculously, we make it to the lobby of the building without incident. Once outside, I start walking down the street toward a busy intersection. It's dark out but the city is bustling with people going to dinner. All too easily, I blend in with the crowd.

My heart is racing, but I attempt to stay calm. I won't relax until we're far, far away from Dad's monstrous grip.

All this would be much easier if I could use my cards. But, since I left all that at home, and I don't have any cash, I have to make my escape the old-fashioned way.

On foot.

Ty lives several blocks away. It's a long and arduous trek, especially carrying a now sleeping child, but I keep going. Even when my feet throb so badly I want to cry. Even when I get lost. Even when a couple of guys say creepy stuff to me that has me running. When I finally make it to the address of the building where he lives, I almost fall to my knees with joy.

So close to real freedom.

For the past hour of my journey, I've constantly had to look over my shoulder. With each passing second, fear rises higher and higher like a swelling tide threatening to drown me. If he were to catch me now, when I was so close to escape, I'd probably die from defeat.

I'd be letting Della and me both down.

The building Ty lives in is nice. Nearly as nice as ours. It makes sense considering he's a Constantine. I make sure to keep my head down and not look too suspicious.

An eternity of a wait on the elevator to his floor ends with a high-pitched ding.

I exhale the stress of the evening and suck in a breath of relief. We've made it. We've really made it. I keep expecting Dad to jump around a corner and drag us back home.

The door to Ty's apartment feels like my last final hurdle of the night. I'll rest and regroup. Then, tomorrow, I'll be on the next leg of my journey.

Disappear with Della.

I knock on the door and then reposition Della's sleeping form. She's heavier than usual now that she's completely passed out and isn't holding on like before. I'm exhausted and my muscles are on fire. I could sleep for days, though I don't have days.

Footsteps thud toward me from the other side and then the lock disengages. Ty opens the door and takes a long look at me.

But it's not Ty.

No, concerned blue eyes don't stare me down. There's no smile or shimmering dark blond hair. No kindness or worry or even relief.

I'm staring at the darkness.

A void.

Deep and soulless.

It's sucking me in though I'm mentally begging my worn-out feet to run.

Black shirt. Black jeans. Black boots. Black soul.

"F-Ford?" I choke out in confusion. "What are you doing at Ty's house?"

Are they friends?

Dark eyes, like melted chocolate, flash at me. There's something sinister in the way he smiles. Triumph. I can see it written all over his handsome face. He's achieved something. I'd seen the same look on his face when he fingered me in the school bathroom, rough and cruelly, and yet I still begged for it. Came all over his fingers shamelessly.

"I don't understand," I murmur.

Move your feet, girl. Run!

"You will soon." The deep timbre of his voice reverberates through me. "Come inside."

I try to take a step back but my sore muscles

don't allow me to move. So he takes the step for me, clutches a possessive hand on the back of my neck and guides me inside. My heart flipflops inside my chest. I want to feel relieved at being in Ford's presence, but something's off. Something's really wrong.

He has secrets.

Dark ones.

Twisted ones.

I know this. I've always known this. I just never understood them. Never could make sense of what they were.

The door closes behind me with a click of finality. It sends a shiver down my spine. Maybe, if I keep him calm long enough, I can get Chevy to surface. I almost sob at the thought of him holding me right now through the anxiety and overwhelming stress. I need that. I need him.

"Who was at the door?"

The voice is Ford's but he's not speaking. He simply watches me in an expectant way. Like he's waiting for a bomb to drop and to see my reaction. My stare finds the man entering the space behind him.

Ty?

Stupid, stupid girl. You know better.

Ford gapes at me. Confused. Horrified.

He has a twin. He has a freaking twin. It makes sense now. All those times when he'd mention his brother…

But that means he's been playing me.

Lying to my face.

Switching out with his brother.

I'm going to be sick. A low mewl crawls up my throat. I'm paralyzed. I can't move and don't know what to say. Betrayal is a knife to my chest—stabbing over and over again, puncturing my lungs and my heart both.

I can't breathe.

I'm dizzy.

"Sully!" one of the Fords shouts.

At first I think he's talking to the one in front of me, but then the unthinkable happens. Another Ford appears. This is a joke. I'm dreaming. I'm stuck in some horrible nightmare.

They're triplets.

Terrible, terrifying triplets.

"What the fuck did you do, Scout?" the one who just entered, and who I think is Sully, snarls. "What the fuck did you do?"

Sully approaches me and I start shaking my head. Tears are spilling down my cheeks, but I'm unable to stop them.

"Hey, honey," Sully says. "Let me take Della.

You look like you're about to fall over."

He reaches for her, but my grip tightens.

"Don't touch her," I hiss. "Don't touch me either. Where's Ty?"

"Ty." Scout, the evil one, grins. "He's at home, I guess."

He's playing with me. I'm nothing but a game. A freaking toy.

"Sparrow," Sully growls at the other brother. "Snap out of it. We have to deal with this."

Sparrow, with eyes like dark maple syrup, stares at me with a mixture of shame and disappointment. Like he's given up on something. I want to shake him and smack him.

Sully is closer now. When he grabs Della, I don't have the strength to keep her in my arms. I watch, helplessly, as he tugs her away from me and disappears with her.

No.

This can't be happening.

Scout grabs hold of my backpack and roughly drags it off my body before tossing it into the floor.

"Chevy," I whisper, pleading with Sparrow. "What's happening? Why are you doing this?"

He closes his eyes and bows his head.

"Don't worry, prickly princess, we're going to

take real good care of you," Scout says, his rumbling voice behind me. "Be a good girl and don't scream."

I do scream.

But the second I do, his hand clamps over my mouth while his other one hooks around me, pinning me to him. I kick out and struggle, fighting this man who's holding me captive—who lured me here by using Ty somehow.

My foot connects with something, or some-one in this case. Sparrow's eyes fly to mine. I expect him to pounce on his brother and rescue me because we slept together. We had a connec-tion. He cares about me.

But he does nothing.

Watches me as his brother drags me away kicking and fighting with everything in me. Scout's limp is pronounced, but it does nothing to deter from his strength. The last thing I see is Sparrow turn his back to me. Then, with a sinister slam, Scout closes a door between us.

I'm trapped with a monster.

Again.

✧　✧　✧

Thank you for reading TRIPLE THREAT! Who do you think will win? Is it possible that Landry can end up with all three of the Terror Triplets? Or will one of them steal her away?

I'm the daughter of a controlling and cruel billionaire, so I understand about power. But I find myself fighting the triplets. I find myself testing them. It's like I have a death wish. I used to have one monster in my world. Now I have three.

DEATH WISH by K Webster is available now!

Want more dangerous romance with multiple heroes?

Once upon a time I was promised to a powerful man. I was raised to be dutiful and innocent. But on my wedding day, I'm stolen by four men. Men who loathe my fiancé. They're going to use me to fulfill their vendetta.

VELVET CRUELTY by Eve Dangerfield is available now!

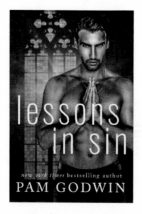

Love forbidden romance that will push your boundaries?

As Father Magnus Falke, I suppress my cravings. As the headteacher of a Catholic boarding school, I'm never tempted by a student. Until her...

I became a priest to control my impulses.

Then I meet Tinsley Constantine.

LESSONS IN SIN by Pam Godwin is available now!

The warring Morelli and Constantine families have enough bad blood to fill an ocean, and there are told by your favorite dangerous romance authors. See what books are available now and sign up to get notified about new releases here... www.dangerouspress.com

About Dangerous Press

The warring Morelli and Constantine families have enough bad blood to fill an ocean, and their scorching hot stories will be told by your favorite dangerous romance authors.

Meet Winston Constantine, the head of the Constantine family. He's used to people bowing to his will. Money can buy anything. And anyone. Including Ash Elliot, his new maid.

But love can have deadly consequences when it comes from a Constantine. At the stroke of midnight, that choice may be lost for both of them.

> "Brilliant storytelling packed with a powerful emotional punch, it's been years since I've been so invested in a book. Erotic romance at its finest!"

– #1 New York Times bestselling author
Rachel Van Dyken

"Stroke of Midnight is by far the hottest book I've read in a very long time! Winston Constantine is a dirty talking alpha who makes no apologies for going after what he wants."

– USA Today bestselling author
Jenika Snow

Ready for more bad boys, more drama, and more heat? The Constantines have a resident fixer. The man they call when they need someone persuaded in a violent fashion. Ronan was danger and beauty, murder and mercy.

Outside a glittering party, I saw a man in the dark. I didn't know then that he was an assassin. A hit man. A mercenary. Ronan radiated danger and beauty. Mercy and mystery.

I wanted him, but I was already promised to another man. Ronan might be the one who murdered him. But two warring families want my blood. I don't know where to turn.

In a mad world of luxury and secrets, he's the only one I can trust.

"M. O'Keefe brings her A-game in this sexy, complicated romance where you're left questioning if everything you thought was true while dying to get your hands on the next book!"

– New York Times bestselling author
K. Bromberg

"Powerful, sexy, and written like a dream, RUINED is the kind of book you wish you could read forever and ever. Ronan Byrne is my new romance addiction, and I'm already pining for more blue eyes and dirty deeds in the dark."

– USA Today Bestselling Author
Sierra Simone

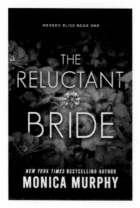

One moment I'm the forgotten daughter of one of the most wealthy families in the country, and the next I'm the blushing bride in an arranged marriage. My fate is sealed in my wedded union with a complete stranger.

"A fiery, slow burn that explodes with chemistry and achingly perfect tension. Monica Murphy has written a sizzling masterpiece."

– USA Today bestselling author
Marni Mann

"Monica Murphy's The Reluctant Bride is a sinful yet sweet arranged marriage romance. I am in love with the Midnight Dynasty series!"

– USA Today Bestselling Author
Natasha Knight

SIGN UP FOR THE NEWSLETTER

www.dangerouspress.com

JOIN THE FACEBOOK GROUP HERE

www.dangerouspress.com/facebook

FOLLOW US ON INSTAGRAM

www.instagram.com/dangerouspress

ABOUT THE AUTHOR

K Webster is a USA Today Bestselling author. Her titles have claimed many bestseller tags in numerous categories, are translated in multiple languages, and have been adapted into audio-books. She lives in "Tornado Alley" with her husband, two children, and her baby dog named Blue. When she's not writing, she's reading, drinking copious amounts of coffee, and research-ing aliens.

You can easily find K Webster on Facebook, Twitter, Instagram, Pinterest, and Goodreads!

Can't find a certain book? Maybe it's too hot! Don't worry because titles like Bad Bad Bad, This is War, Baby, The Wild, and Hale can all be found for sale on K's website in both ebook and paperback format.

Website: www.authorkwebster.com

COPYRIGHT

39791932R00219